Praise for The Sleep R

'The novel is an elegantly constructed psychiatric Gothic, all spires and gargoyles and ghostly echoes – the sort of vast, dread edifice we sometimes build around ourselves when the lights go out'   *New York Times*

'Delivers some wicked chills'   *Publisher's Weekly*

'Layering several familiar elements expertly, Tallis creates a deliciously creepy mood of neogothic suspense'   *Kirkus Reviews*

'[*The Sleep Room*] combines strange, vague occurrences with moments of true power to create a plot which is poignant and unique. Writing as F. R. Tallis, this well-paced shocker builds brilliantly from the start and offers the kind of suspense that makes thrillers so enjoyable'

Hampstead & Highgate Express

'It goes without question that *The Sleep Room* is the best psychological horror of the year. Steeped deep in the tradition of M.R. James and Henry James, it is bound to keep you awake long at night'

upcoming4.me

'I found the novel fascinating . . . Tallis has crafted a skilful exercise in neo-Gothic horror'   *Washington Post*

'Be warned . . . there'll be no sleep until the last page has turned!'

Lancashire Evening Post

'An authentic psychological horror constructed of dreams, reality, perceived reality and the supernatural'   *Scream*

'F. R. Tallis's story charms with its period detail (it's set in the late Fifties) and establishes an effectively spooky setting in its isolated hospital'

SciFiNow

The Passenger

F. R. Tallis is a writer and clinical psychologist. He has written self-help manuals, non-fiction for the general reader, academic text books, over thirty academic papers in international journals and several novels. Between 1999 and 2012 he received or was shortlisted for numerous awards, including the New London Writers' Award, the Ellis Peters Historical Dagger, the Elle Prix de Letrice, and two Edgars. His critically acclaimed Liebermann series (written as Frank Tallis) has been translated into fourteen languages and optioned for TV adaptation. His recent books are *The Forbidden*, *The Sleep Room* and *The Voices*. This novel, *The Passenger*, is his latest.

For more on F. R. Tallis, visit his website
www.franktallis.com
or follow him on Twitter @FrankTallis

BY F. R. TALLIS

The Forbidden
The Sleep Room
The Voices
The Passenger

Writing as Frank Tallis

Fiction
Killing Time
Sensing Others
Mortal Mischief
Vienna Blood
Fatal Lies
Darkness Rising
Deadly Communion
Death and the Maiden

Non-fiction
Changing Minds
Hidden Minds
Love Sick

F. R. TALLIS

The Passenger

PICADOR

First published 2016 by Pegasus Books, New York

First published in the UK 2016 by Picador

First published in paperback 2017 by Picador
an imprint of Pan Macmillan
20 New Wharf Road, London N1 9RR
Associated companies throughout the world
www.panmacmillan.com

ISBN 978-1-4472-3604-7

Visit www.picador.com to read more about all our books
and to buy them. You will also find features, author interviews and
news of any author events, and you can sign up for e-newsletters
so that you're always first to hear about our new releases.

The sea is the favourite symbol for the unconscious,
the mother of all that lives.

(Carl Gustav Jung)

The Crew of U-330

The Officers

Kapitänleutnant Siegfried Lorenz *Commander of U-330,*
addressed as Kaleun, an abbreviation of his full title

Oberleutnant Falk *First Watch Officer*

Leutnant Juhl *Second Watch Officer*

Oberleutnant (Ing.) Graf *Chief Engineer, addressed as Chief*

Leutnant Pullman *Photographer from the Ministry of*
Propaganda. Joins crew for Patrol II.

Warrant Officers, Chiefs, Petty Officers and Seamen

Stabsobersteuermann Müller *Navigator and Third Watch*
Officer

Stabswaffenwart Schmidt *Master-at-Arms. Responsible for*
weapons and crew discipline.

Obermaschinist Fischer *Chief Mechanic*

Elektro-Obermaschinist Hoffmann *Chief Electrician*

Elektro-Obermaschinist Reitlinger *Chief Electrician. Replaces*
Hoffmann for Patrol II.

Obermaschinistmaat Richter *Senior Mechanic*

Maschinistmaat Neumann *Mechanic*

Oberfunkmeister Ziegler *Senior Radio Operator / Medical Orderly*

Funkmaat Brandt *Radio Operator's Mate*

Oberbootsmann Sauer *Boatswain (Bosun) and head of the Deck Department. Addressed as Number One*

Bootsmannsmaat Voigt *Bosun's Mate*

Bootsmannsmaat Wilhelm *Bosun's Mate*

Bootsmannsmaat Danzer *Bosun's mate (control room)*

Matrosenoberstabsgefreiter Werner *Cook*

Obertorpedo-Mechanikersmaat Kruger *Torpedoman*

Torpedo-Mechanikersmaat Dressel *Torpedoman*

Oberhorchfunkermaat Lehmann *Senior Hydrophone Operator*

Horchfunkermaat Thomas *Hydrophone Operator*

Matrosengefreiter Keller *Steward*

Obersteuermannsmaat Stein *Senior Quartermaster's Mate*

Matrosenobergefreiter Krausse *Seaman (compressors, cooling system, water)*

Matrosengefreiter Schulze *Seaman (periscope, oxygen, ventilation system)*

Diesel-Maschinisthauptgefreiter Peters *Seaman (right-hand diesel mechanic)*

Diesel-Maschinisthauptgefreiter Engel *Seaman (left-hand diesel mechanic)*

Elektro-Maschinisthauptgefreiter Martin *Seaman (batteries)*
Matrose Berger *Seaman (deck division)*
Matrose Wessel *Seaman (deck division)*
Matrose Arnold *Seaman (deck division)*

The above are only the named members of the crew.
A Type VIIC U-boat carried fifty men in total.

Patrol

Kapitänleutnant Siegfried Lorenz looked back at the foaming wake. Pale green strands of froth separated from the churning trail and dispersed on the waves like tattered ribbons. The sea surrounding U-330 had become a gently undulating expanse of floating white pavements and the mist was becoming thicker. He had only been on the bridge for a few minutes, but already his hands and feet were frozen and his beard was streaked with tiny glittering crystals. Diesel fumes rose up from the gratings and lingered in the air like a congregation of ghosts. As he turned, his face was lashed by spray and his mouth filled with the taste of salt.

Below the conning tower sailors were hammering at shards of ice that hung from the 8.8 cm gun. Glassy spikes shattered and transparent fragments skittered across the deck. Others were engaged in the arduous task of scraping encrustations of rime from the safety rails.

'Hurry up,' Lorenz called down. 'Get a move on.'

Excess weight made the boat unstable. It rolled, even in the absence of a heavy swell.

Juhl – the second watch officer – moved stiffly towards Lorenz; he was wearing oilskins that had become as inflexible as armour. Icicles had formed around the rim of his sou'wester. 'I hope they don't do any damage,' he muttered.

'It'll be all right,' Lorenz responded. 'They're not using axes.' One of the men swore as he slipped and dropped his hammer. 'I'm more concerned about the state of the deck. It's like a skating rink. If one of them slides off the edge there'll be trouble. We'd never get him out in time.'

'Perhaps we should dive?'

Lorenz considered the suggestion. 'The water temperature will be a little warmer, I agree. But I'm not confident the vents will open.'

Juhl peered into the fog and grumbled, 'And all for a weather report!'

Lorenz pulled his battered cap down low and pushed his gloved hands into the deep pockets of his leather jacket. 'What are your plans – after we return?'

'Plans?' Juhl was puzzled by the question.

'Yes. Where are you off to?'

'Home, I suppose.'

'I've been thinking about Paris again. There's a very fine restaurant near the cathedral. A little place on the Isle Saint Louis – only a few tables – but the food is exquisite.'

Stein and Keller (one fixedly monitoring the south quadrant, the other gazing east) stole a quick, smirking glance at each other.

An iceberg came into view. Even though the sky was overcast the tip seemed to glow from within, emitting a strange, eldritch light.

'I didn't expect the temperature to drop like this,' said Juhl.

'Surprisingly sudden,' Lorenz agreed.

Veils of mist drifted over the bow and the men below became indistinct and shapeless. The gun rapidly faded until only its outline remained and within seconds they were moving through a featureless void, a white nothingness – empty, blind.

'This is ridiculous, Kaleun,' said Juhl. 'Can you see anything: anything at all?'

Lorenz leaned over the open hatch and ordered both engines to be stopped. He then called over the bulwark, 'Enough! Down tools!' The men on the deck were hidden beneath a blanket of vapour. Voigt, the bosun's mate who was supervising the work party, acknowledged the command.

The boat heaved and the collision of ice floes created a curious, knocking accompaniment.

'What are we doing, Kaleun?' asked Juhl.

Lorenz didn't reply. Paris, Brest, Berlin – the steamed-up windows of a coffee house, fragrant waitresses, billboards, cobbled streets and tram lines – umbrellas, organ grinders, and barber shops. They were so far away from anything ordinary, familiar, apprehensible. Eventually Lorenz said: 'We should dive soon.'

'As soon as possible,' Juhl concurred.

'If the vents are stuck,' said Lorenz, 'we'll just have to get them open again – somehow.'

The rise and fall of the boat was hypnotic and encouraged mental vacancy. Lorenz inhaled and felt the cold conducting through his jaw, taunting the nerves in his teeth.

'Kaleun?' The speaker had adopted a peculiar stage whisper. 'Kaleun?'

Lorenz leaned over the bulwark and could barely make out Peters – one of the diesel hands – at the foot of the tower.

'What?'

'Herr Kaleun?' The man continued. 'I can see something . . .'

Juhl looked at Lorenz – tense and ready to react.

The commander simply shook his head and responded, 'Where?'

'Off the port bow, Kaleun. Forty-five degrees.'

'What can you see?'

'It's . . . I don't know what it is.'

Lorenz lifted his binoculars and aimed them into the mist. He was able to detect drifting filaments, a hint of depth, but nothing materialized below the shifting, restless textures. 'All right, I'm coming down.' He squeezed past the lookouts, descended the ladder, and walked with great care towards the bow, where he found Peters standing in front of the gun and gazing out to sea.

'Kaleun,' Peters raised his hand and pointed. The commander positioned himself beside the seaman. 'You can't see it now. But it was just there.'

'Debris, a container – what?'

'Not flotsam. Too high in the water.'

'An iceberg, then. You saw an iceberg, Peters.'

'No, Herr Kaleun.' The man was offended. 'With respect, sir. No. It wasn't an iceberg. I'm sure it wasn't an iceberg.'

They were joined by two others: Kruger, a torpedo mechanic, and a boyish seaman called Berger. All of them were boyish, but Berger looked obscenely young – like a child.

'Ah yes,' said Berger, 'I think . . . Yes, I see it.'

'There! There you are.' Peters jabbed his finger at the mist.

Shadows gathered and connected: a vertical line acquired definition. Like a theatrical effect, gauzy curtains were drawn back until a pale silhouette was revealed. The object was a makeshift raft with barrels attached to the sides. A figure was leaning against a central post – one arm raised, a hand gripping the upper extremity for support, his right cheek pressed against his own bicep. The man's attitude suggested exhaustion and imminent collapse. Another figure was sitting close by: knees bent, feet flat, head slumped forward.

Lorenz's fingers closed around the safety rail and he felt the intense cold through his gloves. He called out: 'You. Who are you? Identify yourselves.'

A blast of raw wind swept away more of the mist. The figures on the raft did not move. Lorenz tried hailing them in English – but this also had no effect. Above the horizon, the sun showed through the cloud, no more substantial than a faintly drawn circle.

Lorenz raised his binoculars again and focused his attention on the standing figure. The man had empty sockets where his eyes should have been and his nose had been eaten away. Much of the flesh on the exposed side of his face was missing, creating a macabre, lopsided grin. A fringe of icicles hung from his chin, which made him look like a character from a Russian fairytale, a winter goblin or some other supernatural inhabitant of the Siberian steppe. Lorenz shifted his attention to the seated man, whose trousers were torn. Ragged hems revealed the lower bones of his legs. The raft was drifting towards the stationary U-boat and Berger whispered, 'They're dead.'

The milky disc of the sun disappeared.

'But one of them's standing up,' said Peters.

'He must be frozen solid,' replied Kruger.

Lorenz settled the issue. 'They're dead all right.' He handed Peters the binoculars.

The diesel hand whistled. 'That's horrible. How did it happen?'

'Gulls,' said Lorenz. 'They must have pecked out their eyes and torn off strips of flesh as the raft was carried north.'

'Extraordinary,' Peters handed the binoculars to Kruger. 'I've never seen anything like it. And one still standing ... poor bastard.'

'Who are they?' asked Berger.

'They're from a liner,' Lorenz replied. 'Look at those life jackets. They're ancient. A warship wouldn't carry life jackets like that.'

The commander and his men stood, captivated, watching the raft's steady approach. Waves slapped against the hull. Lorenz wondered how long this ghoulish pair had been floating around the arctic and he toyed with a fanciful notion that they might, perhaps, have been adrift for years, even decades.

Kruger handed the binoculars back to Lorenz, who raised them one last time. The lopsided grin of the standing figure was oddly communicative.

'Well,' said Lorenz, letting go of the binoculars and clapping his hands together, 'let's move on. We don't want the

Tommies catching us like this – enjoying the weather and mixing with the locals.'

One of the radio men, Ziegler, stepped out of his room and called out, 'Officer's signal.' Juhl squeezed past some petty officers, collected the message, and set up the decoding machine. He did this with a degree of studied ostentation, supplementing his actions with flourishes reminiscent of a concert artist. The machine looked like a complicated type-writer in a wooden case. In addition to the standard keys, there was a lamp-board, three protruding disc-shaped rotors, and a panel of sockets that could be connected with short lengths of cable. Lorenz handed Juhl a piece of paper on which he had already written the daily code setting. The second-watch officer configured the machine and proceeded to type. His brow furrowed and he turned to address Lorenz. Speaking in a confidential whisper he said, 'For the Commander only.' Lorenz nodded, picked up the machine and took it into his nook, where he readjusted the settings according to his own special instructions.

Receipt of a triply encrypted message was an unusual occurrence. Lorenz could hear the muffled whisper of hushed speculation. When he finally emerged from behind his green curtain, he handed the code machine back to Juhl and climbed through the circular hatchway that led to the control room. He stood by the chart table and studied a mildewed, crumbling map of the North Atlantic. Altering the angle of the lamp, he moved a circle of bright illumination across the grid squares. Above the table was a tangle of pipes and a black iron wheel.

There was a sense of expectation and men started to gather, all of them pretending to be engaged in some crucial task. Lorenz rolled up the sleeves of his jumper and pushed his cap back, exposing his high forehead and a lick of black hair. 'How confident are you – about our position?'

Müller, the navigator, cleared his throat: 'It's been a while since I've looked up into a clear sky.' He slapped his hand on the sextant box. 'So it would be difficult to . . .'

'You're always being over-cautious.'

Lorenz stepped forward and examined Müller's plot. He took a deep breath, turned to face the group of men that had assembled behind him, and called out an order to change course. The helmsman, seated at his station, acknowledged the command and adjusted the position of the rudder. 'Full speed ahead,' Lorenz added. The engine telegraph was reset and a red light began to flash.

Müller glanced down at the chart and said, 'Iceland?'

'Thereabouts . . .'

'Why?'

The red light stopped flashing and turned green.

Lorenz shrugged. 'They didn't say. Well, not exactly.' The diesels roared and the boat lurched forward, freeing itself from the grip of a tenacious wave.

The sea was calm and lit intermittently by a low moon that struggled to find gaps in the cloud. Falk, the first watch officer cried, 'There it is.' He had spotted the other boat – a barely visible shadow among scattered flecks of silver. Immediately, Ziegler was called to the bridge and he emerged from the tower carrying a heavy signal lamp.

'All right,' said Lorenz. 'Let them know we've arrived.'

Light flashed across the darkness and after a few seconds this was answered by an irregular winking.

'He wants the recognition signal,' said Ziegler.

'Monsalvat,' Lorenz replied.

'What?'

'Monsalvat.' Lorenz repeated the name, stressing each syllable. Ziegler did as he was instructed and after a brief pause the signal lamp on the other boat began to wink again. 'A-M-F . . .' The radio man identified each letter but before he could finish Lorenz cut in and said, 'Amfortas.'

'Friends?' said Falk, hopefully.

'Well, I wouldn't go that far,' Lorenz quipped before speaking through the communications pipe: 'Half speed, both engines.' He then requested some minor alterations to their course.

'Small, isn't she?' said Falk.

'And no guns,' Lorenz replied. 'Not what I was expecting.'

Lorenz ordered small arms to be distributed on the bridge. Falk and Ziegler looked uneasy. 'A precautionary measure,' Lorenz reassured them. 'I'm sure we'll be welcomed like the prodigal son.'

As they drew closer, a rift appeared in the clouds and moonlight poured through the opening. 'Well, that should make things a little easier,' said Falk.

Lorenz levelled his binoculars. 'What a tub!'

'Do you have any idea what all this is about?' Falk asked. 'Surely you can say now?'

'Your guess is as good as mine.' Lorenz's breath condensed in front of his mouth. 'The message contained very little information. Anyway, we'll all know soon enough, won't we?' He gestured ahead, 'Almost there now.'

It was cold, but not freezing. The temperature had risen and there were no longer any ice floes on the water. Everything seemed muted, preternaturally still.

U-330 halted alongside the rusting hulk, an old cargo ship with two derricks and a dilapidated superstructure. Figures silently watched the manoeuvre from above. One of them leaned over the rail and shouted: 'Kapitänleutnant Lorenz?'

'Yes?'

'Obersturmbannführer Hans Friedrich – permission to board.'

'Permission granted.'

The men on the bridge glanced at each other. *The SS? What the hell are they doing here?*

A Jacob's ladder was lowered and the SS officer clambered down. The skull-and-crossbones insignia on his cap was conspicuously illuminated as he stepped into the moonlight. 'Heil Hitler,' he said, raising his arm. Lorenz responded with the military salute. 'Welcome aboard U-330, Obersturmbann-führer.'

'An honour, Kapitänleutnant.' The SS man studied Ziegler – who was holding the ladder – and spoke softly to Lorenz, 'If I may – a word in private?' Lorenz led Friedrich away from the tower. Friedrich lifted his lapels and in doing so exposed his death's head ring: not a national decoration, but an award bestowed in recognition of the wearer's personal devotion to the brotherhood's ideals. 'Forgive me. We have very little time and I must be brief. I have two prisoners for you to transport: one a British naval officer, and the other a gentleman whom we believe to be in possession of some extremely sensitive intelligence. They must be taken to your flotilla base imme-diately. Neither you nor any of your crew members are authorized to question the prisoners. Indeed, I would suggest that you avoid all but essential conversation.'

'Who are they?'

'The naval officer is Lieutenant Commander Lawrence Sutherland – a submariner like you.'

'What happened to his boat?'

'I'm afraid I can't say.'

'Does he speak German?'

'A little.'

'And the other prisoner?'

'Professor Bjørnar Grimstad – a Norwegian academic.'

'He's a long way from Oslo.'

'Indeed.'

'What's his subject?'

Friedrich grimaced. 'Herr Kapitänleutnant, I must stress that this is a *special operation*. Your orders . . .' Leaning closer, he whispered, 'Your orders originate from a source close to the Führer. It is essential that they are obeyed to the letter. Get these prisoners to Brest safely. Nothing else need concern you.'

'Of course,' said Lorenz.

Friedrich marched back to the ladder, where he improvised a megaphone with his cupped hands: 'Send them down.'

The British naval officer was the first to land on the deck, a tall, lean man wearing a cap, greatcoat and tattered uniform.

His trousers were torn at the knees, his beard was unkempt, and one of his eyes was bruised and swollen. Even in the half-light it was obvious that he had been severely beaten, possibly tortured. He limped slightly when he moved. The second prisoner was small and elderly, perhaps in his late sixties or early seventies. His grey-blond hair was combed back and myopic eyes squinted through round spectacles. He was spry for his age and appeared to be unharmed. Neither of the captives showed any sign of emotion, their faces were fixed masks of impassivity.

Friedrich stood squarely in front of the British naval officer, feet apart, hands on hips, and snorted with contempt. Then, turning to face Lorenz, he raised his arm once again. 'Heil Hitler.' His ascent was reminiscent of a spider running up a web. The ladder was retrieved and the shadowy figures looking down from above dispersed. Lorenz inclined his head. 'Commander Sutherland, Herr Professor Grimstad, I am Kapitänleutnant Siegfried Lorenz, the commander of this vessel. Allow me to escort you to your new quarters.' They remained expressionless, their eyes giving no indication as to what they might be thinking.

The prisoners were ushered on to the bridge and down through the conning tower hatch. Lorenz noticed that Sutherland was attempting to avoid putting weight on his bad leg.

The interior was illuminated by a red light that made the watchful crew look like a troop of demons.

Richter, one of the mechanics, was undertaking minor repairs, and when he turned to gawp at the arriving prisoners he dropped a heavy wrench which bounced on the rubber link matting and came to rest at Sutherland's feet. The British commander moved swiftly for an injured man. He genuflected and was suddenly standing upright with the tool in his hand. The circle of men tensed, but Sutherland simply gestured for Richter to take it back. When the mechanic grasped the dimpled handle he found that he had to pull it hard to free it from Sutherland's grip.

'The English place a very high value on common courtesies,' said Lorenz.

Richter bowed and said, 'Thank you, sir.'

Sutherland studied the mechanic for a few seconds, showing no emotion, and turned away.

'Let us proceed,' said Lorenz. From the control room the prisoners were marched in single file towards the bow, passing along the officer's mess and between the bunk beds beyond. Cured meats and hard cheeses hung from the overhead and these had to be pushed aside to make progress. They arrived in the forward torpedo room.

'Well, gentlemen,' said Lorenz, speaking in English and sweeping his hand around the restricted space. 'I'm afraid that this is all I can offer you. You'll have to sit on the linoleum, but should a hammock or bunk become available you'll be permitted to lie down. It's not ideal, I realize that. But I've troubled to accommodate you some distance from the engine room – so sleep isn't completely out of the question. We are not accustomed to entertaining guests; however, I suspect that you will find us better hosts than the Schutzstaffel, who are not renowned for their hospitality.' Sutherland's injuries were horribly vivid. His right eye was surrounded by livid bulges and his lips were crusted with carbuncles of dried blood. Lorenz noticed a pattern of crossing lines on the man's fore-head and supposed that they would match the underside of Friedrich's boot.

Lorenz continued, 'Your leg has been hurt. We don't have a doctor on board, but one of the crewmen can perform basic medical duties. I can send him to examine you – if you wish?' Sutherland shook his head. 'Very well.' Lorenz looked from Sutherland to Grimstad. 'Are you thirsty?' he asked, reverting to German. 'Do you want something to eat?' Neither of the captives replied. 'All right, suit yourselves. You can have break-fast along with the rest of us in due course. Kruger?'

'Kaleun?'

'Keep an eye on our guests.'

'Should I tie them up?'

'Tie them up? Where do you think they're going to run?'

Lorenz made his way back to the control room, passing men who looked at him quizzically. After calling out instructions for the boat to be turned round, he spoke to the navigator. 'Plot a course for Brest. The most direct route possible.'

Müller picked up the compasses and parallel ruler. 'Really?'

'Both engines, full speed ahead.' The public address system crackled into life. 'Men,' Lorenz continued, 'we have been ordered to return to base. That is all.' The crew were shocked into silence. Then, gradually, expressions changed and before long every one of them was grinning inanely. Excitement and relief had turned U-330 into a ship of fools.

Lorenz was sitting in the officers' mess with Juhl, Falk and Graf – the Chief Engineer. They were all hunched over the rectangular table top, conspiratorially close, their heads bowed beneath a shaded lamp. The steward was serving them coffee.

'We've all heard talk of death rays and the bomb,' said Falk. 'You know, the big one, the one that can destroy whole cites.'

'The old boy's a scientist. Obviously,' said Graf. The chief engineer was dressed casually – a chequered shirt, a sleeveless pullover, and a loosely knotted scarf. On his head he wore a blue peaked cap.

'It seems inconceivable,' said Juhl, 'that a single explosion could cause so much destruction.'

'How does it work?' asked Falk. 'This bomb?'

'Why don't you go and ask the old boy?' Graf suggested.

'He's not very talkative,' said Lorenz.

'Nor is the Tommy,' Juhl observed.

'They don't like us,' Lorenz replied. 'It's inexplicable.'

'Look, I understand why we're not supposed to ask them any questions,' Falk persisted. 'But what I can't understand is why they're being quite so reticent. They haven't said a word. They haven't even asked for a glass of water.'

'I wonder if they were captured separately or together?' Graf mused.

'They might not know each other at all,' Juhl speculated. 'What if they're strangers, thrown together by chance?'

'Oh, I'm not sure about that,' said Falk. 'I think I can sense . . .' The sentence trailed off and he rippled his fingers next to his ear.

'What?' A note of mistrust sounded in Juhl's voice.

'Something,' Falk continued. 'You know . . . *something* between them, an affinity.'

Juhl pursed his lips and replied, 'I haven't sensed anything.'

'Perhaps the Norwegian resistance helped the scientist escape and sailed him out to a British submarine.' Falk's bright blue eyes were like discs of glazed china. 'Perhaps a technical fault prevented the submarine from diving and it was discovered by one of our destroyers. The British surrendered and the two most important prisoners – the officer and the scientist – were whisked away in that rusty merchantman.'

'Yes, but why put them in a cargo ship?' Juhl challenged.

'Safety?' Falk ventured. 'A hulk like that isn't an obvious military target.'

'We haven't received any news of a British submarine being sunk or captured,' said Lorenz, 'not recently and certainly not in these waters.'

'Special operations,' Graf grumbled. 'Who knows what's going on? We're wasting our time thinking about it.'

'Iceland,' said Lorenz. Before he could elaborate, Kruger appeared. Lorenz acknowledged his arrival and added, 'Aren't you supposed to be keeping an eye on our guests?'

'Dressel's taken my place, sir,' said Kruger.

'Is there a problem?'

'The old boy – something's wrong with him. His eyelids started fluttering and now he's talking to himself. It's like he's in a trance or having some kind of fit.'

Lorenz's companions stood to let him squeeze out from behind the table and he followed Kruger between the bunks to the torpedo room. Sutherland was leaning against the torpedo tube doors but Grimstad was seated on the linoleum with his legs stretched out in front of him; between his trembling eyelids only thin white crescents were visible. His lips were moving and he was mumbling quietly. When Lorenz crouched next to Grimstad he was unable to identify what language the professor was speaking, but the pattern of stresses and the vowel sounds suggested a Germanic dialect. Spittle adhered to the old man's beard like threads of cotton. As Lorenz listened he detected regularities, insistent repetitions and an underlying pulse that reminded him of religious chanting. He reached out and shook the old man's shoulder. 'Professor? Can you hear me?' Grimstad's head rolled lazily from side to side.

'Shall I get Ziegler?' Kruger asked.

Lorenz ignored the question and turned to address Sutherland. He spoke in English. 'Does this man have a medical condition?' The British commander communicated his ignorance with a shrug. Lorenz tried again: 'Was he beaten? Did he receive a blow to the head?'

'I don't think so,' Sutherland replied. It was the first time the British commander had spoken and his voice was hoarse.

Lorenz glanced at Kruger and reverted to German. 'How long has the professor been like this?'

'Not long,' Kruger replied. 'I came to get you as soon as he started acting strange.'

'Yes, but how long was that?' Lorenz persisted. 'One minute, two minutes . . .?'

'About two minutes,' said Kruger. 'No longer than that.'

'Professor?' Lorenz shook the old man's shoulder with greater force. 'Wake up!' Grimstad snapped out of his delirium.

His eyes opened and his right hand, moving with unexpected independence and speed, traced a triangle in the air, its simple, inclusive geometry seemed to connect the professor and the two commanders. The movement was too precise to be unconscious and Lorenz was reminded of the sign of the cross, the symbolic unification of the trinity by means of two intersecting lines. This curious association made Lorenz feel uneasy. The old man blinked, drew his legs up to his chest and wrapped his arms around his knees. 'Professor?' Lorenz inquired. 'Are you all right?' Grimstad moistened his lips with the tip of his tongue and whispered in perfect, deliberate German: 'The fetters will burst and the wolf run free, much do I know and more can see.' The old man closed his eyes and his head fell forward as if exhausted by extreme effort. A small flat stone with smooth edges dropped from his left hand. Lorenz picked it up. Something had been scratched on one side: a triangle attached to a vertical line.

Dawn. The waves were the colour of green glass; not the luminous, emerald green produced by light passing through a church window, but the inert, opaque green of a beer bottle. White streamers leapt from rising crests and hung in the air before finally succumbing to the pull of gravity. Lorenz hadn't been able to sleep. He had been too preoccupied. Gazing across the sea, the same unanswered questions were continuously revolving through his mind. He tapped Juhl on the shoulder, indicated that he was about to leave the bridge, and climbed down the ladder which descended through the conning tower to the control room. Graf acknowledged his return and without pausing, Lorenz marched to the forward torpedo room. It looked as if the two prisoners hadn't moved. Blankets had been provided and Grimstad had used his to make sitting more comfortable. His eyes were closed and he was embracing his knees. Sutherland had remained standing and his blanket was untouched. Lorenz inclined his head at Sutherland and extended his arm towards the crew quarters: 'This way, please.' The British commander limped between the occupied bunks, past the officers' mess and into the area between Lorenz's nook and the radio shack. Fresh air from the bridge was passing through the compartment, displacing the ripe stench of body odour. Lorenz noticed how Sutherland was looking around and how he ducked quickly to get a better view of the crowded control room through the hatchway.

'I know what you are thinking,' said Lorenz. 'I would be just the same if I had been captured. But you can't escape.' Ziegler peeped out of the radio shack. 'This is my cabin,' said Lorenz. He pulled a green curtain aside, revealing a bed and small cabinet. 'Please sit.' He offered Sutherland a chair, tugged the curtain along the rail to its original position and sat on the mattress. There was so little space that the curtain was touching the back of Sutherland's head. The British commander removed his cap and placed it on the cabinet. Lorenz opened a drawer, took out a bottle of rum, and poured the dark liquid into a small glass. He swirled the contents, inhaled, and then, after taking a sip, he continued in a breezy, conversational tone, 'So what happened to your boat?' Sutherland pressed his lips together. The pattern of crossed lines on his forehead had faded but his right eye remained discoloured and swollen. 'There is an English expression – what is it now? – "There but for the grace of God go I". Is that right? I am sorry you lost your boat.'

'You have no authority to interrogate me.' Sutherland's delivery was crisp and bureaucratic, a statement of fact.

The two men stared at each other.

'You think I'm interrogating you?' Lorenz smiled. 'You must have a very short memory, Commander Sutherland. The Schutzstaffel interrogated you. What happened to your boat? I'm curious.' He held out the glass of rum. Sutherland's Adam's apple bobbed up and down as he swallowed. 'Go on,' said Lorenz. 'Take it. Nobody's watching.' Sutherland's resolve broke. He snatched the glass and emptied it down his throat. When he had finished he was slightly flushed and breathless. 'Another?' Lorenz filled the glass a second time and Sutherland drank more slowly. 'Well? What happened to your boat?'

Sutherland placed the glass next to his cap and folded his arms. Lorenz sighed. 'How often do opportunities like this arise? How often do we get a chance to speak with our opposites? What harm will it do – a little civilized conversation?' Lorenz poured more rum into the glass. 'Where are you from? London? I know London very well. Kensington, Mayfair, Hyde Park . . . Buckingham Palace. I used to enjoy the changing of the guards.' Lorenz picked up the glass and took a few sips. 'Have you had a good war? I am close to 50,000 tons.'

'You must be very proud,' Sutherland responded with haughty contempt.

'Destruction is *your* purpose – as much as it is mine.'

'It was your Führer who invaded Poland.'

'Come now, since when were we anything but the servants of our political masters?' Lorenz snatched Sutherland's cap, placed it on his own head and repeated, 'There but for the grace of God . . .' The British commander held out his hand, silently requesting the return of his property. Lorenz obliged and said, 'What's wrong with Grimstad?' He pointed towards the torpedo room. 'Did he have a seizure? The Schutzstaffel will be very unhappy if the old man doesn't survive the journey. He must be very important. My crew think he's a physicist. Are they right?' Lorenz showed Sutherland the small flat stone that Grimstad had been holding. 'What's this? Have you any idea? It has some sort of symbol scratched on it? See?

Do you know what it means?' Sutherland remained stubbornly silent.

After a further ten minutes of unproductive questioning Lorenz said, 'Well, I can see that you are finding my company dull. Perhaps we should try again later. We could go up to the bridge for a cigarette. Would you like that?' The British commander stood, put on his cap and adjusted its position while observing his pale reflection in a polished wooden panel. Although Lorenz had brought the interview to a close, he was left with the uncomfortable impression that it was not he who had dismissed Sutherland, but Sutherland who had dismissed him.

In the control room, the men were at their posts, pretending that they were unaware of the illicit conference that had just taken place. Graf stepped closer to Lorenz, but before he could speak, Lorenz said, 'I gave him some rum, that's all. Besides, who's going to report it?'

'What did you find out, Kaleun?' Asked Graf.

'Nothing,' Lorenz replied.

Lorenz, Falk and Graf were sitting in the officers' mess waiting for breakfast to be served.

'Iceland,' said Lorenz. 'The SS sent a group of German scholars there, didn't they? Before the British invaded?'

'Yes,' said Graf. 'They went there to study the people. I can remember reading about it in a magazine. And they were interested in the museums – they took photographs of some of the exhibits.'

'What exhibits?' Falk asked.

'I don't know,' Graf responded. 'Old things – archaeological remains – I've forgotten now.'

'Why?'

'They wanted to *acquire* them. They wanted to put them in our museums – I suppose.' Graf tightened the knot of his neck scarf. 'Where's breakfast? I'm extremely hungry.'

'A few years ago I had to attend a Party function,' said Lorenz. 'There was this SS man there. His name was Schweizer—' Raised voices could be heard coming from the crew quarters. Lorenz looked towards the forward compartment hatchway and a moment later men came stumbling through the opening. Kruger was among them. 'Herr Kaleun, the British officer is armed: he drew a gun and I . . .' Kruger almost fell as the bosun and one of his mates pushed past him.

'Shit,' said Lorenz. The officers stood abruptly – Graf and Falk struggling to get out from behind the table.

'Do you still have your pistol?' Lorenz asked Falk.

'No,' he replied.

'Well get it.'

'Where are you going?'

'Where do you think?'

Lorenz reached into his jacket and pulled out his Mauser. He had been so preoccupied since collecting the two prisoners that he had neglected to put it back in the gun locker. Gesturing for the crewmen to hurry, he waited until they were all behind him before advancing up the narrow gangway between the bunks. The hanging meats and cheeses obscured his view, but he was still able to see the British commander standing in front of the tube doors. Lorenz wondered why Sutherland was standing in such an exposed position: he didn't appear to be aiming straight ahead, he had his gun pressed against his chest with the barrel pointing off to the side.

'Commander Sutherland,' Lorenz spoke calmly in English, 'put down your weapon. We are many in number and you will be overpowered. Put down your weapon, now. My orders are to transport you and Herr Professor Grimstad to France – safely – and that is what I intend to do.'

Two shots fired. Lorenz dived onto one of the lower bunks and aimed his Mauser into the torpedo room. He saw Sutherland sway for a moment and then fall. When Lorenz glanced down he discovered that Falk had crawled up the gangway on his stomach. He was also clutching a pistol.

'Kaleun? Are you all right?'

'Yes, I'm all right.'

'What's he doing?'

'I think he just shot himself.'

'And the other one? Is he armed too?'

'I haven't seen him yet.' Lorenz called out, 'Professor Grimstad? Professor Grimstad?'

Smoke drifted through the air and the smell of gunpowder mixed with the aroma of the foodstuffs.

'Shall I put a bullet in him, just to make sure?' asked Falk.

'We were supposed to be ensuring their safe passage to Brest. I can't help feeling that your suggestion is contrary to the spirit of our orders.'

'What if he's trying to lure us closer?'

'I don't think so, Falk. If I'm not mistaken he's losing a large amount of blood from a hole in his head.'

'I can't see it from here.'

'I can.'

Lorenz climbed out of the bunk and proceeded towards the bow. 'Herr Professor Grimstad?' When he entered the torpedo room he saw the old man sitting on his blanket and leaning over to one side. Lorenz crouched beside him and examined the upper part of his body. The entry point of the bullet was clearly visible and the old man's coat had started to stain. He had been shot through the heart.

'What a mess,' said Falk. The torpedo tube doors and the surrounding pipes had been sprayed with blood. 'It's a miracle he didn't cause any damage.' Men were gathering around the entrance: Juhl, Graf, Richter and the two torpedo mechanics – Kruger and Dressel. 'Keep back,' said Lorenz. He crawled over to Sutherland, who was lying with his face pressed against the linoleum. The back of his skull had been blown away, revealing a glistening, wet, grey-pink interior. Around the rim of the hole were shards of jagged, broken bone. When Lorenz rolled the dead officer over he discovered that the man's eyes were still open and curiously bright. Lumps of matter that had stuck to the overhead began to drop. Something landed on Lorenz's hand and when he brushed it off it left a brown trail. He wiped the slimy residue on his trousers and suppressed the urge to retch.

The dead man was still gripping his weapon. Lorenz pointed it out to Falk and said, 'A Walther PPK: favoured by the SS and party officials.'

'How on earth did he get hold of that?'

Lorenz stood up. 'There was either a double agent on board the cargo ship or Obersturmbannführer Friedrich made a gross error of judgment concerning his estimation of Commander Sutherland's dexterity.' More pieces of brain tissue fell from the overhead and splattered at their feet. Falk looked up and his face shrivelled with disgust. 'They won't be persuaded to part with their secrets now, will they?' Lorenz added as he looked from one corpse to the other.

'The SS aren't going to be very happy, Kaleun.'

'You have a real gift for understatement, Falk.'

'Well, as long as they don't try to blame us for their own incompetence.'

'Yes, God forbid. Lucky there's no chance of that happening.'

'They can't – *can they*? What about the evidence, the PPK?'

'Are you pretending to be naïve for my amusement, Falk?' The first watch officer stiffened. 'No, Herr Kaleun.'

'Good,' said Lorenz, 'because I'm not laughing.'

Lorenz left the torpedo room shouting orders. 'Someone get this place cleaned up. And Ziegler . . . where are you, Ziegler?'

With the radio man's assistance Lorenz sent a message to U-boat headquarters explaining what had occurred. He then retired to his nook and made an entry in his log. It did not take very long for the command centre to respond and their communication was remarkably succinct: BURY PRISONERS AT SEA. RESUME PATROL. PROCEED AT ONCE AND AT FULL SPEED TO GRID AK 21.

As soon as the order was announced the boat became subdued. Fantasies were reluctantly relinquished, imaginary jazz bands fell silent and spectral girls retreated into darkness. The Casino Bar, with its promise of sensual delights and sweet champagne, was reconsigned to memory. Lorenz detected a subtle undertow of nervous agitation flowing beneath the palpable disappointment, and after some reflection, he concluded that the cause was very likely the proximity of the dead. Sailors were notoriously superstitious.

When Lorenz returned to the forward torpedo room he was pleased to find the area clean and smelling of carbolic. The two bodies had been laid out next to each other, arms by their sides.

'What do we do now?' asked Juhl.

'Search them,' Lorenz replied.

Sutherland's pockets were empty but Grimstad had been carrying a small notebook. Juhl stood and handed it to his superior. 'It'll be full of mathematical equations.' Lorenz flicked the pages and a wry smile appeared on his face. 'What?' Juhl inquired.

There were no numbers in the notebook. Instead, it was filled with neatly copied symbols composed of straight lines of varying length. Some of these symbols resembled letters – one was like an 'F', another like an 'R' – and the way they were grouped suggested words and sentences.

'Look,' said Lorenz, holding the notebook open.

Juhl squinted. 'Runes?'

'That's what I think.'

'It could still be a code.'

'But why choose runes?'

'I don't know.'

'Perhaps Professor Grimstad wasn't a scientist after all. Perhaps he was a specialist in old Norse languages – or a historian of some kind.'

'What possible use would such a man be to the SS? What could a historian know that's *so* important?'

'The SS have obscure interests.'

'Even so, Kaleun.'

Lorenz put the notebook in his pocket and ordered Voigt to find some clean blankets. The bodies were wrapped and carried onto the deck. Above the eastern horizon the clouds were aglow with a sickly, putrescent light. Lorenz called for the boat to be stopped and descended the conning tower. He read the burial service and the two bodies were tipped into the ocean. One of the seamen made the sign of the cross and Lorenz was reminded of the professor's odd gesture, the triangle the old man had drawn in the air on coming round after his 'seizure'. The waves were slow-moving and evenly spaced. Lorenz touched the cover of Grimstad's notebook with his fingertips. What had the SS been up to?

Lorenz was dreaming and in his dream he was standing on the deck, observing the slow materialization of an approaching raft in a vertical column of moonlight. The tableau was vaguely familiar: two figures, one standing with a raised arm and the other sitting and slumped forward. Ice floes were knocking together and a frozen mist was depositing crystals on his beard. He looked through his binoculars and expected to see empty sockets and an exposed jawbone. Instead, he found himself looking into the neutral eyes of the British commander. Sitting at Sutherland's feet was Professor Grimstad. Lorenz heard a voice and it was only when the sentence had ended that he recognized it as his own: 'No, I'm not coming with you.' He was no longer asleep and he was breathing shallow and fast. Reaching out, he tugged the curtain aside. Lehmann was turning the hydrophone wheel, his features illuminated by the glowing dial, his ears obscured by headphones. Clearly, he hadn't been disturbed. Lorenz turned on the lamp, listened to the electric motors, and wondered if the wind was still whipping up twenty metre crests on the surface. U-330 was sailing silently through a dark green void, high over submerged summits and valleys that had never known light. An image came into Lorenz's mind. He pictured a monstrous sea creature roused by the sound of the boat's screws: sucker-bearing tentacles stirring ancient sediment, fish with bulging eyes and whiskers scattering in black water.

The following day the cloud-cover was low and oppressive: a sagging canopy of grey beneath which dirty yellow scraps were blown along at high speed. Juhl and his companions gazed out over a sea that looked as if each wave had been cast from iron. An untrustworthy light created a disconcerting illusion of arrested movement, a bleak, metallic uniformity that extended in every direction to the wide horizon and resembled the surface of a dying planet. Raindrops tapped irregular rhythms on the rubberized cloth of Juhl's foul-weather gear. The second watch officer's cheeks had become encrusted with salt and his dry lips were striped with black lines where the skin had broken and bled. His balaclava seemed to offer no protection from the malicious wind.

'This is shit,' said Hoffmann, an electrician with a broad Bavarian accent. It made him stand out because most U-boat men were from the north.

'I don't know,' Juhl responded. 'Things could be worse.'

'Could they, sir?'

'Well, imagine what it would be like if you were in the army. Just think of it, all that square bashing and posturing, getting shot at all the time. We don't have to go on long marches, we don't have to eat dog meat on the eastern front, Werner is an excellent cook, and our service uniforms are really very eye-catching.' Juhl took a deep breath. 'And smell that fresh sea air! Bracing, medicinal, it's like being on a cruise.'

'You've been spending too much time with the skipper,' said Hoffmann.

It was an astute observation. Echoes of the commander's habitual sarcasm could be heard in Juhl's speech, a hint of weary resignation, grim humour. The second watch officer raised his binoculars and studied the livid, pitiless expanse. 'You may be right,' he muttered.

'The wife's pregnant,' said Hoffmann.

'Congratulations,' Juhl laughed. 'When is the baby due?'

'About now, sir.'

'What do you want, a boy or a girl?'

'I already have a son,' said Hoffmann. Suddenly, he seemed embarrassed by his personal disclosures. 'This is shit. How long have we been at sea now, sir?'

'Too long. Sometimes I feel like the flying Dutchman . . .'

The boat continued along its course, the bow carving through the swell and producing two frothy trails. A faint melody drifted up through the hatch. Someone, probably Richter, was playing a ballad on the accordion and Hoffmann croaked along with the chorus, '*Embrasse moi, embrasse-moi.*' The music had the effect of detaching Juhl from his surroundings and he pictured the familiar smoky lounge of a Brest hotel, where a scrawny, aging chanteuse with a taste for revealing dresses frequently enacted the end of love affairs on a makeshift stage. He saw her superimposed on the waves, making violent gestures and shaking her mane of badly dyed hair. The vision absorbed him completely until one of the lookouts screamed – 'Aircraft! Sixty degrees!' – and Juhl was jolted back to reality. Even in the second or two it took to confirm the sighting the plane seemed to become inordinately large.

'Alarm!' Juhl extended the cry until his lungs had no more air in them. The men scrambled into the tower, hardly making contact with the steps, sliding their hands down the ladder rails to guide their fall. Juhl followed. Boots landed on the matting with a loud thud. The bell was ringing, a bright continuous clamour.

In the control room Graf's voice was loud and urgent. 'Flood! Flood! All hands forward.' The diesel engines were shut down and the crew in the stern compartments ran towards the bow in order to increase its weight. Two men near the front stumbled and those running behind simply leapt over the sprawled bodies. The vents were opened and the air that had been keeping the boat afloat was released, producing a bellicose roar, the dive tanks filled and U-330 became heavier. As the hydroplane operators pressed their control buttons the deck angled downwards and the pointer on the manometer began to move. Lorenz steadied himself by leaning against the silver shaft of the observation periscope. There was a loud booming noise as one final, rolling mass of water crashed against the tower and then, apart from the gentle humming of the electric motors, silence prevailed.

In theory, they could achieve 150 metres in thirty seconds, but this assumed optimal levels of performance from the crew, and human beings were not machines.

Depending on conditions a U-boat might be detectable as a shadow even at a depth of sixty metres. A direct hit wasn't necessary to destroy a U-boat. Anywhere within the parameters of a mathematically defined 'lethal radius' the laws of physics would allow a shock wave, travelling though the dense medium of water, to rip the boat apart. Lorenz remembered visiting the Krupp shipyard in Kiel: so many rivets, so much welding. He was agonizingly aware of the numerous weak seams that made the boat vulnerable. The entire crew were cowed in readiness.

Two deafening explosions followed. Deck-plates jumped and water splashed in the bilges. Maps and compasses fell from the chart table and the accordion smashed into the fore bulkhead. The depth charges had detonated over the bow, forcing the boat down and increasing the steepness of its dive.

'Very accurate,' said Lorenz, almost approvingly. 'This one's experienced.'

Graf glanced at the manometer and shouted orders at the hydroplane operators. Now they were descending too fast. 'Motors, full speed.' The additional power failed to pull them out of the dive. 'Damn it!' Graf addressed Lorenz. 'We're not levelling off.' Fear blanched complexions like a rapidly spreading contagion.

There were two more explosions, the lights went out, and the hull rocked from side to side. Lorenz felt a hand on his shoulder. Long fingers tensed and the grip tightened. He couldn't recall a prior instance of the chief engineer choosing to express his solidarity with such a gesture and hoped that it was not intended as a private farewell. Torch beams flashed and Lorenz was surprised to hear Graf's voice over the public-address system, 'We're bow-heavy. All hands astern.' Graf wasn't standing behind Lorenz, he had moved away. The shimmering emergency lights came on as the men from the bow compartment clambered up the gradient and through the control room. Amid the subsequent commotion, Lorenz was not conscious of the exact moment when the hand on his shoulder released its grip; however, he was still curious enough to turn, and when he did so, he was bemused to find that he was staring only at pipes and cables.

The manometer pointer was slowing down and the tilt of the boat was becoming less severe. Graf stepped towards Lorenz and said, 'We're definitely getting back on an even keel. Thank God.' He wiped the sweat from his forehead.

'Ninety metres,' said Lorenz. 'He won't be able to see us now.'

'Well, let's hope we're not leaving a nice oil slick for him to follow.'

A few seconds later the sound of dripping could be heard. Graf produced a torch and directed the beam close to the overhead on the port side. He lowered his gaze and studied the system of complex, serpentine pipes that descended to the matting next to the chart table. With his head tilted and his neck stretched, he looked like a mime artist. The regular beat of the droplets stopped. Graf shrugged, slid the torch back in his pocket, and returned to his former position in order to resume his scrutiny of the instruments.

'We'll stay down here for a while,' said Lorenz. 'He's bound to get bored and fly off. They always do. Airmen have no patience.'

Graf nodded. 'All right, Kaleun, but not for too long.' He touched his ear to draw the commander's attention to a trickling sound that could be heard above the hum of the electric motors.

The deck plates rattled and somewhere in the boat a low creaking began. It recalled an earlier age of maritime adventure, taut ropes and the complaining timbers of a galleon. One of the hydroplane operators looked over his shoulder, his face pinched by a flicker of anxiety. There was a sharp crack, like a gunshot, that seemed to come from the petty officers' quarters. 'The woodwork,' said Lorenz. 'That's odd.'

'We're only at ninety metres,' said Graf.

There was a prolonged rumble like the sound of a distant storm: hammerings and a sudden, sonorous clang. Lorenz struggled to reconcile the depth reading on the manometer with the ominous noises. It was difficult not to think of the cold, dark water, pressing against the 2.5 cm metal hull, weighing down from above – squeezing the gunwales – unimaginable tonnage. It was how most U-boat men died in the end – a long, fatal descent – crushed to death, when the circular frames gave way and the pressure hull collapsed.

A metallic groan increased in volume until it became a horrible yowl. The sound conjured up images of torment, medieval depictions of writhing bodies and winged devils. Then, a jet of water spurted horizontally from a point above the hydroplane operators. It was so powerful that it crossed most of the control room before curving downwards to hit the matting.

Several voices screamed in unison, 'Breach!'

'I'll deal with it.' The control room mate leapt up and with the assistance of Müller, they endeavoured to repair the rupture.

Before calm had been restored a diesel-hand appeared. 'Herr Kaleun, air valve leaking badly.'

Lorenz looked at Graf. 'What's happening? It feels like we're in the cellar.' *The cellar* was the term that they used to describe depths below 250 metres; depths at which the metal casing between the armoured sections of the boat would buckle.

Two thin sprays discharged into the atmosphere. The air misted and haloes appeared around the lights. Graf found the source and beckoned Richter. 'Secure this rivet – quick as you can. If it shoots out it'll travel faster than a bullet.'

Another shout from astern: 'Breach in the diesel room.'

Lorenz struck the conning tower ladder with his fist and swore. 'Shit.'

The pointer of the manometer was quivering slightly. Lorenz leaned closer and, reaching out, tapped the glass with his finger. It was an action that resonated with a distant memory of his grandfather. The old fellow had been in the habit of coaxing a sluggish barometer into life by employing the same technique – a dial mounted on carved wood, a brass rim that had blackened with age – Lorenz could remember the object in minute detail.

The quivering pointer suddenly jumped.

One hundred and fifteen . . .

Yet, the boat clearly wasn't sinking.

'Fuck,' said Graf. 'The pointer must have been stuck.'

They looked on in horror as their actual depth was revealed.

One hundred and twenty, one hundred and thirty metres . . .

The pointer on the dial face moved from the orange arc into the red.

One hundred and eighty metres, one hundred and ninety metres . . .

An eternity seemed to elapse before the pointer finally came to rest at 210 metres – well over twice the depth of the shipyard's safety guarantee.

Lorenz was surrounded by bloodless faces, waxy death masks floating in space. They were all thinking the same thing: so much water above them, so much weight. One of the men was nervously clawing at his skin and another had developed a tic. Yet, none of those gathered around the manometer lost control. The veneer of competence and firmness of purpose did not fracture. Vice Admiral Dönitz's dictum had been drummed into them: the men of a U-boat crew were a 'community of fate' – their lives were in each other's hands.

Joint responsibility strengthened their determination, but every commander understood that indoctrination, even when thorough, could not prohibit fear indefinitely. There would always be a breaking point.

'Prepare to surface,' said Lorenz.

The watch reassembled beneath the tower. Graf issued instructions to the hydroplane operators and compressed air was released into the buoyancy tanks. The manometer pointer remained fixed at 210 metres. 'Come on!' Lorenz growled. He rapped his knuckle against the glass. Metal moaned and the hull shivered, every member of the crew was willing the boat to rise. The manometer pointer started to move, so slowly, at first, that its progress was barely discernible.

One hundred and eighty-five, one hundred and eighty . . .

The men in the control room closed their eyes and sighed with relief, and those among them who believed in a watchful intercessory God offered silent thanks.

Lorenz grinned at Graf.

The chief engineer frowned and said, 'We're not there yet, Kaleun.' His forehead was glistening with perspiration.

'Ever the optimist,' Lorenz replied. 'Take her up to forty-five metres.' He ordered the helmsman to zigzag at this depth before calling out, 'Twenty-five.' Then, Lorenz swung through the fore bulkhead hatchway and crouched outside the sound room. Lehmann was turning his hand wheel this way, then that, and listening intently through his headphones. He was leaning forward, eyes raised, as if he could see through the overhead and all the way to the surface. This looking heavenward might have suggested religious transport, but his gaunt features were lit from below, producing a rather sinister, ghoulish effect.

'Can you hear anything?' asked Lorenz

'No,' Lehmann replied, 'nothing at all.'

'Good.' Lorenz returned to the control room through the

hatchway and called out, 'Periscope depth.' Graf reduced speed to minimize vibrations and Lorenz sat on the periscope saddle. He unfolded the hand grips, closed his left eye, and pressed the orbit of his right eye against the rubber circlet of the ocular lens. After adjusting the magnification and the angle of the mirror he studied the dark bands of cloud. The sky vanished as the periscope dipped beneath the surface. 'Depth-keeping, please,' said Lorenz, mildly irritated. Graf apologized and a few moments later the top of the periscope cleared the waves once again. Visibility could have been better, but Lorenz was fairly confident that the aircraft had gone. 'We live to fight another day. Surface!' Over the hissing of compressed air the crew began conversing normally. 'Equalize pressure,' said Graf. 'Man the bilge pumps.' The dispersal of tension was the cause of much hysterical laughter. Eventually, the sea could be heard outside and the diesel engines were engaged. Lorenz ascended the conning tower ladder and opened the hatch. Fresh air poured into the boat, dispelling the stink of fear. He could hear Juhl coming up behind him, singing 'Embrasse-moi'.

When the boat was back on course and all the routine procedures restored, Lorenz summoned Graf: 'Well? What are we going to do about that manometer?'

'I'll check it, Kaleun,' said the chief engineer.

'Yes,' said Lorenz, 'I think you'd better.'

Later, Lorenz retired to his nook. The entry he made in his

war diary was telegraphic and devoid of drama: '15.35 Attacked by aircraft. Four depth charges. Minor damage.' He lay back on the mattress and remembered the lights going out in the control room, the hand landing heavily on his shoulder. Another sensation had registered at the time, but since then he'd been far too distracted to think about it. Now he closed his eyes and recreated the moment, acknowledging a host of memories that had hitherto been competing for attention among the marginalia of consciousness. The hand had been cold. He had felt frozen tendrils taking root in his flesh and curling around his bones and the coldness had intensified as the long fingers tensed.

The peculiarity of the memory made him doubt its fidelity. It was common knowledge that the brain was an unreliable record-keeper in extreme situations. Everything could become sharp and hard-edged or distant and dreamlike. He pieced together a reassuring scenario: in the darkness one of the crew had mistakenly laid a hand on his shoulder and the coldness of Lorenz's own fear had become localized at the point of contact. Realizing his mistake, the embarrassed crew man, most probably Krausse, had slipped away before the emergency lights had come on. *Yes*, Lorenz thought. He snapped the war diary shut. *That's it. That's what must have happened.* Yet he wasn't wholly persuaded and a feeling of unease persisted.

*

The swell was high and the boat rolled. Two books tumbled onto the rubber matting and the chart chest slipped a few inches. Through the circle of the open hatch it was possible to see black clouds. Howling squalls were accompanied by a rattling assault of hailstones. Lorenz lurched down the gangway to the officers' mess where he found Falk and Graf. Falk was serving potato soup from a tureen suspended above the table. It was impossible to ladle the thin gruel into the bowls without spilling any. The grey liquid collected in wide pools, and when the boat heeled, it flowed under the rails and slopped onto the officers' laps. None of them reacted.

'So,' Lorenz addressed Graf. 'Is the manometer working?'

'Yes, Kaleun,' Graf replied. 'It's fine.'

'What do you mean, fine?' Lorenz protested. By the time the soup spoon had reached his mouth it was already empty.

'I've checked everything.'

'And . . .?'

'It's in perfect working order.'

'Then why did it malfunction?'

'I don't know, Kaleun – just one of those things.'

'One of those things,' Lorenz repeated, shaking his head. The steward appeared and tried to wipe the table with a rag. 'Not now, Keller.' The steward retreated. Above their heads, the tureen swung away from the hull and more potato soup splashed onto their trousers.

'I've been thinking about our guests,' said Falk.

'Really?' said Lorenz, finally transferring some soup from the bowl to his mouth.

'Have you had a chance to look through the old man's notebook?'

'Yes.'

'And did you find anything of interest, apart from the runes, I mean?'

'That's all there is – runes. Perhaps those rumours about death rays and the big bomb are all wrong. Perhaps the SS intend to win this war using magic.'

More soup rained down on the table. Graf swore at the tureen and then said, 'Maybe he put a curse on the mano-meter.'

It was a flippant remark, but it caused discomfort rather than amusement.

'We were . . . unlucky,' said Falk, eager to fill the uncom-fortable silence. 'That's all. Like you said – one of those things.'

'Yes,' Graf's head moved up and down emphatically, 'one of those things.'

When Lorenz went back to his nook he opened his drawer. He reached in for the bottle of rum but was startled by an unanticipated sensation. His fingers closed around the stone Grimstad had been holding when the old man was having his fit. It was definitely warm. Lorenz rubbed it between his thumb and forefinger. He wasn't mistaken – the stone was very warm – almost hot.

The BBC German-language broadcast – relayed over the public-address system – began with a familiar call: 'Attention! Attention! This is Viktor Ferdinand, the chief, speaking.' The men responded with a communal cheer. Viktor Ferdinand purported to be a high-ranking, old guard 'brown shirt', but nobody believed that. It was assumed that he was a bilingual Englishman who spoke extremely good German. He delivered his lines with the panache of a skilled actor. Ferdinand began by vilifying the upper echelons of the Party and then pouring scorn over certain members of the SS. He accused them of dandyism, effeminacy and cowardice. Some fictitious military blunders were reported and Göring was accused of rank incompetence. Curiously, Ferdinand never ridiculed the Führer. Given the messianic psychology of the German people, or at least their *perceived* messianic psychology, the British may have thought that to criticize a demigod was unwise. Everyone was eagerly anticipating the final part of the programme, which was typically dedicated to a salacious exposé. Some of the crew had started to laugh merely thinking about what was to come.

'So,' said Ferdinand, delaying his revelation, toying with his audience. 'So . . . let us now turn our attention to the mayor of Bremen, a dear friend of Himmler and a great supporter of the party, a man who has taken a keen interest in youth projects and has donated a considerable sum of money to the war widows' foundation. What sort of a man is he, this fine, upstanding pillar of the community, this distinguished humanitarian and champion of high culture: this servant of the people, frequently photographed with school children, urging them, like a kind uncle, to aspire to the elevated ideals that he holds so dear – purity, duty and valour? Ah yes, purity, purity.' It was easy to imagine an accompanying sneer. 'Allow me to enlighten you.' There was another dramatic pause. 'For many years now the mayor has been a problematic figure for his party associates on account of his irregular appetites. Be that as it may, his political sponsors have been unstinting in their efforts to conceal his disgraceful predilections. But there is only so much you can do for a man like the mayor of Bremen, a man who has become so inflated with his own self-importance that he no longer feels obliged to exercise discretion. Our sources have revealed that only last week, the good mayor presided over an orgy in the Town Hall, in which he and his guests were excited by the obscene spectacle of five Polish fisherwomen defecating.'

Every compartment in the boat filled with laughter and a hail of swiftly interjected quips.

'Not content with such gross depravity,' Ferdinand's delivery was portentous, 'the mayor then invited several of his female guests to urinate over his manhood, and he subsequently demonstrated that his taste for expensive French wines is complemented by a weakness for an altogether less refined vintage.'

Again the crew were quick to respond. *Sounds just like the Casino Bar – Perhaps we should invite him – But only if he promises to bring those Poles.*

Before long the crew were laughing so much that the broadcast could no longer be heard. Only occasional words – 'degeneracy', 'baseness', 'hypocrisy' – floated above the shrieks and guffaws. Sailors were wiping away tears, slapping thighs, and falling out of bunks. In due course, Ferdinand made his final appeal. 'Comrades, don't let this go on! Report it to Minister Dr Lammers in Berlin. He will be most interested to hear from you!'

Berger climbed through the bulkhead hatchway and halted outside the radio room where Lorenz was seated. 'That was a good one, wasn't it?' His cheeks were glowing.

'One of the best,' said Ziegler.

'Where does he broadcast from?' asked Berger.

'We're supposed to believe that he operates a mobile transmitter on the European mainland,' Ziegler replied.

'But where is he really?'

'The wireless monitoring service has plotted the source of the signal and he is definitely in London.'

Lorenz smiled at the young seaman. 'Ever been to London, Berger?'

'No, Herr Kaleun.'

'A very fine city: I'm particularly fond of the view from Greenwich.'

'Perhaps I'll visit London after we've won.'

Lorenz sighed with satisfaction. The chief had done it again. BBC propaganda was so prodigiously good for morale.

A radio message from the U-boat command centre warned of several British destroyers in the vicinity. Lorenz gave the order to submerge and U-330 began a silent run at forty metres – speed one and a half knots – just sufficient to maintain depth. The subdued atmosphere in the control room was intensified by the red glow of the dark-adaption light. Lorenz and Müller were leaning over the chart table, conversing in low tones, when Hoffmann interrupted them. 'Excuse me. Kaleun? The sound man wants a word.'

Lorenz nodded and climbed through the fore bulkhead

hatchway. Thomas, the younger hydrophone operator, was turning the hand wheel and looking at the large dial located above it. The pointer swept from 220 degrees to 260 degrees, stopped for a moment, then rose until it was vertical. When Thomas saw the commander he said, 'I've been picking up something very odd, Herr Kaleun. I've never heard anything like it before.'

'Odd?'

'Yes. And I've been wondering whether it's some kind of long-distance detection system. There's whistling and a sort of squeaking noise.' Thomas raised a hand and brought his fingers together. 'Like when you squeeze a rubber toy. It's been intermittent. There's nothing there right now.' Thomas offered Lorenz a pair of auxiliary headphones. The captain took off his white cap, wrapped the metal arch around the crown of his head and pressed the circular pads against his ears. Thomas began searching for the sounds again. His hearing must have been very acute because Lorenz saw the hydrophone operator's expression change from neutrality to excitement a few moments before he, Lorenz, detected the first, faint whistle. 'There!' said Thomas. He continued to turn the hand wheel backwards and forwards and as the range of these movements narrowed the volume of the whistling increased.

Lorenz grinned. 'No, Thomas. That's not some fiendishly clever Tommy invention. We're listening to dolphins.' The commander was captivated by the eerie charm of the sounds: clicks, whickering, peeps, and a low churr that accelerated and rose beyond the upper limit of human audition. Occasionally there were loud thuds as the dolphins bumped against the hull. Lorenz imagined the pod weaving through the water, tracing elegant, interlocking ellipses; playful, carefree, curious, circling their discovery. A stark contrast: the natural world, innocent and joyful, and the boat, malevolent and deadly. 'Yes,' Lorenz added while removing the headphones, 'definitely dolphins.' He was about to leave when he noticed Thomas was frowning. 'What?'

'It's just . . .' The youth seemed about to raise some objection but changed his mind. 'Thank you, Kaleun.'

The hydrophone operator lacked experience and Lorenz supposed that Thomas's natural diffidence might make him overly reticent: he might feel foolish for having mistaken dolphins for a detection system and consequently fail to report something significant. Lorenz rested his palms on both sides of the doorway and leaned forward into the sound room. 'What's bothering you, Thomas?'

An inner struggle was taking place, and it was only after a lengthy pause that the youth finally mumbled, 'I thought I heard words.'

'Words?'

'Yes, English words.'

'Well, that's not possible, is it? The microphones wouldn't have picked up a radio signal.'

'Exactly.' Thomas looked relieved, as though he was pleased that Lorenz had been so blunt. 'Sometimes, when you're concentrating hard, you start to hear things.'

'Maybe you need a rest. Perhaps we should get Lehmann to take over?'

'No,' said Thomas defensively, 'I'll finish my watch, sir.' His response was curt, clipped. Realizing that he had been too abrupt, he offered Lorenz a placatory smile. 'Sorry.'

Lorenz dismissed the apology with a benign hand wave. 'Thomas?'

'Kaleun?'

'Do you speak English?'

'A little.'

'So what did you hear?'

'I really can't say, sir.'

Lorenz wasn't sure whether Thomas was being coy because he had been unable to translate the English or because he felt foolish saying aloud words that he must have imagined. The youth's expression had become pained. Lorenz felt a strong urge to clarify Thomas's meaning, to resolve the ambiguity, but he was forced to query his own doubtful motivation. 'All right,' said Lorenz, withdrawing. 'Carry on.' He ducked, stepped back through the bulkhead hatchway and surveyed the control room: ladder, periscope, torpedo-tube indicators, engine telegraph, the large white cylindrical air compressor. All was calm, the crew focused, yet he felt mildly unsettled, as if he had just walked through a spider's web in the dark.

The moon hovered above a pyramid of cloud and shone with exceptional brilliance. A broad avenue of silver ridges fanned out from the horizon, and, at its edges, glittering threads broke away and floated across the water. On either side, the sea darkened through shades of slate grey and charcoal to deepest black. The tanker was conspicuous, a silhouette enlarged by a smudge of smoke. Even without binoculars it was possible to discern a shadowy shape interrupting the continuity of the horizontal crests. U-330 was ideally positioned, approaching the tanker from behind, facing the moon and upwind of its target. Lorenz knew that under such conditions the low, narrow outline of a U-boat was virtually invisible. Falk had been down to the forward torpedo room and when he emerged from the conning tower he could barely contain his excitement. 'How big do you think she is?'

'Ten thousand tons or thereabouts,' Lorenz guessed. One of the ratings turned to take a look. 'You're supposed to be keeping watch, don't forget,' Lorenz admonished.

'Apologies, Herr Kaleun.' The man sounded meek and ashamed.

'We don't want any nasty surprises at this stage,' Lorenz remarked to Falk.

U-330 circled into position sixty degrees forward of the tanker's starboard beam. Juhl and Müller came up onto the bridge and stood next to the attack periscope housing like ceremonial guards. Sauer, the bosun, disappeared into the conning tower.

'They still haven't seen us,' Falk observed with glee and disbelief.

'All right,' said Lorenz. 'Let's see if we can get as close as possible.'

Falk expanded his chest and affecting a somewhat studied, martial pose, readied the crew. 'Stand by for surface firing.'

A voice in the bow compartment reported through the communications pipe: 'Tubes one to four ready.'

Falk looked through the aiming device which was mounted on a pedestal and connected to the firing system. He started reciting figures that were acknowledged by Sauer. The bosun was at his station in the tower, entering relevant data into the computer which would, with superhuman efficiency, calculate the gyro angles for each individual torpedo.

'Their helmsman must be blind,' Müller laughed. It was a

dry, humourless laugh that suggested astonishment rather than satisfaction.

Falk recited a list of figures that described the position, speed and distance of the tanker. He then specified the operational parameters of the torpedoes. 'Thirty knots: depth ten metres.' The target was perfectly quartered in the cross hairs of the view finder. Falk licked his lips and called out, 'Tubes one and two, fire!'

There was no recoil, tremor, or loss of momentum, U-330 simply continued slicing through the waves. 'Hard a-port,' Lorenz hollered. He gave a new heading and added: 'Ahead full.' The deck inclined steeply as the boat changed course. It was essential to get out of the tanker's way. The U-boat was no longer invisible. If the torpedoes missed and the U-boat was discovered then the tanker would soon try to ram them.

Stopwatches were ticking.

'Fifteen seconds,' said Falk.

Lorenz imagined the torpedoes running silently towards their destination. As they passed beneath the tanker's keel a pistol fuse set off by the hull's magnetic field would detonate over a thousand pounds of explosives. Most of the men on board were probably asleep. A few might be reading or playing cards. Some, perhaps, were lying on bunks and making plans.

'Come on . . .' Falk crossed his fingers and growled. 'Come

on.' Two roaring explosions followed, the first separated from the second by a heartbeat. The tanker was raised by the double blast and when it sank back down again there was a mighty splash and an ear-rending metallic crack. The spectacle resembled a toy being subjected to playful violence in a child's bath. It was as though the brain, unaccustomed to witnessing the release of such colossal energies, demanded a reduction of scale to facilitate comprehension. 'Got you,' Falk punched his fist in the air. 'Did you see that? Fantastic! We actually blew it out of the water!' Orange flames leapt out of the buckled superstructure and columns of smoke climbed high enough to discolour the moon.

Falk was looking at Lorenz, his eyebrows raised, expectant. 'Shouldn't we finish her off?'

'She isn't going to recover from that,' said Lorenz. 'Believe me.'

'We mustn't waste our torpedoes.' Juhl ventured his opinion in a subdued monotone. 'We haven't got many left.'

'Yes,' Lorenz agreed. 'There's no need to deliver a *coup de grâce*. We've snapped her in half – she'll go down in no time.'

Lorenz gave orders for the boat to turn and reduce speed. The tanker was burning with such fierce intensity that the clouds beneath the moon were reflecting red light. The wind carried with it an acrid smell that left a bitter taste at the back of the throat. Brandt's head appeared through the hatch and the radio operator handed Lorenz a slip of paper. On it was the British code signifying that the tanker had been attacked by a submarine, the tanker's name – *Excelsior* – some position coordinates and a three-word communication: *Torpedoed. Sinking fast.* Lorenz read the message out aloud, translating the English into German.

'He used the international frequencies,' said Brandt.

'Is he still signalling?'

'No.'

'Good.'

Someone gave Brandt the Lloyd's register and the radio operator passed it up to Lorenz. Juhl shone a torch over the text as the commander flicked through the pages. On finding the tanker's entry Lorenz declared, 'Eleven thousand, three hundred and nine tons.' He then gave the register back to Brandt who dropped from view. There was a cheer and some applause from below.

Most of the tanker was hidden by billowing smoke. Occasionally, a fountain of sparks would ascend to a great height and volcanic showers made the water hiss and steam. When the holds exploded the noise was formidable and Lorenz shielded his face from successive blasts of hot air. Metal twisted and groaned and a blazing oil slick made the swell incandesce. The scene seemed too sensational, too terrifying to be real. It resembled the brimstone daubing of some melancholy nineteenth-century painter irresistibly attracted to the theme of Biblical catastrophe. Lorenz had seen canvases of this type in art museums, always immense nightscapes the size of a gallery wall, enlivened by forked lightning and ruinous eruptions.

U-330 was slowly getting closer to the conflagration. The faces of the men on the bridge had become florid as they stared over the bulwark with oxblood eyes. It was like being exposed to an open furnace. The only visible part of the tanker, the stern, began to list.

'It's going,' said Falk.

Against the constant crackling and popping of the burning sea the sound of screams and cries could now be heard. Lorenz looked through his binoculars. Men were vaulting over the safety rails. Some of the figures were surrounded by glowing coronas and trailed fiery tails like meteors as they plummeted into the water.

Juhl produced a handkerchief and coughed into it. The air was barely breathable. 'We're getting rather close, don't you think?'

Lorenz, roused from awful fascination, leaned over the hatch. 'Reverse diesels. Back one-quarter.' The smoke was still thickening. More detonations and flashes made the clouds transparent. There was something biological about their appearance, a hint of internal organs and vasculature. The screams were becoming intolerable. Why were they making such a racket, Lorenz wondered. It was physically impossible. The firestorm should be using up all of the available oxygen and the men should be suffocating in silence. If they opened their mouths the burning air would rush into their mouths. Why were they still screaming?

'Poor bastards,' said Müller. No one contradicted him. All were sharing the same thought.

Eventually, the smoke enveloped the tanker completely. Only the moon was visible: its argent purity soiled and dimmed to a dun haze.

Lorenz glanced at the phosphorescent dial of his watch. If a British destroyer operating in the area had picked up the distress call then it would now be speeding towards them. Yet Lorenz felt disinclined to leave. He found himself giving orders for U-330 to manoeuvre slowly around the stricken tanker. Its demise was compelling.

'What's that?' Juhl pointed into the black fog. 'I don't believe it.'

Looking through his binoculars Lorenz saw a lifeboat coming towards them. The haze was layered and in constant motion. When veils of obfuscation overlapped the boat faded and all but disappeared. It maintained a steady course, becoming less spectral and more plainly material as it neared.

Falk was incredulous. 'The sea is on fire . . .'

'There must have been a way through,' said Juhl.

The merest suggestion that something inexplicable had occurred made the men on the bridge uneasy. They displayed an alarming readiness to interpret the world in terms of portents and signs – bad omens.

Lorenz ordered the engines to be stopped. Falk looked at the commander askance and then turned his attention to the others. They seemed tense, fidgety – like a pen of domesticated animals sensing the proximity of an abattoir. When the diesel engines fell silent it was possible to hear the regular rhythm of rowing strokes and the creaking of oarlocks. The occupants of the lifeboat were coughing like a ward full of consumptive patients. This unequivocal declaration of human frailty caused the atmosphere on the bridge to change. The supernatural aura formerly surrounding the lifeboat was dispelled by the evident vulnerability of the men on board.

'Brandt!' Lorenz shouted into the hatch. 'Someone get Brandt.' A few seconds later the radio operator reappeared. 'Survivors, Brandt. About twelve men, I'd say.' The radio operator was also responsible for provisions. 'Can we spare something?'

'I'll see what I can find.'

'And a compass – see if you can dig out a compass – there's one under the chart table. I have no idea what it's doing there

– a cheap toy – the sort of thing a schoolboy might own. Even so: better than nothing on the open sea.'

There were more detonations but the screaming had ceased.

Red and yellow flashes penetrated the sooty pall and the effect was horribly infernal. The approaching lifeboat might have been navigating through the waterways of hell.

Brandt returned with a bulging sack.

'What's inside?' Lorenz asked.

'Water, some cans of condensed milk: the cook wasn't happy – but there we are.' Brandt spread his fingers out. 'Ten cans of boneless chicken meat and a piece of cheese.'

'Good.'

'And the compass, Kaleun.'

'Thank you.' Lorenz threw the sack over his shoulder and looked around at his companions. 'Stay here.' Falk exempted himself from the order and started to follow. 'No,' Lorenz added, 'I'll do this on my own.' The first watch officer stepped back. Lorenz's precise motivation was unclear, but he was aware of some scruple that demanded he accept full responsibility for his command. To do anything less would be cowardly. His rank obliged him to look directly into the eyes of these 'poor bastards' without flinching. He climbed down the conning tower ladder and walked along the deck, past the 8.8 cm gun, and towards the bow. As the lifeboat drew closer he noticed that the woodwork was striped with scorch marks. A coxswain was seated at the tiller and six oars rose and fell in rough synchrony. The wind cleared some of the smoke and the ruddy light of the burning tanker revealed a gang of filthy men who were either completely bald or possessed only patches of singed hair. None of them had eyebrows. They looked very similar, as if they all shared a common congenital abnormality. The coxswain issued some final directions and the lifeboat scraped to a halt against the iron bow. Some of the men were retching so hard it seemed that they meant to expel their innards through their mouths.

'I'm sorry,' Lorenz said in English. 'I can't take you on board; however, I can inform you that your radio operator succeeded in sending out a distress call, so someone may come to your assistance. Otherwise, you might consider maintaining a north-easterly course and there is a reasonable chance that by tomorrow afternoon you will be sighted by an aeroplane or encounter a fishing boat. Here, take this.' Lorenz took the compass from his pocket and tossed it into the lifeboat. 'Iceland isn't far and the weather forecast is good. We aren't expecting any more storms for the next few days at least.' Lorenz became aware of a familiar smell, a whiff of grilled meat blending with the pungent, oily fumes. There was another detonation and the tanker flames flared. Some of the seated men had suffered terrible burns. Beetroot-coloured flesh sagged and ran down their faces like melted candle wax. Lying in the lifeboat were other men with charred heads and smouldering clothes. They had obviously been pulled out of the water too late. Lorenz was thankful when the tanker flames died down again. 'I have some provisions for you,' he continued. 'Food, water, milk: not much, I know, but it will be enough to ease your discomfort for a day or so – should that prove necessary.' He lowered the sack and two men reached up to receive it. They were close enough for him to see the whites of their eyes. None of them said anything. It would have been easier had they shouted abuse. Their neutrality, their dignified silence, their refusal to judge, made him profoundly uncomfortable. 'Good luck.' Lorenz did not betray his feelings. His voice was firm and steady. 'I hope that someone finds you soon.' And with that, he turned and began walking back to the tower. He heard the lifeboat casting off, oars striking the hull and producing gong-like reverberations.

Another cloud of smoke, perhaps produced by the final detonation, rolled across the water. It was thick and advanced in collapsing folds. Within seconds, Lorenz couldn't breathe. Each inhalation seemed to excoriate his windpipe and fill his lungs with tar. The smoke was all around him and impenetrable. Ahead, the conning tower was no longer visible and the gun was fading. He found himself isolated and benighted, choking on foul, bitter smuts. He needed to escape asphyxiation but he quickly became disorientated and couldn't decide which way to run. There seemed to be someone standing ahead of him, an outline in the obscurity. It was odd that Lorenz could see anything at all, because in all other respects he was blind. Somehow, a shaft of moonlight must have penetrated the murk because the figure was faintly luminous.

'Falk?' Lorenz spluttered into his hand. 'Is that you, Falk?' Even as he repeated the first watch officer's name he did so without conviction. Falk hadn't been wearing a long coat. A short delay – filled with mounting disquiet – was followed by the recognition of further peculiarities. Why hadn't the man made any noise? And why was he seemingly immune to the effects of the polluted air? There was something challenging about his stance, as if he meant to hinder Lorenz's progress.

'Who's there?' Lorenz demanded. 'Speak, damn you!' But there was no reply. Smoke made Lorenz's eyes sting and everything became distorted. The figure became a grey-blue smear against the roiling darkness. Another gust of wind pushed the smoke across the deck and out onto the water on the other side of the boat. The smear of luminosity seemed to become enfolded in the turbulence and when Lorenz regained his focus the figure had disappeared. Lorenz supposed that the poisons he had inhaled had been the cause of some kind of hallucination. A scarcely perceptible breath of warning had passed through his ribcage. The sensation was subtle and it had vanished before he had had the opportunity to ascertain its significance.

Falk appeared from behind the gun and came forward.

'Did you say something, Herr Kaleun?'

'I told you to stay up there.' Lorenz pointed at the bridge.

'Kaleun: the smoke came over and we couldn't see what was happening.' Lorenz nodded and their eyes locked. 'I bet they were grateful,' Falk added, smiling.

'Grateful?' Lorenz sighed. 'For torpedoing their vessel and killing their comrades? I doubt it.'

'I meant for the food,' said Falk.

'Ah yes, the food.' Lorenz wiped some moisture from his eyes. 'They were delighted. They couldn't thank me enough. Indeed, they expressed particular satisfaction when they discovered the tinned chicken. It was as much as they could do to stop themselves from ripping the cans open and devouring the lot there and then.' The first watch officer appeared dispirited. 'How long have you been loitering there, Falk?'

'I've only just got here, Kaleun.'

'And you're on your own?'

'Yes.'

'There's no one else?'

Falk, puzzled, looked around. 'No, sir – just me.'

There was a monstrous creaking sound followed by rusty screeches. The stern of the tanker rose out of the water and for a moment the ship held an almost vertical position, as steep as a cliff. Then, with a great roar, it dropped beneath the waves and the sea closed over it.

'We'd better get going,' said Lorenz.

On the bridge, Lorenz took one last look through his binoculars. The lifeboat was surrounded by flotsam, lots of objects – all roughly the same size – creating a regular pattern on the surface. It took him a few seconds to appreciate what he was looking at. Each element of the pattern was a dead body.

The miasma in the bow compartment was almost overwhelming: bilge water, mouldering food, body odour, and the cloying smell of decomposing lemons. Two naked light bulbs seemed to intensify rather than relieve the gloom. Hammocks were suspended between the upper bunks requiring those passing through to stoop or crawl. Conditions were horribly cramped and it was difficult to make even relatively small movements without hitting a rail, a locker, salted meat or a slimy green cheese. Some of the berths were occupied by sleeping off-watch men and one of them was snoring loudly. Occasionally he would stop breathing and a lengthy pause would be followed by a loud, protracted gasp. They were hemmed in like livestock and made nauseous by the perpetual roll of the boat. Belches, fetid exhalations, flatulence – there was no escaping the indignities of the body in the bow compartment.

Berger was lying on his side, propped up on his elbow, staring at a blank sheet of paper and trying unsuccessfully to compose a letter to his girlfriend. He repositioned his body on the mattress but was still uncomfortable.

'What's her name?' asked Peters.

'Rosamunde,' Berger answered.

'How old is she?'

'Seventeen.'

Kruger leaned out of his bunk into the feeble light. His face was covered in red rashes and boils caused by the grease he was obliged to work with. A torpedo man could always be identified by his bad skin and the tang of iodine ointment. Kruger leered at Peters and said, 'Just seventeen. Think of it . . .' Leaning out a little further, he added: 'What have you got there?'

Peters rolled over so he was facing the hull. 'Nothing.'

'Yes you have.' Kruger got out of his bunk and wrestled with Peters. After a short struggle he triumphantly held up a bra. 'Oh, will you look at this!' Kruger pulled the shoulder straps apart and let the cups dangle. 'Who does it belong to?'

'Just a girl,' said Peters sheepishly.

'You stole it?' Kruger feigned shock.

Stein appeared and snatched the bra from Kruger. He held it against his face, inhaled and said, 'I can smell her.'

They all froze when they heard Lorenz say, 'How cosy it is in here.' His approach had been silent. Kicking an empty can of tinned fruit aside he advanced a few more steps. He was wearing a jumper and his white cap was rakishly askew. 'Obersteuermannsmaat Stein, if you'd put that fetching female undergarment down for a moment I'd like to offer you a drink.'

'Kaleun?' Stein handed the bra back to Peters.

Lorenz produced his bottle of rum and filled two small glasses. He handed one of them to Stein and said, 'I believe it's your birthday. And my birthday wish for you is . . .' he hesitated for a moment, 'is that you have a future. Any future, frankly, let alone a happy one.'

'Thank you, Herr Kaleun,' said Stein.

They touched glasses and knocked back their measures. Stein coughed. The rum was particularly strong. Lorenz reached out to Peters and indicated that he wanted to examine the bra. Peters handed it over and Lorenz gazed down at the brocade trim which had become slightly soiled with oil. The atmosphere became a little tense as the men wondered what the skipper was thinking. After a lengthy pause he looked up, scanned the expectant faces and burst out laughing. 'Good for morale, is it? Perhaps I should advise Admiral Dönitz to make bras standard issue. One never knows. It could prove to be the difference between victory and defeat.' He threw the bra at Peters and sauntered back towards his nook. 'If the Führer knew what his sea-wolves were really like he'd sleep like a baby, wouldn't he? Truly, the fate of the Reich is safe in our hands.'

The message from U-boat headquarters was brief: ALL U-BOATS IN GRID AD INTERCEPT CONVOY HX IN AD 79. ATTACK WITHOUT FURTHER ORDERS. The helmsman changed course and the diesels ran at full speed. In the forward compartment, torpedoes were removed three quarters out of their tubes – batteries recharged, instrumentation checked. Reserve torpedoes were greased and serviced. When Lorenz was satisfied that everything was in order, he retired to his nook where he dozed periodically. For an indeterminate length of time he was returned to the black waters of his nightmare and he saw, once again, a raft carrying two figures floating towards him. The image dissolved when the hull started juddering loudly. Thereafter, sleep became elusive and he rose from his bed and went to collect his jacket from the radio room where he had left it draped over the heater to dry. The leather was still damp and patterned with stains that exuded a horrible rotting smell caused by a prolific mould that had also colonized his shirt, belt and shoes. Lorenz put on his jacket and tried to remove the larger patches with a penknife. He soon abandoned the exercise on account of its sheer futility. The mould was everywhere: on the crew's clothes, in their bedding, and growing immoderately on the meat and cheese. There was no point in trying to halt its proliferation.

Werner, the cook, was preparing breakfast for the second watch and the clatter of his plates carried through the boat. Lorenz crossed the control room, climbed through the aft hatchway and, stepping over a man sleeping on a mat, walked onwards to the galley, eager for a large, restorative coffee. He would have made some polite conversation with Werner, a popular, good-humoured man, but the engines were making too much noise. Standing in the petty officers' quarters Lorenz marvelled at how the men in the bunks were able to sleep in spite of the din. He had only just swallowed the bitter dregs from the bottom of his cup when Graf appeared and said, 'You're wanted on the bridge, Kaleun.'

Lorenz emerged from the hatch, said good morning to the watchmen, and positioned himself by the bulwark. He nodded at Juhl: 'I have the conn.' Beyond the dipping bow the sea was a restless, prehistoric immensity. If a great marine lizard had broken the surface and extended its sinuous neck to scream at the pewter sky he would not have been wholly surprised. Juhl handed Lorenz a pair of binoculars and gestured in a south-westerly direction. 'There they are.' Lorenz adjusted the thumbscrew and observed a smear of darkness on the horizon. 'Yes,' Lorenz agreed. 'That's a convoy all right.' As he studied the smoke it expanded outwards. Lorenz removed the stopper from the communications pipe and directed a slight alteration of course. Spume arced over the bridge and the boat veered towards the spreading cloud. Mastheads peeped over the flat grey line of the sea and their slow ascent presaged the appearance of two ships; escorts, travelling ahead of the convoy. More mastheads came into view and then the funnels of the cargo ships. Lorenz estimated that these merchant craft would be within firing range in approximately one hour. 'So,' he said, returning the binoculars to Juhl and clapping his hands together. 'Let's make Dönitz happy. Clear the bridge!' Immediately the lookouts and Juhl descended the ladder. Lorenz shouted through the communications pipe, 'Prepare to dive!' before following the others and dogging the hatch.

Submerging was invariably accompanied by a sense of wary expectancy. Human beings were not meant to survive under water and every man understood – at some level – that he was party to an infringement, a transgression that might not be readily overlooked. They were defying Nature or Neptune or some other proprietary Personification and when the pointer on the manometer revolved, it measured not only depth, but increments of dread. The pounding of the diesels ceased and it wasn't until the manoeuvre was successfully completed that the tension in the atmosphere finally dissipated. Their hubris had gone unnoticed or some kindly god had granted them yet another dispensation.

Lorenz sat at the attack periscope in the conning tower, securing his position by clamping his thighs either side of the shaft. He switched on the motor and tested the pedals, rotating the column and saddle to the right and left. His fingers found the elevation control and he raised the periscope. Conditions were very favourable, the 'stalk' was travelling in the same direction as the sea and the waves were washing over the hood from behind. He was able to keep the objective low in the water, reducing the chances of being spotted while simultaneously benefitting from a clear view. Falk was standing by the computer, lightly touching its dials and buttons as if he needed to reacquaint himself with their function. There was something superstitious about his redundant movements. He seemed to be performing a private ritual.

The hatch in the deck that separated the conning tower from the control room was supposed to be closed during an underwater attack, but Lorenz always kept it open because he liked to feel in direct contact with the men below. He liked to hear Graf's instructions and to monitor the steady flow of reports. As they drew closer to the convoy he called out, 'Half speed ahead,' ensuring that the size of the periscope's wake would be reduced. A U-boat's principle advantage was stealth. Without stealth, there was only vulnerability.

Several cargo ships were now visible. Employing 6X magnification Lorenz examined each one in turn and selected his target. He then ordered another minor change of the submarine's course. Reverting to 1X magnification he watched the two escorts sail past.

'Flood all tubes.'

Another escort, flanking the convoy, was very close; however, U-330 was already inside the protective perimeter.

'Open torpedo outer doors. Course twenty. Bow left. Bearing sixty . . .'

Falk began feeding the information into the computer. When he had finished he addressed Lorenz, 'Tubes one and two ready to fire.'

The electric motors seemed to hum more loudly. Lorenz could feel the release lever in his hand. The cargo ship was positioned perfectly in the cross hairs, when, quite suddenly, it vanished, and Lorenz was gripping the periscope shaft tightly to prevent himself from falling off the saddle. The entire column had rotated forty-five degrees and stopped abruptly. Yet, he had not been conscious of applying any pressure to the pedals.

'Kaleun?' Falk sounded worried. Was the flanking escort preparing to ram?

The motor laboured when Lorenz tried to correct the periscope. It felt as though the column was encountering some kind of resistance. When the cargo ship finally appeared in the viewfinder it had changed course slightly. 'Damn!'

'What?'

'We'll have to start again.' The automatic update system depended on the variables remaining constant.

Lorenz revised the figures and for the second time Falk declared, 'Tubes one and two ready to fire.' The cargo ship was back in the cross hairs, the detail of its superstructure clearly visible. Lorenz was hesitant, almost expecting the periscope to swivel round again. It had moved just as he was about to fire. The timing had been curiously precise and optimally disruptive. Indeed, it had felt more contrived than contingent, a purposeful interference, and, for an instant, it had seemed as if someone were snatching the periscope out of his hands, wresting control away from him. He tightened his hold on the firing lever and as he did so, he heard an exhalation close to his right ear, an expulsion of air, but imbued with a faint vocal quality, enough to suggest the emotions of frustration and regret. Although disconcerting, Lorenz dismissed the phenomenon. He could not afford to be distracted.

'Tube one – fire! Tube two – fire!'

Falk counted off the seconds and Lorenz kept his gaze fixed on the target. Graf was still giving orders. To maintain depth and keep the boat level it was necessary to fill the trim tanks with sea water weighing exactly the same as the torpedoes that had just been discharged. The adjustment was subtle but perceptible nevertheless. Lorenz felt strangely detached, like an ancient god dispensing casual destruction. He saw the cargo ship transformed into a blazing fire ball and the absence of sound made the conflagration appear like an event in a dream. Lehmann, who was manning the hydrophones, must have reacted and signalled success, because a chorus of triumphal exclamations preceded the arrival of the shockwave.

'Did we hit it?' asked Falk.

'Yes,' said Lorenz. 'We hit it.' He was obliged to evaluate the feasibility of undertaking another attack, but when he looked for the flanking escort he discovered that it was already turning towards them. 'Close torpedo doors, new course 180 degrees, seventy-five metres, ahead slow: silent routine.' In the control room, men grabbed the handles of the leverage valves and their feet left the matting as they used all of their bodyweight to pull them down. The ballast tanks flooded and the boat tilted while Falk and Lorenz were still negotiating the ladder. Hand wheels were being rotated with furious, concentrated energy, and members of the crew who were not seated had to reach for the overhead pipes to stop themselves from falling. Anything unfastened slid towards the bow: cans, sou'westers, books and boxes.

The first detonation was like a sledgehammer landing heavily on the hull. It produced a reverberating clang, all of the lights blinked and the metal began to shriek. There then followed a terrifying roar, even louder than the initial strike. An enormous quantity of water, blasted outwards by the force of the explosion, was rushing back to fill the void. Men staggered, others lost their footing and fell, and the boat's angle of descent steepened. In the confusion that followed, Lorenz heard a voice shouting: 'Obermaschinistmaat Richter badly injured.'

Before Lorenz could react there were two more massive detonations that accelerated the boat's descent. Graf's response was swift and effective. The aft compartment dropped and the deck became level again. When the noise subsided there was absolute silence. Even a cough would conduct through the hull and betray their location, so all of those who were not seated swapped their boots for slippers. Men crept into bunks and attempted to breathe slowly and remain calm. The boat could not remain submerged indefinitely: it was imperative to conserve air. Only essential lighting was retained to save power. They waited – and waited – until the stillness was infiltrated by the repetitive thrashing of high speed propellers.

A mechanic lowered himself to the matting and knelt next to the master gyro compass. Another seaman crouched beneath the chart table. It seemed that the crew were trying to escape danger by making their bodies occupy less space. Fear had impoverished their thinking and their irrational behaviour betrayed a return to infantile logic, the reappearance of semi-magical beliefs. They folded their arms and shortened their necks, as though it were possible – by the exercise of will – to shrink to a vanishing point and elude the destruction promised by the relentless thrashing above. Lorenz looked at his men and hoped that their sanity would be protected by some vestige of pride or honour, that their training and count-less practice dives would make the approach of the escort bearable.

Six splashes – an agonizing interlude of fraught expect-ation – succeeded by six detonations. With each boom the manometer pointer jumped and the boat was pushed lower. Lorenz closed his eyes and translated what was happening into a reduced mental representation. In his head, a tiny U-330 was travelling in one direction while a miniature escort sailed transversely above it. He guessed the current positions of the forward escorts, estimated their speed and courses, and intro-duced them into the trigonometry of his mental representation. 'Hard a-port,' said Lorenz. The tiny U-boat in his head began to turn. He opened his eyes and climbed through the forward hatchway.

'There's another escort coming towards us,' the hydro-phone operator whispered.

'Just the one?'

'Yes.'

'Bearing?'

Lehmann rotated his wheel: 'One hundred and sixty degrees.'

'Interesting,' Lorenz closed his eyes and reconstructed his model. He repositioned the first forward escort, made the second vanish, and tried to determine his next move. It was like playing three-dimensional chess. His concentration was broken when the steward and Berger appeared carrying Richter. They were having difficulty getting the unconscious mechanic through the hatchway; one of his arms kept catching on the bulwark. When they finally succeeded, Lorenz saw that Richter's face was divided by a deep, diagonal gash. Blood was still streaming from the ugly wound.

'What are you doing?' Lorenz asked.

'Taking him to the bow compartment,' the steward replied.

'Why?'

'There's a strong smell of chlorine in the petty officers' quarters.'

'That's all we need. Look, just lay him down in my nook for now. What happened?'

'Slipped and went flying. He took off and smacked his head against one of the diesels.'

'Took off?'

The steward nodded. As they attempted to rotate Richter's body, Berger tripped. He dropped Richter's legs and fell onto the deck, producing a loud crash.

'You fucking idiot, Berger!' The steward's stage whisper was despairing rather than angry.

'Shit,' the young seaman hissed, 'I'm sorry.' He looked up at Lorenz who simply gestured for him to hurry. Berger grabbed Richter's ankles and helped the steward manoeuvre the unconscious man onto the mattress.

Lorenz tapped Lehmann's shoulder. 'Are their screws getting louder?'

'Yes, sir.'

'Altering their course?'

'One hundred and fifty five degrees: they heard that.'

Lorenz leaned into the control room. 'Take us down another fifteen metres. Hard a-starboard.'

Soon, they could all hear the forward escort's approach; propeller blades churning water. There were more splashes, so many that it became difficult to count them. Lorenz pictured the lethal dispersion of depth charges: trails of air bubbles, slow descent. A moment later they were being attacked by raging Titans. Enormous cudgels were pummelling the hull, buffeting the boat this way and that, battering the conning tower, bashing the ballast tanks. The deck plates jolted painfully against the soles of feet; wood panels split and splintered;

iron growled. Then came the roaring, excessively prolonged as the ocean came crashing back into the numerous empty blast spaces. When the cacophony ended, there was no longer absolute silence. The men were hyperventilating. Graf levelled the boat and Lorenz climbed back into the control room. 'See,' said Lorenz. 'They missed. Even with Berger's generous assistance, they missed. I hope they appreciate how sporting we've been.'

The crew were staring at him with the rounded, protuberant eyes of nocturnal animals. Extreme terror had made them appear even younger than they did ordinarily. For a fleeting moment it seemed that the boat was being piloted by school-children. Only Graf and Müller looked like adults. Several of the men were trembling and one of them had bitten his lower lip so hard that his chin was now cleft by a glistening, crimson stripe. The seaman beneath the chart table had put his fingers in his ears. Even though Lorenz could feel fear gnawing away at his own innards, he adopted an air of indifference and remarked, 'We'll shake them off in the end, don't you worry.' The quality of his performance was vital. Under conditions of such appalling, unspeakable dread, anyone might snap and become hysterical. Lorenz had seen it happen. *Let me out, let me out! For God's sake, let me out!* Fortunately, there had never been an incident of this kind under his command. His men had always lived up to Dönitz's ideal: the community of fate – each component held in place by adjacent parts, the teeth of every cog locked into the rotation of another.

Lorenz remembered reading a story to his little niece and nephew. It was a gruesome tale but they had insisted that he continue even though they were obviously very frightened. Before switching off the light he had kissed their sweet-scented hair. 'It's only make-believe,' he had reassured them. 'Nothing bad will happen to you.'

More explosions brought him back to the present: a truly shocking tumult. A continent was breaking up above their heads, mountain ranges were crumbling into the sea, avalanches of rock were raising monstrous tsunamis. How could it go on for so long? How many drums was it possible to drop in a single location? A seaman in the bow compartment was vomiting into a bucket. The boat twisted like a living creature trying to free itself from the teeth of a trap, glass shattered and the submarine was plunged into darkness.

'What's happened to the auxiliary lights?' Graf's question was really a command. 'Well?'

The sense of being entombed was overwhelming; the claustrophobic darkness pressed against their bodies, thickened in their windpipes and clogged their airways. As the roaring subsided, torch beams appeared, one after another, sweeping through the void, crossing like swords and creating consoling roundels of visibility. Objects flashed into existence

– the air compressor, the chart table, the main gyrocompass. Reports were made, one of which was instantly verified by the sound of gushing water. 'Flooding in diesel compartment, request help.' Lorenz crossed the control room and shone a torch through the aft hatchway. The petty officers' quarters were empty, everyone who had been lying on the bunks had responded.

Although the boat was equipped with pumps, these could only be employed when the depth charges were exploding. As soon as the roaring stopped, the pumps would have to be switched off again or their noise would give away the boat's location. If the boat admitted too much water it might grow too heavy. It would become impossible to surface, an increasingly likely possibility given that evading destruction would almost certainly require diving deeper. Lorenz consulted his mental model of the engagement and struggled to make a decision. He didn't have much time – a few seconds, perhaps. The air smelt badly of oil, sweat, urine, and vomit. Wafts of chlorine, which meant that the batteries had been damaged, were much stronger by the aft hatchway. His order owed more to instinct than the exercise of judgement. 'Down another fifteen metres, hard a-starboard.'

Graf aimed a beam of light at the manometer and issued commands that should have resulted in the boat levelling out after its descent, but the deck remained stubbornly angled.

The hydroplane operators turned to look back at Graf, their eyes almost comically super-enlarged. Peering at the mano-meter needle, the engineer registered each fateful increase: *One hundred and five, one hundred and ten, one hundred and fifteen, one hundred and twenty* . . .

'Are the dive planes jammed?' Graf asked.

'Not responding,' one of the operators replied.

One hundred and twenty-five . . .

Graf placed a clenched fist against his mouth and withdrew it an instant later. 'Switch to manual.'

The power-assisted system was switched off and the hydroplane operators gripped their big, heavy wheels. Each movement was effortful.

One hundred and thirty, one hundred and thirty-five . . .

'Please, please . . .' Graf addressed the submarine as if it were sentient.

One hundred and forty, one hundred and forty-five . . .

Finally, the angle of the deck changed and the boat levelled off twenty-five metres lower than intended. The emergency lights began to glow and produced dull yellow haloes. Some of the crew were on all fours while others had squeezed them-selves into tight corners. A few of them, suddenly self-aware, began to stand, but before they were upright, they were all knocked off their feet again when the raging Titans returned. More dial covers shattered and an overhead lamp burst.

Fragments of glass rained down on the matting. When the detonations stopped the humming of the electric engines was lost beneath the hiss of continuous spraying.

'Very tenacious,' said Lorenz. The gaskets and seats of numerous valves had loosened and were letting in water. Countless rivulets were trickling into the bilges.

The control room mate had started to whisper a prayer.

Lorenz laid an avuncular hand on Danzer's shoulder. 'Think of it this way: back home, your coffin would have been cheap, a horrible little wooden box. This coffin costs four million marks. Kings settle for less.'

In spite of the gravity of the situation a few of the men managed to smile. Lorenz *had* to keep the confidence of his crew to retain his authority; he had to make them believe that he could think clearly even when the merciless, rolling thunder was at its loudest. He was obliged, like all commanders, to service the myth of his own infallibility. The beneficial effect of his bravado was brief. He watched the smiles fade as a strange, eerie sound penetrated the hull, a high-pitched, short pulse, the timbre of which suggested extreme, shivering cold. Its repetition felt like a form of psychic water-torture, every frigid note dropping like a shard of ice directly into the soul.

'Asdic,' said Falk.

Although the British underwater detection system couldn't

determine depth, it could certainly determine bearing and distance.

'Hard a-starboard,' said Lorenz. 'Both motors, full ahead.'

The barrage that followed was protracted and unimaginably violent. It left the crew stupefied, their faces devoid of expression. They had retreated so far into themselves that the connections between mind and body had become attenuated. There was only vacancy, blank staring – transcendent terror.

Lehmann craned out of his room. When he spoke, his voice quivered: 'Sounds bearing two hundred and fifty degrees. Getting louder.'

The attack continued. It was no longer possible to distinguish one detonation from the next. Everyone was cowing now, expecting the boat to break in two and the North Atlantic to rush in. The steel ribs were under so much pressure that they howled, hydraulic oil spouted across the control room, and all the motor relays tripped. A faint reverberation seemed to persist after the bombardment. Someone had the presence of mind to throw the relays back and Lorenz reduced speed to dead slow.

Three hours later the British were still attacking at regular intervals.

'Seventy-eight charges,' said Graf.

'Is that all?' Lorenz replied. 'And I thought they were going to make a *serious* attempt to sink us.' He looked around at the figures inhabiting the boat's preternatural twilight. None of them returned his smile. Perhaps they had lost faith in him? Lorenz climbed through the forward hatchway. Poor Richter was groaning but at least he was still alive. Bending to speak to Lehmann, Lorenz asked: 'Louder or weaker?'

'Staying the same.'

'They're circling?'

'No, Kaleun.' Lehmann paused. 'No, they're coming back again.'

Lorenz returned to the control room. 'Take us down another thirty metres.' Alarm animated expressions that had become pale and mask-like. Would one of them go mad now? Lorenz tried to make eye-contact, albeit momentary, with every man in his vicinity. Which one of them would succumb, which one of them would run through the boat screaming? He could feel the tension mounting, the swell of communal panic. Thankfully, Graf declared his support with an obedient affirmative – 'Yes, Herr Kaleun' – and the sense of having reached a decisive, critical moment dissipated.

One hundred and fifty, one hundred and fifty-five, one hundred and sixty . . .

The woodwork cracked and the hissing of the leaks became louder. Condensation dripped from the overhead. There were more explosions, more showers of broken glass. Another fountain of spray appeared above the water gauge.

'One hundred and seventy-five metres,' said Graf.

Men were attending to the breaches, undertaking repairs like automatons, but the mood of the boat had changed. Lorenz could feel it, a profound shift, as fundamental as the ground moving during an earthquake: fatalism, resignation. The shivering Asdic pulses were like the grim reaper flicking the hull with his bony finger to make it ring. They had become Death's plaything.

'Sound bearing two hundred and ten degrees,' said Lehmann. 'Growing louder.'

And so it continued, explosions, manoeuvres, explosions: lurching, staggering, rolling and pitching – darkness, light – the reek of bodies and the slow accumulation of poisonous fumes. The passage of time became meaningless.

'What now?' Lorenz asked. He had been listening to the steady drip of condensation for some time.

Lehmann adjusted his headphones. 'I think they're going away.'

'Really?'

'Yes. Their screws are fading.'

Graf poked his head through the hatchway. 'We've got to surface.'

The hull was still complaining: pained murmurings, shudders, occasional shrieks. Cracks and snaps issued from the woodwork in the petty officers' quarters, a constant reminder of how much weight was bearing down on them.

'Not yet,' said Lorenz.

'We've made an awful lot of water, Kaleun.'

'Not yet.'

'We can't use the pumps.'

'I know.'

'Kaleun: why have they stopped attacking us?' asked Danzer. 'Do you think they've run out of munitions?'

'No,' said Lorenz, 'I doubt it.'

'Then why?'

'Why? Because they think we're dead.'

Lorenz spent the next twenty minutes inspecting the compartments, assessing the damage and congratulating his men. Most of them were so shaken by the ordeal that they could barely respond. They looked weary, close to the point of collapse. The breach in the engine room had been cataclysmic and the water level had risen above the matting. Fritz Fischer, the chief mechanic, splashed through the gloom. His shirt was torn and his exposed skin was streaked with oil.

'Will it hold, Fritz?' Lorenz asked.

'Not for much longer,' Fischer replied, wiping his face with a rag. A tattoo on the mechanic's right bicep showed a scroll on which the word 'Hope' was emblazoned in Gothic letters.

On returning to the control room, Lorenz ordered Graf to

take the boat up to periscope depth. The tanks were flushed and the hydroplane operators rotated their wheels but the manometer pointer failed to move. U-330 should have been ascending at a rate of one metre per second.

'We're too heavy and too deep,' Graf said bluntly. 'We'll have to use the pumps.'

'I'm not risking that,' said Lorenz. 'Let's try going a little faster.'

Apart from a slight tremor, the manometer pointer remained inert.

'What do we do now?' asked Falk.

'Patience,' said Lorenz. 'We're only going at four knots.'

'I'm not sure we can go any faster in our current state,' said Graf.

'Nonsense,' said Lorenz. 'Of course we can.'

Slowly, the manometer pointer started to move.

Graf exhaled forcefully. 'Thank God.'

'I suspect,' said Lorenz, 'that He had very little to do with it.'

Falk grimaced. The first watch officer considered such provocations unwise when the scales were so finely balanced.

One hundred and seventy, one hundred and sixty-five, one hundred and sixty . . .

The boat was perilously deep; however, the ascent – once it had begun – was sustained, a tentative, gentle engagement with acclivity. Each second dragged and eager faces were enamelled with perspiration. Some dared to entertain the possibility that they might actually survive. At twelve metres Lorenz ordered a reduction in speed. There was an anxious moment when the bow dipped, but it rose again almost instantly. The observation periscope was raised and Lorenz looked through the viewer. 'I can see them.'

'What are they doing?' asked Graf.

'They appear to be waiting for us.'

'Maybe we left some oil behind.'

'Let's creep away while we can. Both motors, ahead slow.'

Half an hour later Lorenz raised the periscope again. There were no escorts. All that he could see was a smudge of discoloration high in the sky: smoke that had risen from the cargo ship they had torpedoed. 'Gone,' said Lorenz. 'Prepare to surface.' He gazed around the control room which looked as if it had recently confined an enraged bull. The matting was littered with tools, broken glass, discarded oilskins, shoes, and a crucifix. He picked up this last item, contemplated the diminutive Christ (whose features were remarkably expressive for such a small object) and laid it on the chart table. 'Start the bilge pumps,' he said. 'Chief: ahead one half.' Ordinarily, the grinding of the pumps was irritating, but at that moment they sounded sweeter than a lullaby. The second watch were already assembling. As soon as U-330 broke the surface the diesels started up. Lorenz climbed into the conning tower and opened the hatch. Cool, fresh air rushed into the boat and for a moment he was arrested by its purity. He stepped up onto the bridge, scanned the horizon and leaned against the bulwark. Juhl and the rest of the watch followed. None of them spoke. They were all enjoying the private ecstasy of being alive. The sea was a heaving mass of molten lead bathed in a jaundiced light. It would be dark soon. Waves smacked against the bow, raising geysers.

Lorenz turned the bridge over to Juhl and went back down to his cabin to get his war diary. Richter was still lying on his bed and being treated by Ziegler, who in addition to being a radio operator was also the boat's medical orderly. The gash across Richter's face had been cleaned but this made it look worse, rather than better. It was now possible to see how wide and deep it was. Spikes of bone were clearly visible. The injured man was silent, his eyes closed.

'I'm sorry I dropped Richter.'

Lorenz turned to see Berger standing close by, evidently expecting a stinging reprimand. 'Yes, you certainly chose your moment. When did you decide to change sides, Berger? Had you been thinking about it for a while or was it a spur-of-the-moment decision?'

'Kaleun?' The boy looked horrified.

'Go and make yourself useful, Berger,' Lorenz didn't want

to berate the young seaman any further. 'There's plenty for you to do.'

Berger sketched a salute and made a swift retreat.

Having escaped annihilation the men felt indestructible and went about their business with fierce enthusiasm. They reminded Lorenz of the 'heroes' who appeared in the U-boat propaganda films that the Party showed back home. There was banter, jokes – robust high spirits. Yet, the outcome could so easily have been very different, the boat, broken, resting on the sea bed and these same men harassed by fishes with sharp teeth, perpetual night.

Looking down at the injured man, Lorenz addressed Ziegler. 'How is he?'

'Not good.'

'Kaleun,' Richter groaned.

'Yes, it's me,' Lorenz responded. 'You banged your head rather badly. Just rest for a while, eh?'

Richter's eyelids flicked open. They were red with irises like discs of jet. He looked like something that had clambered out of a fissure in hell.

'Kaleun?'

'Rest. You're going to be fine.'

'I saw him.'

'What?'

'I saw him.'

'You saw who?'

'The British officer.'

'Well, we all saw him, Richter. He was our prisoner.'

'No, Kaleun. He was in the diesel room. I saw him.'

The men who were standing nearby might have laughed, but none of them did. Lorenz wanted to believe that this was because they were feeling sorry for their comrade, but their uneasy expressions suggested otherwise.

'You've had a nasty knock on the head, Richter.'

'I saw him.'

'Ziegler,' Lorenz whispered, 'can you give him something? He's lost a lot of blood. He's in shock. We don't want him agitated like this.'

'Yes,' said Ziegler. 'I'll do that.'

As Lorenz moved to walk away Richter's hand shot out and grabbed his commander's sleeve with surprising strength. He gripped it so hard Lorenz couldn't free himself. 'I saw him,' the injured man insisted. 'And he pushed me.'

While repairs were being undertaken the weather became progressively worse. A belligerent wind flayed the waves and raised curtains of foam. Green mountain ranges with frothy peaks appeared on either side of the boat and storm clouds gathered at every compass point. By the following morning conditions were appalling. Men were vomiting into cans and one of the petty officers was thrown from his bunk. Lorenz went up to the bridge and leaned against the periscope housing. The ocean resembled a winter landscape; wherever he looked the surface had been agitated into uniform whiteness. As the saddle tanks rolled out of the turbulence he was hurled against the bulwark. Lorenz tapped Müller on the shoulder. 'Enough! Clear the bridge.' He gesticulated at the open hatch and shouted 'Dive!' into the communications pipe. The watch clambered into the tower, and, after taking a quick look around, Lorenz followed them down.

In the control room Lorenz sloughed off his oilskins and said, 'Forty metres.' The vents were closed and there was the customary burst of activity prior to the boat's descent. As the manometer pointer revolved, the reeling, yawing, rocking and swaying subsided and a grateful hush spread through the compartments.

Lorenz proceeded to the radio room where he undertook a leisurely perusal of the boat's record collection. Strauss waltzes, Wagner overtures and the complete Mozart horn concertos; traditional naval marches (rarely played); tangos and foxtrots arranged for a small dance band; hits performed by Zarah Leander, Marika Rökk, and Lale Andersen; French cabaret songs and illicit American jazz – Cole Porter, Glenn Miller and Benny Goodman. Although the Party had banned jazz, this prohibition wasn't enforced on U-boats. Indeed, the popularity of jazz among U-boat crews was common knowledge in Berlin and considered, with weary disapproval, as another example of their tiresome eccentricity.

'Put this on,' said Lorenz, handing Brandt a Benny Goodman record. The public-address system transmitted the thump of the connecting stylus and the boat filled with lively syncopations. Lorenz retired to his nook, but left the green curtain open. Lying on his bed, he listened to Goodman's agile clarinet, the irregular leaping intervals, the growling low notes, the sweet high notes. It was such paradoxical music, powerful and driving, yet at the same time fleet and fluidly inventive. How bizarre, thought Lorenz, to be travelling under the sea in an artificial air bubble, while listening to jazz! The vibrations would be transferred through the hull and out into the deep, providing a musical accompaniment for passing squid and porpoises. When the music came to an end, he called out: 'And another.'

Lorenz got up and walked to the officers' mess where he found Graf, sitting alone, finishing a coffee. The chief engineer had exchanged his grey leathers for British standard-issue khakis. He had acquired the uniform from captured stocks abandoned by the British Expeditionary Force prior to their departure from the northern French ports. Such spoils were much sought-after.

'Repairs complete?' Lorenz asked

'Almost,' Graf replied.

Lorenz sat down beneath a portrait of Vice Admiral Dönitz. 'What about the hydroplanes?'

'They seem to be working very well.'

'So what happened? Why did we have to switch to manual operation during the attack?'

'I checked the system.' Graf's sentence was irresolute.

'And . . .'

'Thoroughly, you understand.' The chief engineer sipped his coffee. 'I checked the system thoroughly and I couldn't find a fault.'

'But there must be an explanation, a cause?'

'Not all causes are readily identifiable, Kaleun.'

'Just one of those things, then, eh?' Lorenz repeated Graf's favourite maxim.

'Yes,' Graf shrugged, his voice flat. 'Yes, Herr Kaleun.'

A tin of vitamin-fortified chocolates caught Lorenz's attention. He prised the lid off, selected one and popped it into his mouth. As he chewed, his expression became contemplative. 'There was a problem with the attack periscope.'

'Was there?' Graf leaned forward, concerned. 'You didn't say . . .'

'It suddenly rotated and I hadn't used the pedals.'

'Do you want me to take a look?'

'The machinery functioned well enough,' he paused to scratch his beard, 'in the end . . .'

Benny Goodman's clarinet soared above the chugging brass and the drummer produced a striking beat that suggested a reversion to the primitive.

'The boat's been very temperamental lately.' Graf's expression was full of meaning. He began to nod his head slightly, encouraging Lorenz to speculate.

'Everything was working when we left Brest.'

'Still . . .' Graf continued to nod.

Rumours of sabotage had been circulating for some time. 'Nothing has been tampered with,' said Lorenz dismissively. Graf accepted Lorenz's rebuff with stoic calm. Only the fractional elevation of his right eyebrow betrayed his mild irritation.

They sat in silence for a while, both listening to a bright, blaring trumpet solo. When the full orchestra returned, Lorenz addressed Graf in a low, confidential register. 'The crew . . .' He hesitated before continuing, 'Are the crew all right? Do you think?'

'I had a chat with Sauer. He thinks Richter may have unsettled them,' Graf replied.

Lorenz took another chocolate. 'Do you remember that old story about Günter Leidland?'

'What story?'

'His boat was scheduled to leave Lorient on Friday the thirteenth. As the date approached his men were getting more and more on edge, so he cast off on the twelfth and sailed to the other side of the dock, where he and his crew waited for a whole day before continuing their patrol.' Lorenz studied the second chocolate before putting it in his mouth. When he spoke again it was as though he was thinking aloud. 'It's possible to convince yourself of certain things . . .'

'They'll be all right,' said Graf. Then, indicating the chocolates he added, 'Have you finished with these, Kaleun?'

'Yes,' Lorenz replied, standing up. Graf pressed the lid back onto the tin and Lorenz walked off. He found Richter lying on a bunk in the bow compartment. The injured man was feverish and talking in his sleep. A bandage had been wrapped around his head and only one of his eyes was visible. Lorenz noticed the iris oscillating beneath the papery lid. He tried to make sense of what the mechanic was saying, bending down so that his ear was close to Richter's lips. A single, clear phrase interrupted the stream of poorly articulated syllables. 'Stay away from me, you devil!'

Lorenz drew back.

'What did he say?' asked Voigt.

'Nothing,' Lorenz replied. 'He's delirious.'

*

Juhl handed the decoded message to Lorenz who accepted it with a curt nod. His expression gave away nothing. As always, after a message had been received, the men watched him closely. He fancied that he could feel their frustration when, albeit for only a few seconds, he disappeared behind the curtain of his nook. When he emerged his features were still uninterpretable and set hard, like plaster of Paris. He marched resolutely to the petty officers' quarters where he found Hoffmann. sitting on a bunk, reading a damp, disintegrating newspaper. Torn strips hung out loosely from the front page. The electrician sensed Lorenz looming over him and stood up. 'Herr Kaleun?'

'Well, Hoffmann.' Lorenz steadied himself by reaching out to grip a rail. 'How are you feeling today?'

'As good as can be expected, sir.'

'Yes, filthy weather.' The electrician folded his newspaper. 'We just got a message from headquarters,' Lorenz added.

Hoffmann looked bemused. He wasn't accustomed to being taken into the commander's confidence. His brow wrinkled as he tried to work out what was expected of him. Feeling obliged to respond, he made a guess: 'Is it about the batteries, sir?'

'No,' said Lorenz. 'However, it *does* concern you.'

'Me, sir?' Hoffmann looked over Lorenz's shoulder at Juhl, who was as inscrutable as his superior.

'A personal communication from Admiral Dönitz,' said Lorenz.

Hoffmann's face showed confusion and incredulity. 'Admiral Dönitz?'

'Indeed.'

'Are you sure there hasn't been a mistake, sir?'

'Quite sure.'

'Admiral Dönitz?' Hoffmann repeated the name in an uncomfortable, higher register.

'The Lion himself!' Lorenz produced a sheet of paper and held it up ceremoniously as if he were about to read from a scroll. 'You are informed, Elektro-Obermaschinist Hoffmann, of the arrival of a submarine,' Lorenz looked over the top of the paper, 'without periscope.'

'Without periscope . . .' Hoffmann echoed.

Lorenz handed Hoffmann the paper and pulled a bottle out of his pocket. 'Congratulations.' Suddenly, men began to crowd into the petty officers' quarters. They extended their arms to shake Hoffmann's hand and reached in to slap him on the back. 'I gather from Juhl here,' Lorenz continued, 'that you were hoping for a daughter.'

'Yes, I was.' Hoffmann looked at Juhl. 'How did you know?'

'You told me.'

'Did I?'

'Maybe not explicitly: on the bridge.'

'I don't remember that.'

Lorenz filled two glasses and handed one to Hoffmann. 'To your daughter, may she enjoy a long life of unprecedented health and spectacular happiness.'

'Thank you, Herr Kaleun,' said Hoffmann. His eyes glittered with emotion.

After touching glasses they downed the rum.

Werner emerged from the galley and made a lewd remark about Hoffmann's potency, which provoked laughter and quick exchanges of competitive vulgarity.

'Have you thought of a name?' Lorenz asked.

'My wife likes Dorothea,' said Hoffmann.

'And so do I,' said Lorenz. 'Congratulations.'

The men parted, giving him enough room to leave. On returning to his nook, Lorenz observed, with considerable attendant regret, that his bottle of rum was now almost empty.

The lights had been dimmed in all compartments. Lorenz stepped out of the forward torpedo room and made his way between the occupied bunks. He passed the officers' mess, the sound room, the radio shack – climbed through the forward compartment hatchway – and arrived in the control room. Graf was standing by the periscope and Müller was studying charts. The crew looked at Lorenz but their expressions were curiously untenanted. Lorenz crossed the control room and ducked into the petty officers' quarters where the bunks were also fully occupied with sleeping men. As he passed through the galley Lorenz saw Werner at his stove. The cook was beating a thick red mixture with a whisk. His skin shone with a porcelain glaze and the ticking revolutions of his wrist made him resemble a clockwork dummy. Lorenz continued, along the narrow gangway between the motionless diesel engines and then into the motor room. Because the motors were relatively small and mostly concealed beneath the deck, this part of the boat appeared spacious and uncluttered. The lights flickered into darkness and when they came on again they emitted a weak glow: a slow luminescence that diffused through the air like an expanding ink blot. Beyond the panels of the motor room Lorenz could see the rim of the rear torpedo tube. He paused and found that he was reluctant to go forward. Why was this part of the boat empty? Where had everyone gone? The sound of Werner's whisk suddenly stopped. Its abrupt termination created an odd impression, like stepping off a precipice. Everything seemed wrong, misaligned, disturbed by subtle discords. He tried to remember what he had been meaning to do, the purpose of his nocturnal wandering, but his memory was opaque – misted over with undefined anxieties. Unease made him turn on his heels and the next instant he was looking into the eyes of the British commander. Sutherland's hands came up quickly and closed around Lorenz's neck. Weakness and terror made retaliation impossible. Lorenz tried to call for help but his windpipe was being crushed. Sutherland swung him round, pushed him against one of the electric motors and tightened his grip. Their noses were almost touching.

'Destruction is *your* purpose,' said Sutherland, repeating the words that Lorenz had used during their brief parley. 'Destruction is *your* purpose as much as it is mine.' His voice was fortified by an echo, the final iterations of which survived the dissolution of the dream. Lorenz stared at the overhead. He was breathing heavily but he could still hear waves breaking against the conning tower.

'Herr Kaleun?' Brandt sounded anxious.

Lorenz's answer was poorly articulated. 'Bran— ... Brandt?'

'Did you call for something, Kaleun?'

'Yes,' Lorenz improvised. 'I've got a murderous headache. Go and get Ziegler for me, will you? I need some pills.'

Lorenz sat up and swallowed with difficulty. He undid the top button of his shirt and pressed the flesh around his neck. It felt tender and sore. How could that be? Had he harmed himself in his sleep? Had the blanket twisted around his body as he tossed and turned?

'Kaleun?' It was Ziegler. Lorenz raised his collars before pulling the curtain aside. 'You wanted some aspirin?'

'Yes,' said Lorenz hoarsely. 'Thank you.'

The wind had abated and a dull, dejected light filtered through a ragged canopy of cloud. White lines spaced at regular intervals travelled across a malachite sea. Falk was looking through his binoculars, listening to Engel and Krausse's conversation. He was about to remind them of the need for constant vigilance, when curiosity got the better of him and he chose to remain silent.

'So,' said Engel. 'I was lying on a sofa in the Casino Bar, and Hauser – do you know him? – Commander of U-395 – he asked Madam to show us one of her films. I'd heard about them but I'd never seen one. Hauser was very drunk and waving a bottle of champagne in the air. Madam said no and made some excuse or other; something about the girls not having had an opportunity to perform, I don't know. Anyway, Hauser wasn't put off. He kept on and on at her, begged and pleaded, said that his men had been at sea for so long they'd all forgotten how to fuck. "We need to be reminded," he said. Eventually, she gave in and when Hauser and his crew went upstairs I followed them, just tagged along. Madam set up the projector, the lights went out, and the film started. Well, how can I put this? It was a real education. Perhaps the women in this film were freaks, you know? Like you'd find in a circus? Because they got themselves into positions that I didn't think were possible. And there was this incredible scene, set in what looked like a respectable drawing room, in which several large objects were laid out on the floor in front of this little brunette, she was tiny, no bigger than a child, and she . . .' Engel stopped. 'Are we turning?'

'I believe so,' said Falk.

'Shit! I hope we're not going back into that storm.' Engel spat over the bulwark.

'What's that?' said Sauer. 'Starboard quarter forty-five degrees. In the water.'

The watchmen turned so that they were all facing in the same direction.

Falk raised his binoculars. 'I can't see anything, Number One.'

'Nor me,' Krausse agreed.

'What did it look like?' asked Falk.

Sauer hesitated. 'I thought I saw something . . .'

'What?'

'I'm not sure.'

'But not a periscope,' said Falk.

'No,' Sauer responded, 'definitely not a periscope.'

'All right,' said Falk. 'Probably just flotsam. Stay alert.'

After a few minutes of silent observation had elapsed, Sauer heard the ladder thrumming – the sound of someone ascending. He stiffened and announced: 'Captain on the bridge.' Lorenz climbed out of the conning tower and stood next to Falk: 'New instructions from headquarters.'

Falk wiped the lenses of his binoculars. 'A convoy?'

'Over twenty ships. *All U-boats: maximum speed.* We're likely to get there first.'

'How long will it take us, sir?'

'Fourteen hours. Twelve hours if we're lucky. The weather forecast says the storm is moving north.'

'Will you look at that,' shouted Engel. 'God in heaven! Look at the size of it!'

Next to the boat the waves had been parted by something immense, rising up from below the surface – shiny, bluish-grey. It arched out of the sea and produced a waterspout that rose higher than the conning tower. A small dorsal fin preceded the appearance of broad, notched flukes. Within seconds the whale had disappeared leaving only a transparent mist over a wide eddy.

Falk called down the communications pipe. 'Hard a-port!' Lorenz nodded his approval and said, 'A sensible precaution. We should give that monster a very wide berth. One swipe from that tail and our rudder will be off. Very good, Falk, I have the conn.'

The boat veered away but the creature almost immediately closed the gap. It could be seen through the transparency of the waves, a long, aquamarine shadow almost thirty metres in length. Once again, it surfaced and forced air through its blowhole.

'Shoo, shoo,' said Engel, flicking his hands in the air as if he were trying to discourage a troublesome fly. They were all still laughing when Krausse hollered, 'Aircraft, dead astern!'

Lorenz was about to shout 'Alarm!' but the pilot had already commenced his attack run and it was far too late to dive. He grabbed the communications pipe: 'Right, full rudder.' Falk leapt to the rear platform and manned the 2 cm flak cannon. The plane was coming at them low.

'Oh, fuck,' hollered Falk. 'The cannon's jammed.' He worked the charging mechanism to load the new round in the chamber. It still didn't work. Sauer calmly detached the magazine, smacked it on the breach and re-seated it in the well: Falk jacked the action and swept the weapon around to track the fighter. With uncharacteristic agility, Sauer skipped out of the way and retrieved a spare magazine.

'Evasive manoeuvres,' Lorenz shouted into the hatch. The boat turned sharply and crashed into a high wave as the useless cannon traced a silent arc. Through a curtain of shimmering spray they watched the unhurried descent of four bombs. Three of them exploded off the starboard saddle tank, creating a line of tall fountains. The effect was ornamental, like a water feature in an eighteenth-century landscaped garden. A loud splitting noise made Lorenz look down from the bulwark in horror. The fourth bomb had landed on the painted wooden grating and was now bouncing towards the bridge. A shower of splinters followed each impact and the bomb's progress was recorded by a trail of gouges in the deck. As the boat heeled and rolled, the lethal device slowed, swerved and slid off the port side, its nose propeller still spinning madly. The pilot had flown so low that their faces had been momentarily warmed by hot exhaust fumes. So low, that the bomb hadn't fuzed. Lorenz gazed at the receding plane in stunned silence. He had expected it to bank and return, but instead the pilot followed a straight course over the sea.

'Why isn't he coming back?' asked Engel.

'He's used up all his bombs,' Lorenz answered.

'God, that was close.' Engel took off his woollen hat and raked his hair.

'It certainly was,' Lorenz agreed.

'That last one,' said Sauer, 'fancy it being a dud.'

'A miracle,' said Engel.

'Well, I wouldn't go that far,' said Lorenz. 'However, I . . .' As Lorenz looked up he was struck dumb by the appearance of another Martlet dropping out from beneath the cloud cover.

Krausse was screaming: 'Aircraft astern!'

Again, it was too late to dive. Lorenz called into the communications pipe: 'Hard a-starboard!'

Falk repositioned the flak cannon, took careful aim, depressed the firing lever and swore: 'You fucking hopeless piece of shit!' In frustration, he smacked the top of the breach with his fist and was rewarded with a satisfying clunk. When he depressed the firing lever again the cannon roared into life and a quick three-round burst was directed harmlessly into the ocean. He raised the barrel and emptied the rest of the magazine without even bothering to aim as the fighter flew past. The boat was turning quickly enough to ruin the pilot's attack run and the plane passed at a safe distance. No bombs were released. The pitch of the plane's engine suddenly altered. There was a spluttering sound, then some distinctly unhealthy mechanical coughing, before the engine cut out altogether.

'I got it!' Falk exclaimed. 'I fucking got it!'

Lorenz watched, transfixed, as the Martlet's canopy slid back. 'Get out,' he whispered. 'Get out!'

The pilot negotiated a tight circle as he fought to maintain control, but the plane lost altitude and one of its wing tips touched the water. It tumbled across the surface, disintegrating, and the pilot was ejected from his cockpit. He was still airborne when the fuel tanks exploded and his body was engulfed by flames. Burning debris showered the bridge.

'Full ahead,' shouted Lorenz.

They all scanned the sky, tense, and ready for the appearance of a third plane, but no more came. Some smoking wreckage bobbed up and down on the sea.

Falk pointed beyond their frothy wake. 'Remarkable!' The great dark back of the whale was still visible. They could hear the blast of its waterspout before the massive tail sprang up and fanned the air. 'We shouldn't let that monster distract us again.'

'Quite,' said Lorenz. 'Perhaps he's working for the British.'

'Why didn't the bombs scare him?'

'Perhaps he's deaf.'

'I've a good mind to blow it out of the water. Werner could do with some fresh meat.' Falk rotated the flak cannon. 'Let's have a feast tonight.'

'No,' said Engel. 'Don't do that, sir. Poor beast: he doesn't mean us any harm. He probably thinks our boat is a female, that's all.'

'Really, Engel,' said Falk. 'You're completely preoccupied with sex!'

'When I was Rylander's first watch officer,' said Lorenz, 'we shot a polar bear and ate it.'

'Did it taste any good?' asked Falk.

'I've had worse meals in Hamburg,' said Lorenz. 'Well done, Falk. Good shooting.'

'That fourth bomb,' said Sauer, still trying to make sense of its provident failure to explode. 'Unbelievable. That's what I call lucky.'

'Like I always say,' said Falk. 'When your number's up, your number's up.' He secured the flak cannon and tapped the rail a few times. 'Our number wasn't up.'

War Diary

12.50   Light swell. Cloudy but clear. Reasonable visibility.
Smoke shadow bearing 115° true. Course around
120°. An aircraft in sight at bearing 115° true, roughly
the same course.

13.30   Aircraft in sight, possibly a Sunderland. Bearing 180°
true, course 130°. The aircraft turns and retraces its
course.

13.40   A U-boat in sight at bearing 60° true. Closing.

15.03   Plume of smoke at bearing 100° true. Within minutes
further plumes of smoke appear over the horizon.
A total of six.

15.50   Some distance away, an aircraft in sight bearing 130°.

16.30   The convoy's air escort has been flying over with some
regularity. On one occasion two Martlet fighters were
observed together. There is a British carrier escorting
this convoy; identity unknown.

23.21   Minimal wind and sea, sporadic clouds, night rather dark. Advance to attack. Battle stations. Our intention to fire four bow torpedoes, and, after turning, to fire a stern torpedo; however, the bow caps for tubes I and II do not open.

23.31   We fire with tubes III and IV at two steamers, and then, after turning, we fire a third torpedo from tube V at another steamer separated from its column. No detonations heard. We withdraw to reload torpedoes and reposition on the opposite side of the convoy. The escorts are firing star shells but these are so poorly directed there is no danger of being detected.

Explosions. Tanker ablaze.

00.10   Run in for second attack. Just before we are about to reach our firing position a U-boat appears between us and the convoy. We turn away because the field of fire is obstructed. As we retreat we see a burning tanker. In front of it is a damaged steamer listing badly. Destroyers continue to launch star shells indiscriminately and the horizon is well lit. We see the convoy sailing past the burning tanker. 23 vessels.

03.32   We run in to attack once again.

03.40   Two torpedoes fired from tubes II and IV. After 3 minutes and 20 seconds we see a torpedo detonation and a great flash. A burst of star shells follows. This time they are directed with greater accuracy but our boat is still unobserved.

03.50   I withdraw from the convoy. As we head off we hear the sound of depth charges.

04.15   No more torpedoes. Report to B.d.U. via W/T, requesting permission to return to port.

Siegfried Lorenz

All of the bunks and hammocks in the bow compartment were occupied by sleeping sailors whose constant growling, huffing and wheezing confirmed the fundamental brutishness of the human condition. The effect suggested a cave of hibernating bears. In the last of the starboard bunks, Richter was raised up slightly on some pillows, looking at Lorenz with the aid of his single, serviceable eye. A yellow-brown stain had seeped through the mould-speckled dressing that had been wrapped diagonally around his head. The wound underneath, Lorenz supposed, was probably infected and would take a long time to heal. Richter might not survive, especially if the infection was spreading through his body or blood was clotting in his brain. The air was noisome, sulphurous, like rotten eggs, and what remained of the suspended foodstuffs had turned black. Incessant dripping made everything permanently damp.

Lorenz shifted his gaze from Richter to Graf. 'The caps are working now?'

'Yes,' Graf replied, 'one and two, fully operational.'

'This is getting ridiculous.'

'I really have no idea—'

'—what went wrong,' Lorenz cut in, making a dismissive gesture.

'I'm sorry, Herr Kaleun.' Graf's apology received no acknowledgement.

The torpedo doors were arranged squarely like the four dots on a die. Surrounding them was a chaotic arrangement of large and small conduits, wheels and metal boxes.

'So,' said Lorenz, turning to speak to Kruger and Dressel, the two torpedo men. 'What happened to our first batch of torpedoes?'

'They were properly maintained, Herr Kaleun,' said Kruger. His unsightly rashes were particularly vivid and his nose was misshapen by outcrops of boils.

'What about the calculator connection?' Lorenz asked.

'No problems there, sir,' Dressel answered. Like his colleague, his skin had been disfigured by exposure to toxic chemicals.

'They missed altogether – or didn't explode?' Lorenz raised his eyebrows, inviting the two torpedo men to offer an opinion.

Kruger cleared his throat and said, 'I'd checked the gyros, and – with respect, sir – as you know – with these torpedoes premature detonation is the more common problem.'

The boat rolled and the hoist chains rattled. Dressel raised his finger to indicate that he wished to speak. 'They say there's a tendency for the G7e Type II to fail if you go too far north. Once you've crossed the sixty-second parallel you can expect trouble, something to do with the earth's magnetic field.'

'That's all very interesting, Dressel, but we weren't above the sixty-second parallel.'

Dressel pulled off his hat and toyed with the badges that he had attached to the material. One of them was the boat's emblem, a crudely cut scorpion that he had fashioned himself from a tin can. 'It's not clear yet, sir. The science . . .'

Lorenz saw that Dressel was uncomfortable and adopted a less challenging tone of voice. 'True.'

'The firing pins could have been damaged,' said Kruger.

'Three of them?'

Graf nodded. 'Abnormally high interior pressure – that could have damaged the pins.'

'And the tubes haven't been watertight since we got hammered that last time,' said Kruger.

'Disturbed depth-regulation mechanisms?' Dressel addressed Kruger.

'If so,' Kruger continued, 'the torpedoes could have run so far under the targets the pistols wouldn't have fired.'

One of the sleeping sailors made a fearful cry, called out a name and sank back into his nightmare.

'We've been at sea for thirty-eight days,' said Dressel.

'Storing torpedoes for too long can cause difficulties, even if they are well-maintained.'

'Remember what happened to U-39?' Kruger shuddered. 'The torpedo pretty much exploded as soon as it left the tube. That was because they'd stored their torpedoes for too long.'

'But ours didn't explode at all,' said Lorenz. He looked at their blank faces and paraphrased Dressel. 'Things aren't clear yet? An inexact science?'

Kruger shrugged.

'Kaleun,' Richter raised a feeble arm. 'Kaleun? It was him.'

'Oh, for God's sakes, Richter,' said Kruger. 'Just take it easy. Go to sleep.'

'I saw him,' Richter continued. 'The British officer.'

Kruger spoke to Lorenz in a whisper. 'He's driving me mad with all this talk, Kaleun.'

Richter strained to sit up. 'He tried to strangle me. While I was asleep . . .'

'Get Ziegler,' said Lorenz.

'I think the poor sod has already had too much morphine,' said Graf.

'Something bad will happen,' Richter cried.

'It already has, Richter,' said Lorenz. 'We're at war.' His attempt at levity was ineffective. Graf, Kruger and Dressel fidgeted uneasily and looked away. Lorenz marched off, annoyed. Richter's words were still resonating in his mind. *He tried to strangle me. While I was asleep* . . . As Lorenz weaved his way around the clutter between the bunks, he accidentally kicked a book which skidded over the linoleum. When he picked it up, he discovered that his boot had made contact with the Bible. Usually, his men read collections of obscene jokes or adventure stories. The fact that one or more of them was seeking solace in scripture did not bode well. Richter's utterances were fraying nerves, not least of all his own.

Once again, the weather worsened and waves crashed against the conning tower. The hull of U-330 resounded like a metal drum being repeatedly struck with a mallet. There were rasps, scrapes and screeches, and occasionally the entire structure would shake so violently that the agitation threatened to rearrange internal organs and loosen joints. The perpetual, dizzying motion was intolerable. When the diesel intake vents were submerged the engines drew air from inside the boat. Wild pressure variations caused ears to ache. Water poured through vents and the pumps worked ceaselessly. No one could eat. The mere thought of food caused bile to rise in the throat. Crewmen became rigid and jerked backwards through the air as the boat heeled. Some sank to their knees, mimicking the revolving descent of marionettes with relaxed strings, while others, overwhelmed by nausea, clung to pipes and valve wheels. Casualties mounted: twisted ankles, bloody faces, knocked-out teeth – a suspected fractured rib, a sprained wrist, grazes and bruises. Vomit collected in the bilges and sailors retired to their bunks, clutching their stomachs and mumbling curses.

Lorenz ordered as many dives as possible. Sixty metres below the roiling surface, U-330 was able to follow a largely untroubled course, heading south towards Brest, both electric motors running slow, its trim scarcely disturbed by deep currents; however, this relative calm did not allow for a return to normality, there were none of the usual card games and salacious stories, no jazz records on the turntable. The crew were enfeebled by starvation and exhausted by sickness. Only Richter broke the silence with sudden, brief outbursts, during which he voiced oblique warnings about the British devil.

The boat could not remain submerged indefinitely; only one or two hours when travelling at maximum speed. Then it was necessary to surface in order to run the diesels and recharge the batteries.

On the eighth day of the storm, within seconds of arriving on the bridge, Falk was thrown against the bulwark and knocked unconscious. Lorenz took his place, joining Hoffmann, Berger and Arnold for the returning first watch. It was difficult to negotiate the ladder dressed in oilskins, and even harder getting Falk below; whenever the hatch was opened water cascaded into the tower. Lorenz had to hang on tightly to prevent himself from being dislodged. He struggled out and immediately secured his safety belt to the aiming-device pedestal with a snap hook. The world had become a place of extravagant savagery. Black clouds were boiling over the horizon, mounting towards the zenith, while sheer, perpendicular faces of grey-green water collided and shattered, saturating the air with icy spume. The boat yawed and lurched forward.

Water flooded onto the bridge through the rear railings and its sucking retreat dragged Lorenz until he fell. He hauled himself upright and when he peered over the bulwark a rising geyser delivered a powerful uppercut that snapped his head back. The foul-weather gear was almost useless in these extreme conditions. Freezing water dripped down his back and legs and filled his boots, the oilskin collar chafed his neck, and the salt water made the sensitive, broken skin burn. His gloves were heavy and soaked through.

U-330 tilted and glided around the outer rim of a whirlpool. It reminded Lorenz of Charybdis, the legendary scourge of ancient Greek maritime heroes. For a few heart-stopping seconds he thought that the boat was going to slip into the vortex and spiral towards its deep centre of attraction. The diesels throbbed, the screws turned, and the boat fought free of the swirling precipice. U-330 chugged up a steep swell, teetered at the summit and then slid down the other side. The entire forward section of the upper casing was invisible and covered in hissing foam. Even the 8.8 cm gun was completely submerged.

The swell lifted them again to a point of vantage that revealed an astonishing vista of jagged peaks and valleys; the entire ocean appeared to be escaping from the earth's gravitational field. They were surrounded by leaping, thrusting upheavals.

'Chaos,' Lorenz whispered to himself. He looked back at his companions and registered their terror.

The boat began to descend at a steep angle.

'Hold fast,' Lorenz hollered. The next wave reared up in front of them, a monstrous wave, the crest of which curved over their heads. 'Hold fast, we're going under.'

The bow cut through the water and the sound of the lashing wind died. Suddenly, there was only green and cold and gurgling and the jarring shock of total immersion. Lorenz felt his boots rising off the platform, the restraining band of the safety belt biting into his waist. How many metres were they under the surface? Ten? Twenty? And still going down? He couldn't breathe and the acute cold became pain. Thirty metres? Slowly, the boat levelled and began to ascend. The pain from the belt was excruciating. He was reminded of officer training, when he was made to lift a heavy, electrified iron bar and ordered not to drop it. A shadowy curtain dropped and he supposed that he was about to lose consciousness. His memories deserted him and he was reduced to a state of rudimentary awareness – a sensory trace, raw nerve endings. And then the tower was out of the water and he was lying on the bridge coughing and aching and gasping beneath a blazing arc of lightning. He pulled himself up again and turned to face his companions. Berger was clinging to the periscope housing and the control-room mate was on all fours spluttering over the hatch. Hoffmann wasn't there.

'Hoffmann?' he screamed, 'Hoffmann?' And then: 'Man overboard!' But even as he screamed these words he knew that Hoffmann was lost. The boat was pitched from one wave to the next and sheets of sleet swept over the bow. Shaking, Lorenz looked out across the retributive water and shook his head in despair. Even if Hoffmann was close, shouting for help and waving his arms, they wouldn't be able to see him. Berger and the control-room mate were standing up, wiping their eyes, trying to stay on their feet. The seething water rose to their chests and pulled them all towards the stern. Lorenz found Hoffmann's dangling snap hook and held it in his hand, like a clairvoyant might: trying to establish contact with a departed spirit by caressing a once-treasured trinket.

What must it be like, to be out there now? Sinking, weighed down by the foul-weather gear, or carried away by frozen currents? Lorenz judged that Hoffmann might still be capable of thought – although only just. There might still be a final flickering before the light went out: memories of his wife, wishes for the daughter he would never see.

Lorenz had once been told that the final stages of drowning were peaceful, that when the struggling was over, the battle lost, there was only serene acceptance. He hoped that Hoffmann was experiencing this sublime state. When Lorenz looked up into the roaring, flashing sky, he found it difficult to believe such things. Hoffmann had been ripped off the bridge and transported to hell. How could such a cruel, harsh and lonely death be so comprehensively mitigated by the weightless compensations of a dying brain?

Letting go of the snap hook, Lorenz seized the communications pipe and shouted, 'Hard a-starboard.' They would undertake a search, regardless of its futility.

Lorenz was sitting with Falk and Graf in the officers' mess beneath a swinging lightshade, observing a luminous circle that oscillated from one side of the table to the other. Although the boat was still pitching and rolling the weather had improved a little. Graf was eating some sliced sausage and a chunk of bread that was so hard he was obliged to clench his jaw until a corner separated from the whole with a loud 'crack'. When he began chewing it sounded as though he was grinding gravel with his molars.

'I've never known it to happen before,' said Falk. He scratched at the bandage that covered his swollen forehead.

Graf grimaced as he swallowed. 'It happens . . .'

'But how?' Falk communicated his bemusement by showing his empty palms.

'The leather disintegrated.' Graf loosened a sliver of meat that had become stuck to the plate with his thumbnail and lifted it to his mouth.

Falk paused, considered the chief engineer's answer and said, '*Someone* would have noticed. *Hoffmann* would have noticed.'

'There must have been a tear then. A small tear: small enough to be overlooked.'

'Our safety belts are ten centimetres wide.'

'That makes no difference.'

'And reinforced with steel cable . . .'

'Steel cables can break.' Graf was getting tired of the persistence of Falk's questioning. He glared at his inquisitor.

The first watch officer sighed. His gaze shifted from Graf to Lorenz and back again. 'It's just,' his speech was hesitant, 'we seem to have been getting more than our fair share of bad luck lately.'

Graf tightened the knot of the kerchief that he had tied around his throat. 'Accidents happen.'

The boat heeled and the engineer's plate slid down the table. Lorenz prevented it from hitting the rail. 'Luck?' he said, without looking up. 'What about the fourth bomb – when we were distracted by the whale – the fourth bomb that hit us and didn't explode? *That* was luck.'

Falk took a slice of sausage, studied it for a moment and then put it back on the plate. 'Well, Kaleun, that's just about the only bit of luck we've had on this patrol.'

'Yes,' said Lorenz. 'But it came at the right time. We wouldn't be sitting here now if that bomb had gone off. You and I would have been blown to bits – and this boat,' he struck a wooden panel with his fist before continuing, 'this boat would have gone straight to the bottom.'

Falk grunted his assent.

Placing a finger on one of his front teeth, Graf investigated its stability. There was a distinct wobble. He tossed the bread onto the table and swore.

'Could be worse,' said Lorenz. 'Some crews have had to eat their shoes.'

Juhl appeared and handed Lorenz a message from headquarters. It was a brief communication concerning three aircraft attacks on U-boats, none of which were close enough to merit action. The second watch officer withdrew discreetly like the head waiter of a high-class restaurant.

Lorenz addressed Falk: 'How's your head?'

'A lot better,' Falk replied.

'It doesn't look a lot better,' said Lorenz sceptically.

'The pain is . . .' Falk pressed his dressing and completed his sentence, 'tolerable.'

'You're not going to end up like Richter then?'

'Occasionally I see spots in front of my eyes,' Falk smiled, 'but nothing else, Kaleun.'

Graf put his elbows on the table and clasped his hands together. 'Richter isn't helping matters.'

'No,' said Lorenz.

'Shame we couldn't have transferred him to another boat.'

'I agree.'

'Do you think he'll make it?' asked Falk.

'I don't know,' Lorenz replied.

'What does Ziegler think?'

'Ziegler is a radio operator. He attended a thirty-six-hour first-aid course. We can't expect him to make that kind of prediction.'

'They should provide us with a doctor next time.'

'Doctors are more trouble than they're worth. They get sick as soon as they're on the open sea, they take up valuable space, and when they're finally well enough to get to work they complain incessantly about the conditions.'

'Won't be long now: once we're out of this storm . . .' said

Graf. His voice sounded distant and reflective, as though he were talking to himself.

'Ten days without a fix,' said Falk.

'Müller's dead reckoning is exceptional,' said Lorenz.

'Home . . .' said Graf.

Their conversation became disconnected and degenerated into a series of non sequiturs that preceded a long hiatus. Eventually, Lorenz rose from his seat and said, 'I'm going to get some sleep.' His companions, momentarily roused, nodded before sinking back into their respective states of self-absorption. He left them staring blankly at the table top.

Lorenz retired to his nook and closed the green curtain. A gap remained through which he spied Brandt in the radio room. Another tug of the curtain created a comforting illusion of privacy. Someone opened and closed the door to the diesel compartment and there was a sudden blast of engine noise. Lorenz took off his cap, lay down on his mattress and pulled a blanket that stank of oil over his body. He rested his head on the pillow and when he closed his eyes he became acutely aware of the boat's movements, the continuous rising and falling, the listing, sometimes sustained, that threatened to tip him out of bed. In the absence of any distractions he discovered that he wasn't feeling very well. His mouth was dry and an odd shivery sensation seemed to have settled around his shoulders. Demonstrating a sailor's faith in the restorative properties of rum, he propped himself up, retrieved the bottle from his bedside cabinet, and poured himself a generous final measure. He stared into the open drawer at the flat oval of Grimstad's stone. Pressing his fingertips onto the marked surface, Lorenz registered heat. Once again, he judged that the stone was warmer than it should be. Perhaps it was something to do with the iron content? This hollow speculation did nothing to quell a host of liminal anxieties. He drank slowly, savouring the flavour of the fragrant liquid, and when he had finished he put the bottle and glass back in the drawer. Pulling the blanket up to his chin, he allowed the falling boat to carry his unravelling mind towards sleep.

Before long he was walking by the cathedral of Notre-Dame in Paris with an attractive woman by his side. She was wearing a pillbox hat with a transparent veil that covered half her face. Her lips were sensual and as red as a cardinal's cassock. They talked and laughed and held hands as they made their way around the Hôtel Dieu and along the Quai de la Corse. Presently, they were crossing the Pont Neuf and heading towards the Right Bank. The woman stopped, drew him into a bastion and pointed towards the setting sun. Above, the sky was the same colour as the woman's lips and divided by thin, horizontal slats of purple cloud. Between the Pont Neuf and the Passerelle des Arts the black back of an enormous whale arched out of the Seine. Its motion was unhurried, almost sluggish, and when the woman turned to face Lorenz they embraced. Her perfume was familiar. He knew her well, this woman. They were lovers, but at the very same time she seemed to be a total stranger. This jarring contradiction was comfortably accommodated by the errant logic of the dream world and its resolution seemed as irrelevant as it was unnecessary. Paris melted away and they were no longer locked in a stationary embrace but dancing at a grand ball. There was a large orchestra on a raised stage and it was being conducted from the podium by Vice Admiral Dönitz. The surrounding décor was palatial: gilt mirrors, classical busts, and a painted ceiling overpopulated with gods, shepherds and cavorting nymphs. As Lorenz and the woman waltzed beneath glittering chandeliers, Lorenz spied his niece and nephew among the watching crowd. His niece waved as they passed. The tempo of the dance accelerated and Lorenz and the beautiful woman revolved faster and faster until everything blurred. When they finally stopped and parted, they were standing in a dry dock surrounded by cranes. The woman raised her hat and removed the pins from her hair. 'I'm going to need a complete overhaul,' she said, shaking out her tresses. Her German was softened by a French accent. 'It's going to take months.' The fact that she was naked seemed a perfectly natural development. The light changed and her pale skin began to darken. The process continued until she had turned the camouflage grey of a U-boat. When Lorenz reached out and touched her cheek he discovered it was hard and cold. She was no longer human but an iron statue. The scene changed abruptly and all that had gone before seemed vague and inconsequential. Lorenz was now on the deck of U-330, looking out over black water. He circumvented the 8.8 cm gun and stepped over the loading hatch of the forward torpedo room. When he could go no further he paused and waited. He knew they were out there. He knew they were coming. As expected, the raft drifted out of the night, materializing only a few metres distant. Once again, the British commander was standing by the central post and the old man was sitting at his feet; however, they had now been joined by a third person attired in oilskins and a sou'wester. This newcomer was standing behind the British commander, his head lowered and his posture suggesting dejection. The foul-weather gear was wet and when he moved forward the rubberized material glistened. Halting at the raft's edge the sailor removed his sou'wester. It was Hoffmann. He opened his mouth and water spilled out before he said, 'Permission to board, sir?'

'Permission denied, Hoffmann,' Lorenz responded. 'You're dead.'

'I know, sir.'

'Then be reasonable. Surely you must understand that I can't let the dead onto my ship.'

'But sir, you already have.'

The storm had subsided and all that remained was a squally wind that made the sea choppy and filled the air with twisting braids of spume. Juhl looked through his binoculars and tried to fight off the drowsiness that made his eyelids feel heavy. Endless rocking, sombre light and the unrelieved tedium of the flat horizon had already induced a temporary absence, but luckily this brief dereliction of duty had not attracted anyone's notice. Juhl had remained standing even though he had effectively abandoned his post for a minute or perhaps even more. It was unacceptable behaviour for a watch officer and he endeavoured to make sure that there would be no further lapses by sinking his front teeth into his lower lip until the pain made him alert.

'Aircraft dead astern,' cried Voigt. Juhl wheeled around and saw the approaching silhouette, which was sizeable, and immediately screamed 'Alarm!' The bell rang and the watchmen leapt through the hatch. When Juhl landed in the control room the stampede to the forward torpedo room was already underway. Graf was at his post behind the hydroplane operators, issuing orders. 'Clear air-release vents.'

Lorenz found Juhl and asked, 'What was it?'

'A Sunderland.' Juhl steadied himself by grabbing the halyard of the observation periscope.

Graf was hollering 'Flood!'

'Good,' Lorenz grunted.

'Good, Kaleun?' Juhl queried.

'Yes. Nothing to worry about – they're very slow . . .' But before he could continue his sentence there were several explosions and the hull was jolted by the shock waves. The pens and instruments on the chart table fell to the matting and a light bulb shattered. Lorenz stepped over Danzer, who had lost his balance, and positioned himself next to Graf. 'Take her down to seventy metres.' The manometer pointer revolved at a steady rate – *forty, fifty, sixty, seventy* – and when the boat levelled out Lorenz ordered two course changes. Two more explosions followed but they were distant and caused no damage. Müller picked up the items that had fallen from the chart table and the control-room mate, now back on his feet, started clearing the broken glass.

They waited for the Sunderland to return and more bombs to explode but the silence continued.

'Is that it?' said Graf, puzzled, almost disappointed.

'I believe so,' said Lorenz. 'They just wanted to annoy us. Even so, we'd better stay submerged for a short time at least.'

Perspiration prickled on his forehead. He still wasn't feeling very well.

Thirty minutes passed and Lorenz ordered Graf to take the boat up to periscope depth. He unfolded the handgrips, looked through the eyepiece and saw only green water. The tube was vibrating too much. 'Dead slow. Up scope . . .' A moment later he could see an expanse of sea and sky. He changed the viewing angle and increased the magnification but the boat dropped again. 'Watch your trim! Right so. Down – no, too much! Up-up-up . . . down, right so.'

His view consisted entirely of cloud, a pale grey canopy crossed by streaks of darker grey. When he had studied each quadrant and was satisfied that there were no aircraft he said, 'All clear. Prepare to surface.' He could hear the watch assembling, Juhl chivvying one of the ratings. Just as he was about to raise the handgrips, Lorenz noticed a tiny black speck flying low over the sea. It only took him a few seconds to determine that he was looking at a bird, most probably a seagull, and not a Sunderland in the distance.

'Kaleun?' Graf had noticed Lorenz's hesitation.

'It's all right. Go ahead – surface.'

The buoyancy tanks hissed and the boat began to rise.

'Bow planes up ten, stern planes up five.' There was a great splashing sound and Graf added, 'Conning tower free.'

Lorenz was about to raise the handgrips for the second

time, when he experienced a troubling qualm. Was the black speck really a seagull? Had he been too hasty? He undertook a final, cursory sweep of the horizon and it was only after the bow had flashed past that he paused and tried to make sense of what he had seen. His heart was expanding uncomfortably in his chest and his blood quickened. Even though he had received little more than a fleeting, blurred impression, there had been sufficient detail to permit interpretation; however, Lorenz concluded that he must be mistaken, because what he thought he had seen was clearly an impossibility. His intellect proffered a rational alternative: an illusion created by spray and perfidious light? But logical platitudes could not persuade his gut that there was nothing to fear. The periscope motor hummed as the objective rotated back so that he could view the bow once again. Waves slapped against both sides of the hull creating spires of foam. Lorenz could see the forward deck, receding, slightly raised above the horizon by the swell, and situated about halfway between the 8.8 cm gun and the prow was a man, dressed in a long coat, standing with his legs apart, facing away. He was wearing a cap and his hands were deep in his pockets. Lorenz closed his eyes, but when he opened them again the man was still there – a lone figure, inexplicably undisturbed by the boat's motion, the swash and backwash of the dismal sea. A panicky sensation spread through Lorenz's body, weakening his limbs and threatening to find expression in an involuntary cry. Words formed in his head, *I must be losing my mind*. He was suddenly seized by a desire to confront the phantom, regardless of its provenance.

Lorenz dashed to the ladder and brushed Juhl aside. Graf and the second watch officer exchanged confused glances. The agitated commander did not wait for the pressure to equalize and when he opened the hatch he was almost lifted onto the bridge by the escaping air. The watch followed him, perplexed by his urgency. Lorenz launched himself at the bulwark and leaning over the curved ridge, he stared at the empty forward half of the boat. The watch men gathered nervously behind him.

'Did you see something, Kaleun?' asked Juhl.

Lorenz took a deep breath. Spray hit his face and he licked the salt from his lips. It was strangely reassuring, the sharpness of the sensation, because it authenticated reality and seemed to impose a stricter limit on what was, and what wasn't, possible. 'I thought,' Lorenz began, 'I thought I saw a smudge on the horizon – see – over there – but it's just cloud – just darker cloud.'

'We haven't got any torpedoes left,' said Juhl. It was not a challenge. He was simply interested in what action his commanding officer would have taken had the 'smudge' turned out to be a steamer.

'I intended to use the deck gun,' Lorenz replied.

Juhl, seemingly content, nodded. The wind was freezing and cut straight through Lorenz's jumper: he had forgotten to put on his jacket in his rush to get up on the bridge. The fast beating of his heart coincided with a throbbing pain behind his eyes. 'Carry on,' he said, before lowering himself down the hatch. 'Carry on . . .'

War Diary

20.10   Minimal swell, mainly overcast, average visibility, freshening. At a bearing of 90° true several plumes of smoke. 15–20 nm distant. Qu BE 2374.

20.35   Flying boat at bearing 90° true, heading straight towards us. Alarm dive.

20.43   Surfaced.

20.45   Flying boat at bearing 90° true, heading straight towards us. Alarm dive. Two bombs. Minor damage.

21.15   U-boat heard through hydrophones at bearing 260° true.

21.32   Surfaced. To the south a fiery glow.

22.00   Test dive and performed essential repairs to the diesel-reverse mechanism, exhaust pipe and compressors.

2.35   We surface. Moderate swell, clearing from west, intermittent moonlight, visibility 6–7 nm.

3.10   Several shadows appear ahead. Battleships, range 6 nm. We alter course to 120° so as to avoid being seen by this group in the path of the moon.

3.35   Dive. Course altered to 300°.

4.50   We surface. Resound, then, foaming waves, And coil yourselves around me! Let misfortune rage loud around me, And let the cruel sea roar!

Siegfried Lorenz

The horizon was visible but indistinct. The inky perimeter of the sea and the hem of the night sky had fused together and it seemed to Lorenz that the boat had left the world behind and they were now soaring through the vast immensity of the universe. Tilting his head back, he gazed upwards at the constellations and the softly glowing arch of the milky way and he wondered if there were other planets orbiting stars similar to the sun, and if, at that precise moment, there might be another commander, standing on the bridge of another boat, crossing an equally benighted ocean, contemplating the existence of a counterpart elsewhere in the cosmos.

The sense of space, extending infinitely from the bridge in all directions, diminished the significance of human affairs. It imposed scale, a measure of such awesome magnitude, that nothing, not even the constant threat of annihilation seemed to matter very much. Even a Reich that lasted a thousand years would be forgotten with the passage of time.

Lorenz's thoughts were interrupted by Müller. The upper half of the navigator's body had risen through the hatch.

'Allow me,' said Lorenz, relieving Müller of his sextant.

'Thank you,' said Müller, scrambling onto the bridge. Lorenz immediately returned the instrument to Müller who surveyed the heavens before aiming the telescope at a conspicuously bright star. The navigator muttered to himself, turned a screw and held the graduated arc over the hatch so that the red glow emanating from the dark adaption light below would illuminate the figures. He repeated the process of observation and adjustment and then delivered his results by calling into the tower. After 'shooting' two more stars, his task was complete. He hissed a sailor's name and presently a hand reached out of the luminous well. 'Be careful with it,' said Müller, passing down the sextant.

'Are we in the right place?' asked Lorenz.

'More or less, within ten minutes of arc – a sun shot would be better.' A quicksilver meteor dropped from the zenith. 'Permission to have a cigarette, Kaleun?'

'You still have cigarettes, Müller? Extraordinary.'

'I have one cigarette. I've been saving it.'

'For the return journey?'

'Yes, sir.'

'Very well, I have no objection.'

Müller crouched so that his flame would be concealed by the bulwark. He then lit his cigarette, sighed with pleasure, and stood up again. Wessel, who was the youngest member of the crew, altered his position to inhale the slipstream of tobacco smoke. 'Here,' said Müller, offering Wessel the cigarette. 'One drag – do you understand? And cup it behind your fingers.'

Wessel was so overwhelmed by Müller's generosity that he could only express his gratitude with utterances that barely qualified as language. As soon as Wessel had passed the cigarette back to Müller the navigator held it out again for Lorenz to take.

'No,' said Lorenz, shaking his head. 'It's yours.'

'Only a cigarette, Kaleun.'

'Tell that to Wessel.' Lorenz raised his arm and pointed at a dense cluster of brilliant pinpoints. 'Do you think, Müller, that there's intelligent life up there?'

'No. There isn't any down here,' Müller replied, 'why should there be any up there?' He released a twisting ribbon of smoke from the corner of his mouth.

'We don't even know what lies at the bottom of the ocean yet,' Lorenz continued, undeterred. 'And what's the ocean compared to the enormity of all this!' He rotated his outstretched arm like a drunk. 'It's just a puddle. No more than a puddle. Who knows what's out there, eh? Who knows what's possible?'

'How distant are the stars, sir?' Wessel asked.

Lorenz smiled. 'Tell him, Müller.'

'Trillions of miles,' said the navigator.

'But how do we know that?' the inquisitive youth persisted.

'We know that because of Friedrich Wilhelm Bessel,' Müller replied. 'He measured the parallax of 61 Cygni and proved that the star is some 64 trillion miles away. He was the first astronomer to make such a calculation and he succeeded in beating his British rival, Thomas Henderson, by two months.'

'Do you think Reich Minister Goebbels knows this?' Lorenz said with straight-faced sobriety. 'I'm sure he'd be very interested.'

'Our universe,' Müller continued, 'proved to be very much larger than anybody had previously imagined.' He drew on his cigarette and added, 'Unimaginably larger.'

'What do we know?' mused Lorenz. 'What do we really know?'

'There are more things in heaven and earth, Horatio . . .' Müller stubbed his cigarette out on the bulwark.

'Ah,' said Lorenz, '*our* Shakespeare.'

'I thought Shakespeare was English,' said Wessel.

'Well,' Lorenz said, his voice acquiring the whine of an equivocator. 'That's not strictly true. One must never forget that the English are Germans really, and that they are ruled by a German royal family.'

'Then why are we fighting them, sir?' asked Wessel.

'A good question,' Lorenz replied.

'Herr Kaleun – don't confuse the boy,' said Müller.

The steward had set up an impromptu barber shop in the forward torpedo room and his services were much in demand. His scissors seemed to be clicking incessantly. Hair was cut, beards trimmed and the heady scent of cologne was almost overpowering. Be that as it may, the undertow of rancid sweat and mould could not be entirely mitigated. It was always there, like an indelible stain. Heroic efforts were being made in the petty officer's quarters to clean grubby uniforms as Zarah Leander's contralto warbled over the public-address system. A number of men joined in when she reached the sentimental chorus and their voices achieved the resonant unity of a monastic order singing plainchant.

At dawn, U-330 surfaced and Lorenz climbed onto the bridge. Two minesweepers were waiting to escort the returning submarine past the Ouessant islands, around the Pointe de St Mathieu, and through the Goulet de Brest. The sea was calm, almost flat, and a thin mist made the air luminescent and gauzy. Members of the crew who had no duties to perform were permitted to relax on the deck, to ventilate their clothes and enjoy the freshness of the air. The boat's churning wake was long and effervescent – as though the rear ballast tanks were leaking champagne.

Lorenz inhaled, filling his lungs to their full capacity. 'Can you smell it?'

Falk was standing beside him on the bridge. 'Land?'

'Yes,' Lorenz replied. Victory pennants, snapping in the breeze, had been attached to a line running from the rear safety rail to the top of the periscope. Added together, the figures amounted to 31,000 tons. It was a respectable total (many boats returned with no pennants flying at all). But it would have been a lot higher if all the torpedoes had worked.

Lorenz climbed down to the deck and milled around as though at a social gathering, telling jokes and engaging his men in banter. They were all so excited at the prospect of visiting the Casino Bar that virtually every exchange contained a lewd double meaning. Hoffmann was already forgotten – although not quite. Lorenz had written a letter of condolence to Frau Hoffmann and he was carrying it in the inside pocket of his jacket. He intended to post the letter as soon as he was given an opportunity to do so.

Gazing up at the conning tower, Lorenz noted how weather-beaten the structure looked. The bulwark was streaked with rust and much of the grey paint was peeling due to the abrasive Atlantic salt and prolonged exposure to depth-charge explosions. In some places, the bright red undercoat was showing. The scorpion emblem was faded and the sting at the end of its curving tail had been completely worn away. Lorenz supposed that in addition to having all of her machinery checked and serviced, U-330 would also need extensive rust treatment. He wondered how long it would take. Six weeks? Maybe more . . .

The elevated coastline of Brittany came into view and soon they were negotiating the narrow entrance to the harbour. A pale sun was beginning to dispel the thinning mist. They followed the old sea wall which was mounted with pillboxes. Set back on higher ground was the naval college – a massive central block flanked by three-storey wings. The brickwork facade had been painted with irregular patches to camouflage it from enemy aircraft. Over the sea wall Lorenz could see the U-boat-bunker complex. The austere concrete edifice appeared low and flat and the individual pens were like a row of dark windows. Much of the building was covered in a mesh of scaffold and it was clearly still far from finished. The sound of industry carried across the water. In front of the pens was a ramshackle barricade of expendable hulks fitted with extended masts to deter low-flying allied bombers. Some were being used to anchor barrage balloons that floated above the harbour like giant kites.

A launch came out to meet them. On board were an administrative officer and the 1st Flotilla surgeon, who immediately attended to the ailing Richter. A bottle of brandy was produced and Lorenz was asked to wait for further orders before docking. Apparently, the preparations for the boat's reception were not quite finished and the Ministry of Propaganda had sent a cameraman. 'I hope you understand,' said the officer. Lorenz concealed his annoyance and poured himself another drink. He knew that his crew's high spirits could easily result in some unruly behaviour if they were delayed indefinitely; however, he need not have worried, because after thirty minutes or so Ziegler brought a brief and informal message to the bridge: U-330 PROCEED.

Before reaching the pier head Lorenz ordered Graf to switch from diesel to electric power. A great crowd had gathered in tiers against a backdrop of picturesque buildings with conical turrets and tall chimney stacks. He saw immaculately accoutred officers, a military band, a naval guard of honour, troops dressed in grey and blue, the mayor and his wife, and a horde of port employees waving their hands and cheering. In front of the pier was a large barge which they could tie up to, and on this vessel stood Hans Cohausz, Commander of the 1st Flotilla, accompanied by his aide and a pretty blonde female auxiliary who was holding a garland of flowers. Another man was on the barge, equipped with a cine camera, aiming it first at the crowd and then swinging the lens round to film the incoming boat. Small bouquets began to rain down on the bridge, and the port employees began to clap.

U-330 arrived alongside the barge and the two vessels came together with a slight bump. A shrill whistle sounded and the mooring crew set to work fastening the hawsers. At that point, the band struck up a rousing march. 'Stop motors,' Lorenz shouted above the din. 'Assemble on the aft deck: fall in.' The men lined up to be presented to the flotilla commander and Lorenz climbed down the tower followed by Graf, Falk and Juhl.

Cohausz marched over the gangplank and Lorenz cried 'Attention!' He could sense his crew responding, a tension transmitted through the air. The commanders saluted each other and Lorenz said, 'Report U-330 returning from patrol, Herr Kommodore.' Cohausz took Lorenz's hand and shook it with forceful energy. 'Congratulations, Lorenz. Welcome back.' The aide removed a case from under his arm and opened it to give the commodore access to the medal inside: an Iron Cross First Class. Cohausz lifted the decoration from a bed of blue velvet and pinned it on the left side of Lorenz's chest. There was more saluting, more handshaking, and the pretty auxiliary stepped forward, curtsied, and hung the garland around Lorenz's neck. Sauer led a chorus of hurrahs. When

Lorenz looked up, into a bright, dazzling sky, all he could see was a flock of swooping seagulls and an endless shower of bouquets.

Furlough

That evening a traditional celebration banquet was held at the naval academy. It was a grand affair and the tables were laid out with fine linen and chased silver. A number of distinguished officers had been invited and all of those assembled were in service dress. Embroidered gold-eagle and swastika breast emblems shone vividly against worsted blue wool. Lorenz was seated next to Cohausz whose cheeks were aglow even before the second course had arrived.

'Do you know anything about our special operation, sir?' Lorenz asked.

Someone on their table had just delivered the punchline of a joke and most of Lorenz's sentence was lost in the uproar that followed.

'What did you say?' Cohausz cupped his hand around his ear and leaned closer towards Lorenz.

'I said: do you know anything about our special operation, Kommodore?'

'What special operation?' Cohausz's eyes were bright but without intelligence.

'The British commander and the Norwegian academic,' said Lorenz. 'We had to pick them up off the coast of Iceland. There was an SS officer – Friedrich.'

'Ah yes,' Cohausz swallowed more wine. 'I heard about that. Unfortunate – most unfortunate – but never mind.' The flotilla chief angled a bottle over Lorenz's glass. It was not a controlled movement and some of the Burgundy spotted the table cloth. 'Keep up. You're falling behind.'

'Where did the orders come from, sir?' Lorenz had to raise his voice to be heard.

Cohausz's expression soured, his features curdling into an exaggerated grimace. 'Not now, Lorenz. Not here. Tomorrow: leave it till tomorrow. You can talk to the Lion about it directly.'

'He's coming to Brest?'

'Yes, tomorrow.'

A large white dish appeared in front of Lorenz. On it were several thick slices of pork loin, steaming potatoes and a heap of boiled cabbage. Condiments in small bowls were deposited around the rim of the dish with such deft discretion that the waiters might have been stage magicians.

'Sir,' said Lorenz, conscious of his new decoration. 'My crew . . . There are several men who should be rewarded for good service.'

'Of course, of course,' Cohausz responded. 'Just fill out the forms and submit them to my aide for disposition.'

A disembodied voice spoke the words 'bon appétit'.

When Lorenz placed the pork in his mouth it seemed to melt away to nothingness, as though he were eating spirit food, and the flavour that lingered was so rich and sweet and wholesome, so free of canker and rot, that he almost swooned. All thoughts concerning the special operation were immediately wiped from his mind.

'Good?' asked Cohausz.

'Wonderful, sir,' Lorenz replied.

The next day was cold and a tenacious frost made the world sparkle beneath a wide and cloudless sky. Dressed in their number-one blue uniforms, the crew had assembled in two ranks on the parade ground. At ten o'clock precisely a black limousine rolled into view. The back doors flew open and Vice Admiral Dönitz jumped out accompanied by several aides. He was remarkably tall for a former submariner and the flapping of his coat suggested the emergence of a large, predatory bird. As he approached, his features clarified: he possessed a high forehead and a mouth that in repose had a tendency to wilt at its extremities. His expression was serious, perhaps even grave, and his wiry body moved with determined energy.

'Attention!' Lorenz saluted. When Dönitz came to a halt Lorenz stepped forward. 'Sir: report the safe return of U-330.'

Dönitz nodded and said, 'Put your men at ease.' Lorenz called out, 'At ease.' Adopting a more casual attitude, Dönitz shook hands with all of the officers, and as he turned to face the troop Lorenz called, 'Eyes right.' Dönitz walked slowly along the first line with Lorenz following a few paces behind him. Occasionally, the Vice Admiral stopped to engage a particular individual in a little friendly conversation, but the intensity of his expression was constant. When he had completed his inspection, Dönitz distanced himself from the ranks, folded his arms, and raised his chin. 'Well,' he began, 'this last patrol has cost us dearly. One man lost and another badly injured. But . . .' He paused and the corners of his mouth curled upwards, 'thirty-one thousand tons.' His head began to rock backwards and forwards, 'Not bad at all.' Before continuing, he allowed a brief silence to encourage thoughtful reflection. 'Sometimes we must pay dearly for our accomplishments. Comrades, the fate of the German Reich hangs on your successes. This war will not be decided in Russia. This war will not be decided in Great Britain. This war will be decided in the waters of the Atlantic Ocean. Know *that* – and be proud.'

Turning abruptly, the vice admiral marched off in the direction of the waiting Mercedes. The aides, surprised by his sudden departure, rushed after him. Lorenz called the crew to attention but Dönitz didn't look back. He got into the limousine and when his aides had caught up with him, the doors slammed and the driver turned on the ignition. Gravel crunched under the tyres as the Mercedes pulled away.

'When are you seeing him?' Graf asked Lorenz.

'Later this afternoon,' Lorenz replied.

'Rather you than me, Kaleun,' whispered Graf.

Spending time in the company of a 'lion' was inevitably a fraught and complicated experience.

Lorenz was obliged to supervise the transport of U-330 to one of the dry pens. He descended the ladder into the control room and found that the stink of bilge water, body odour, and mould still persisted. There were some sacks by the chart table. Two of them were bulging with refuse: disintegrating newspapers, paperback books with split spines, broken crockery, and a pair of Zeiss binoculars with cracked lenses. Another sack contained miscellaneous personal possessions: torn photographs, scarves, a pair of braces, and, somewhat incongruously, a single silk stocking. Lorenz peered through the forward hatchway and saw Uli Wilhelm, one of the bosun's mates, standing outside the sound room. There was something odd about his attitude, unbalanced, as though the movement of his limbs had suddenly been arrested before an action was completed. His eyes were wide open and the irises surrounded by disproportionately large amounts of exposed sclera. He did not look like a man who had been simply taken by surprise.

'Wilhelm?' Lorenz inquired, concerned.

'Kaleun?' Wilhelm's voice was tremulous. He continued to stare at his commander for a few moments before he blinked and repeated 'Kaleun', this second time with greater confidence and certainty, as if he were now satisfied that the evidence of his senses could be trusted, whereas before he had been doubtful.

Wilhelm's presence was not unexpected. He was responsible for the final tidying of the compartments and removal of personal property after the boat had returned to port.

'What on earth's the matter?' said Lorenz.

Slowly, Wilhelm's limbs settled into a more natural position and he performed a somewhat belated, perfunctory salute. 'Nothing . . . Kaleun, I . . .'

'Yes?'

'I've almost finished.'

'Good.' Wilhelm looked over his shoulder. 'Are you all right, Wilhelm?'

'Yes, Herr Kaleun.'

'You seem a little . . .'

'Too much to drink last night, sir.' The swiftness of Wilhelm's trite justification betrayed an absence of thought.

Lorenz climbed through the hatchway, walked over to his

nook and pulled the curtain back. He was about to open his cabinet but was conscious of the fact that Wilhelm hadn't moved. 'Shouldn't you be taking those sacks up to the bridge?'

The bosun's mate didn't answer the question. Instead he said, 'I haven't looked in there. I assumed that you wouldn't leave anything behind.'

'Well,' said Lorenz, 'I'm grateful that you are of the opinion that my rank entitles me to greater privacy than the rest of you, but I'm a member of the crew, just like everyone else, and you are equally obliged to remove any of my possessions if I fail to take them away.' Lorenz opened the bedside cabinet and felt along the shelves. Wilhelm remained standing in the same position.

'Kaleun?'

Lorenz closed the cabinet door. 'What is it, Uli?'

'I . . .' Wilhelm put his hand into his pocket. 'I found this.' When his hand appeared again he was holding a coin between his thumb and forefinger.

Lorenz took it and studied the relief image of Britannia, the warrior queen, wearing her plumed helmet and tilting her trident forward in a manner that suggested casual belligerence. The date beneath the personification was 1937.

'A British penny,' said Lorenz. 'Where did you find it?'

'In the torpedo room,' Wilhelm replied.

Lorenz flicked the coin over. The head of King George VI was shown in profile, surrounded by a Latin inscription.

'Yes, but where exactly?'

'On the linoleum, sir.'

'In full view? '

'Yes. In front of the tubes.'

Lorenz held the coin up to the overhead light. 'Why wasn't it noticed before? I wonder.'

'He – the British officer . . .' Wilhelm offered his faltering hypothesis with an accompaniment of awkward gestures. 'He must have lodged it somewhere – between the pipes – and eventually the coin must have worked itself loose.' He shifted as though the deck plates beneath his boots were becoming hot. 'I think I heard it fall out.'

'Did you?' Lorenz drew back.

'No, perhaps not: I heard something.' Wilhelm immediately looked as if he regretted this admission. 'But I don't know what it was, not really.' After picking up the half-full sack he had left in the hydrophone room, Wilhelm squared his shoulders and said, 'Permission to continue clearing the boat, sir?'

'Permission granted,' said Lorenz.

The bosun's mate saluted and stepped through the hatchway and into the control room.

Once again, Lorenz studied the image of Britannia on the

coin. The patriotic British anthem sounded in his mind: *Rule, Britannia! Britannia, rule the waves. Britons never, never, never shall be slaves.* He had visited London many times in order to improve his English, and, when attending public events and ceremonies, he had thought nothing of joining in when the chorus came around. Now those same words were like a bleak prophesy.

Lorenz put the coin in his drawer and sat down on the mattress. *Uli,* he thought. *You are such a bad liar.* He could hear Wilhelm collecting the sacks together before making his departure. The rapid rattle of the mate's ascent up the ladder communicated his eagerness to get out of the boat. He was clearly very frightened.

Lorenz was ushered into a regal room with a high ceiling where he found Dönitz standing by a window, his profile silhouetted against the strong light. Glittering motes floated around his head like the stars mounted on the metal halo of a religious statue. The vice admiral gestured towards a semi-circle of chairs that had been arranged in front of the impressive fastness of his oversized desk. Lorenz sat down and his superior began pacing back and forth before finally stopping to say, 'The need for sacrifice continues, but this need will not continue indefinitely.' It was as though Dönitz were participating in an ongoing conversation that only he had been able to hear. 'Our new boats, when they come out of the shipyards, will be lauded as miracles of advanced engineering. It's just a question of holding on until then. A little longer, that's all.' He sat down behind his desk and tapped a pile of papers that he had evidently been reading. It was Lorenz's war diary. Not the scrawled original, but a more legible typescript prepared by Ziegler. Dönitz turned the pages, slowly, one by one, stopping occasionally in order to look up and ask Lorenz a question. The vice admiral was capable of exceptional pedantry. He was not content to wage war from the safety of the U-boat command centre, moving small blue flags around a map; he wanted to feel close to the action and he could only achieve this by perusing war diaries and interrogating the men who wrote them.

Lorenz was aware that Dönitz was approaching the point in the diary where he, Lorenz, had acknowledged receipt of the triply encrypted special order. He felt a frisson of excitement and hoped that he would soon discover more about Sutherland and Grimstad. Yet he was also braced for a reprimand on account of having failed to return the prisoners safely to Brest. The SS would almost certainly have registered a complaint. He sat up straight, ready to defend himself, but Dönitz passed over the relevant sheets and became somewhat preoccupied with the malfunctioning torpedoes.

'What do you think went wrong?' Dönitz leaned forward, hawkish.

'I don't think we missed,' Lorenz replied. 'We were in close. The most likely explanation is firing-pin damage.'

'Due to high pressure?'

'Yes, sir.'

'I'm inclined to agree.'

The vice admiral continued reading the diary and discussing technicalities; however, the flow of conversation halted when he arrived at a page that seemed to cause him some concern. Ominous creases appeared on his forehead. 'What's the meaning of this?' Dönitz pointed to an entry. As Lorenz craned forward the vice admiral began to recite: 'Resound, then, foaming waves, And coil yourselves around me . . .'

'Ah yes,' said Lorenz. 'It's from a poem by Ludwig Tieck, sir.'

'Let misfortune rage around me,' Dönitz continued, 'And let the cruel sea roar!'

Lorenz sat back in his chair. He had forgotten writing these lines in the solitude of his nook. It hadn't seemed a particularly odd thing to do at the time, but now that he was sitting in front of Dönitz, he regretted having been so flippant. 'I'm sorry, Admiral. I hadn't had much sleep.' He attempted to trivialize his idiosyncratic behaviour by laughing. 'The lines came into my head when I was making a note of the conditions – after we surfaced – stupid of me.'

Dönitz was not amused. 'If the swell was moderate – then please write *moderate swell*. That is quite sufficient.'

'Indeed,' said Lorenz. 'My apologies, sir.'

When the last page of the war diary had been turned, a lengthy silence followed. Dönitz drummed his fingers on the table. He was absorbed by his own thoughts and his gaze was distant and unfocused. The end result of the vice admiral's extended period of concentrated thought was a single word, murmured rather than spoken: 'Unlucky.'

Lorenz was unsure how to respond. 'Yes, Admiral,' he said. 'Losing Hoffmann was very unlucky.'

'I was thinking more about the air attacks,' Dönitz continued. 'Wherever you went, you seemed to run into the British air force.' Motes winked around his head.

'It was as though they knew where we were,' said Lorenz. 'And where we were going, sir.'

Dönitz's eyes narrowed and his expression became disapproving. Lorenz's suggestion accommodated too many challenging possibilities and the vice admiral was loath to engage in speculative discussion. 'You were unlucky, Kapitänleutnant,' said Dönitz, stressing each syllable with deliberate emphasis.

Lorenz decided that it might be wise to change the subject.

'Sir, may I ask a question?' The vice admiral made a permissive gesture. 'The prisoners that we took on board . . .'

'Ah yes.'

'Who were they?'

'You were told, weren't you?'

'I was told that Sutherland was a British submarine commander and Grimstad a Norwegian academic. But who were they? Why were they important?'

'That need not concern you, Lorenz. Thank you for returning the professor's notebook, by the way.'

'And the stone, sir?'

'Ah yes, the stone. It was marked, wasn't it?'

'With a rune, I believe.'

'The notebook and the stone have already been dispatched to Wewelsburg.'

'The British commander was armed. He was carrying a Walther PPK.'

'I know. I've read your diary.'

'How did the SS react when they learned about what had happened? If I may ask, sir?'

'You have nothing to worry about, Lorenz. No one has suggested you were at fault.'

'I'm surprised, Admiral.'

'You may well be; however, that is – thankfully – how things stand. Now, I would suggest we move on.' Dönitz suddenly appeared uncomfortable. He sighed and sat back in his chair. 'Look: between you and me, Lorenz, I wasn't happy about this escapade. There's no such thing as a spare boat and I wanted U-330 elsewhere at the time. Be that as it may, I was not able to refuse the request. Do you understand?'

'It wasn't good for the crew, sir,' said Lorenz. 'They're sailors, they don't like Fridays and they touch their collars for luck. Sutherland killed a man and then took his own life – on *our* boat! The men were . . . unsettled, Admiral.'

Dönitz lifted the war diary and turned it over so that the title page was facing upwards: a clear indication that the matter was closed. Twitches around his lips resulted in an unconvincing smile. 'Thirty-one thousand tons, all things considered a good total. But I know that you can do better.'

'I'm sure I can, sir.'

'Another twenty-eight thousand, Lorenz, that's all that stands between you and a Knight's Cross. I trust that when you return from your next patrol, you will have given us good reason to celebrate.'

'Thank you for your confidence, sir.' The sun edged into view and the window pane behind Dönitz's head was instantly transformed into an oblong of white brilliance. Lorenz shaded his eyes.

*

The Hotel Café Astoria functioned as an unofficial social club for the 1st U-boat flotilla. It was patronized largely by those who eschewed the dubious pleasures of the Casino Bar and tended to attract the higher ranks: officers, warrant officers, and very occasionally a visiting commodore. Conversations took place against a constant background roar of battle re-enactments and immoderate, drunken hilarity, while the statutory chanteuse, whose ruined voice resembled a foghorn, competed for attention with the assistance of a surprisingly energetic trio of elderly musicians.

Lorenz was standing at the long, brightly lit lounge bar, stooped over his beer, eyeing his own reflection: a well-groomed man with a clearly defined jaw and dark slicked-back hair. Behind his shoulders, the mirror revealed a large, crowded space of peeling gilt and threadbare fustian receding into hazy obscurity. Overhead, an ostentatious chandelier manufactured miniature rainbows

'How was it in the Lion's den?' asked Graf.

'He growled a bit,' Lorenz replied. 'But on the whole he was perfectly civil.'

'Did he say anything about – you know – our little errand for the SS?'

'Not a great deal. It's as though the whole episode never happened. Or at least that's how they want it to appear now.'

'Perhaps someone important blundered.' Graf raised his

glass and after taking a few sips, licked the foam from his upper lip.

'That seems very likely,' Lorenz nodded.

'I'd still like to know what it was all about, though . . .' Graf was distracted by a loud crash. A chief petty officer had fallen to the floor and his companions were trying to get him back on his feet again.

'Where are you taking your leave?' asked Lorenz. He was glad of the opportunity to change the subject.

'My wife's coming here at the end of the week,' Graf replied. 'And then we're going to spend some time at the chateau.'

'Which one?'

'De Trévarez. Have you been yet?'

'No.'

'It's right out in the Breton countryside, overlooking Châteauneuf-du-Faou – rolling hills – beautiful.' Graf seemed to be absorbed by recollections of the picture-postcard retreat, where, between patrols, U-boat men could stay and relax with their wives or paramours. Embarrassed by his temporary absence, Graf excused himself and added, 'Then we're going back to Dresden. The children are staying with my mother-in-law until we get back.' Tilting his head to one side, he inquired: 'And you, Kaleun?'

'Paris.'

Graf gave a sly smile and nodded knowingly. For a brief, passing instant, Lorenz was tempted to disclose something more, but he found that he could not speak openly about his private life. Consequently, their conversation became disjointed. Graf yawned and said that he was going to bed. Lorenz stayed on, drinking alone, thinking of Paris and Faustine – her little apartment in the Marais, and their intense, desperate lovemaking. When he finally stumbled out of the Hotel Café Astoria at an hour much later than he had originally planned, he discovered that he had drunk too much and the cobbles felt springy and buoyant underfoot. He needed to walk in order to sober up and he found himself, without much consideration, heading off in the direction of the naval harbour.

The massive steel doors of the bunker were wide open. Painted over the cavernous entrance was a stylized, angular eagle clutching a swastika in its talons and beneath this totemic emblem was a slogan, rendered in blockish, utilitarian lettering: *Through Struggle to Victory.* Two armed guards acknowledged Lorenz's approach and an administrator wearing a uniform decorated with silver trim looked up from his clipboard.

Once inside, Lorenz marched along a corridor that passed between workshops. The air was permeated with dust and the stench of burning rubber. Men in dungarees operated lathes and milling machines – acetylene torches hissed, sparks fell in glittering cascades, and carpenters sawed, hammered and hollered: the din was unremitting. Near the firefighters' room a throng parted respectfully to allow Lorenz through and he continued to penetrate the bunker complex until he arrived at the entrance to pen 'A'.

The dimensions of the structure inspired a reaction akin to religious awe. Lorenz registered converging perspective lines, huge planes of damp concrete, and an inestimable volume of empty space. There was something about its size, its airy vastness, that invited comparison with a cathedral, even though the interior was entirely functional and without ornament. High above the wooden crates on the quayside the ceiling was covered with panels of corrugated steel and spanned by the gantry of a mobile crane. Two hinged, overlapping metal doors provided defence against the sea and upwards of these was an opening through which Lorenz could see a slab of black sky.

U-330 had been lowered onto stocks and the harsh glare of the surrounding lights exposed every detail of its distempered skin, eruptions of blistering paint and florid outcrops of rust which, like soft-tissue ulcers, appeared to be producing runnels of brown discharge. A stab of pity caused Lorenz to catch his breath. To him, the boat did not look like an inanimate object, but rather a great wounded leviathan. Schmidt and Krausse were guarding the footbridge: fear of sabotage had become so great that only crew members and authorized personnel were permitted on board. As Lorenz approached, Schmidt saluted. 'The repair team were called away, Herr Kaleun. Some kind of emergency in the next pen and they needed extra hands.'

'Well,' said Lorenz, 'there's no hurry. We're not going anywhere for a while. Anything I should know about?'

'Nothing specific,' said Schmidt. 'They say there's a lot to do.'

'That's hardly surprising,' Lorenz responded. 'We took a few knocks this time, didn't we?'

'Yes, sir – we certainly did.'

Gesturing towards the boat, Lorenz continued, 'I'm going to take a look.'

He set off down the footbridge and craning over the hand rail observed that the floor of the pen was still mottled with puddles of seawater. He also noted some conspicuous dents in the bulging fuel tank. On reaching the other side of the channel that separated the deck from the quayside he climbed the conning tower and lowered himself through the hatch.

The fetid odours that lingered from the patrol were finally beginning to dissipate and other smells, such as cleansing agents and wood polish, could now be detected in their place.

Portable lamps had been fixed on tall tripods in the control room but only one of them had been left on. Its reflective silver dish was directed at the numerous dials surrounding the hydroplane wheels. Lorenz walked from compartment to compartment, switching on lamps and trying to work out what problems the repair team had uncovered. Several deck plates had been lifted, exposing cables and accumulators. Both of the boat's batteries had been disconnected and abandoned tools and toolboxes confirmed that the electricians had made a sudden departure. Lorenz found the absolute quiet disconcerting. At sea there were always noises: pounding engines, humming motors, voices, creaks, waves slapping against the tower. Now, there was only a solid, unyielding silence. Lorenz drifted through the diesel room, past the tiny galley and between the tiers of bare bunk beds.

In his nook, Lorenz sat on the mattress, opened his drawer and gazed down at the British penny. If it had been concealed between pipes, as Wilhelm had suggested, then it would have almost certainly become dislodged while depth charges were exploding around the boat. How, then, could it have been passed over in a busy torpedo room? How could it have been ignored until Wilhelm chanced to find it? Lorenz's troubled contemplation of the coin was succeeded by more diffuse anxieties. *Why*, he asked himself, *did I decide to come back here tonight?* The absence of ready answers heightened his discomfort, yet eventually he concluded that he had returned to clarify matters – although what he truly meant by this remained imprecise. Gently, he pushed the drawer and the penny disappeared from view.

The long walk from the hotel to the military harbour had been bracing but he still felt slightly drunk. He lay down on the mattress, closed his eyes and surrendered to the illusion of movement. Tiredness paralysed his limbs and dragged on his thoughts. Was he sinking? A fleeting recognition of mental dissolution preceded his descent into sleep.

Once again he was standing on the deck of U-330, looking out over slow-moving water that had the consistency of an oil slick. Red light seeped over the horizon and the benighted ocean was dotted with small, flaring conflagrations. The raft appeared in the middle distance as a silhouette, revealed only momentarily by the fires in its locality. With each burst of illumination it materialized a little closer. Lorenz realized that he was dreaming but this did not lessen the pervasive sense of menace. His very soul seemed at risk. A rising panic made the dream unsustainable and he found himself awake, his heart knocking against his ribs and his mouth sucking in air. It was as though he had surfaced after very nearly drowning. Although his body remained still, his eyes darted around his nook, piecing together reality: loudspeaker, leather panel, cabinet. His heartbeat slowed and he felt the tension flowing out of his limbs. Resting his hand on his sternum he released the air that he had been retaining in his lungs.

At the periphery of his vision Lorenz registered something crossing the gap between the curtain and the edge of the recess. Its transition had caused a fractional dimming of the light. There had been no accompanying sound. Lorenz propped himself up and called out 'Hello?' There was no response, so he called again. 'Hello, who is it?' The silence seemed to intensify.

Warily, he swung his legs off the mattress and pulled the curtain aside. He looked across the boat into the darkened radio room. The sense of danger he had experienced in the dream returned and the atmosphere became overcharged with a kind of electrostatic imminence. His sure knowledge that something was about to happen did not prevent him from starting when a loud clanging noise sent a reverberation through the hull. Lorenz judged that its source was located in the forward torpedo room.

'Schmidt?' Lorenz called. 'Krausse?'

Pressing down on his mattress, Lorenz stood up and began walking towards the bow. He stepped through the bulkhead hatchway and made his way down the gangway between the bunks. The lamp in the crew's quarters emitted a weak yellow light but it was enough to illuminate the torpedo room. As soon as the tube doors came into view he was aware that something was not quite right. Advancing slowly, he saw that one of the upper tube doors was open and he was certain that it had been closed before. He reached out and checked the hinges, moving the door backwards and forwards. Perhaps someone had come on board and opened it while he had been asleep? The silence was dense and suffocating. Once again, he sensed imminence, a feeling of things being strained to an absolute limit. He heard a crack and the tinkling of broken glass.

Lorenz walked back towards the control room, and when he got as far as the officers' mess he saw that the framed photograph of Vice Admiral Dönitz was askew. The glass had been smashed and the shatter pattern consisted of radial cracks emanating from a central point. A few shards had fallen onto the linoleum and reflected the light with unusual brilliance. Lorenz lifted the frame off its hook and pressed his hand against the wooden panelling. It was warm, but not exceptionally so. He placed the photograph on the table and proceeded to the control room where he waited in a state of alert, uneasy preparedness.

The sound that followed made his limbs go rigid and a tingling sensation passed over his scalp. He could hear someone coming towards him from the empty compartment he had only just left: a slow, measured step. It crossed his mind that the phenomenon might be caused by a returning member of the repair team walking along the upper casing, but no sooner had this thought formed than he recognized it as yet another desperate attempt to cling to a remnant of normality. There was a buzzing sound, the lamp flickered and he was enveloped by darkness.

The footsteps were getting louder.

Lorenz remembered the vivid dream he had had of being attacked by Sutherland, hands closing around his throat, terrible weakness and being unable to call for help – their noses almost touching. Was it prophetic? Had he been vouch-safed a preview of his own demise? He felt blindly for the chart table and then the locker above it. After opening the door he reached inside where, next to the sextant, his searching fingers discovered a torch.

Sliding the switch he was rewarded with a bright circle of light. He did not turn. The footsteps had stopped and he found that he was unable to move. He remained perfectly still, facing the locker, but said with cold deliberation: 'This is *my* boat – *my* command.' Then, very slowly, he looked over his shoulder and aimed the torch beam into the darkness. There was no one there. He moved his feet to ease the discomfort of his twisted waist and observed the circle of light warping as it passed over the uneven surfaces.

From the aft end of the boat there was another resonant clang. Lorenz immediately set off, marching briskly through the petty officers' quarters and continuing into the diesel room. The stillness was particularly unnerving in this part of the boat because it was usually filled with the roar and clatter of the engines. He proceeded more cautiously but froze when the door behind him slammed shut. Suddenly, he felt in great danger, as if he had been lured into the diesel room for a specific purpose. He struggled to overcome an irrational conviction that he was entombed and that he would never feel the warmth of the sun's rays again. Even more terrifying was the creeping conviction that he was not alone, that he was being closely studied. Richter claimed to have been pushed. A displacement of air chilled the back of Lorenz's neck. Would he 'slip' and bang his head on a diesel engine too?

Turning sharply, Lorenz traced wild arcs through the air with his torch. For a glaring instant, halfway through its trajectory, the beam illuminated a face beneath a peaked cap. It had been close, alarmingly close, and Lorenz drew back, producing an atavistic cry of horror. When he aimed the torch at the location where he thought he had just seen the face, the passage of the beam was unobstructed. Anger made him address the shadows: 'Get off my boat!'

Lorenz felt confused and divorced from reality. It was as though when he had awakened from his brief sleep he had not been fully delivered from the dream and that he was still subject to its influences. The concession he had made by accepting the ghost's existence had shaken the edifice of his intellect to its very foundations. He felt unhinged, no longer confident that he could trust his own perceptions. How could the boat be haunted? Such was his resistance to accepting what he had hitherto considered impossible that the idea of his own mental infirmity was now almost attractive. If ghosts were real then there might also be a heaven, a hell, judgement and eternal damnation.

He staggered forwards and opened the door that had slammed shut. At once he could hear voices and the thrumming of the ladder. Through the aft hatch of the control room he detected activity. Someone said, 'The lights aren't working.' A gruffer companion swore and complained, 'What? Have the batteries gone flat already?'

A man in oily overalls stepped into the petty officers' quarters. 'Kapitänleutnent Lorenz?' He was followed by two younger men also dressed like mechanics.

'Gentlemen,' said Lorenz.

'What happened to the lights?' The senior mechanic's face was criss-crossed by deep creases filled with dirt.

'They just went out,' Lorenz replied.

The mechanic shrugged. 'Did you want to talk to us about something?'

'No,' Lorenz shook his head. 'I just wanted to see how things are progressing.'

'Not very well, I'm sorry to say.' The mechanic grimaced. 'We had to deal with an emergency on U-685. Anyway . . . your engine mountings are in a terrible state. And you'll need a new propeller. One of the blades is badly out of true. But don't you worry,' he smiled revealing large, asinine teeth, 'we'll get your boat ready for action as soon as we possibly can. I can promise you that.'

'Thank you,' said Lorenz, knowing all too well that such pledges were invariably honoured.

On the express train to Paris, his head resting against the window, Lorenz watched the French countryside flashing past through the transparent wraith of his own reflection. The landscape was dotted with isolated farmhouses and the boundaries between the fields were softened by a pale pink mist. Lorenz listened to the rhythm of the wheels on the track and was reminded of hammering diesels. Repetition lulled him into a state of drowsy abstractedness and the sound seemed to change until it began to resemble exploding depth charges. He lifted his head away from the glass, picked up a newspaper and turned the pages until he came to an article that accused President Roosevelt of indefensible duplicity. The propagandists were clearly readying the German people for a declaration of war. More U-boats would be needed; a lot more than the shipyards of Kiel and Hamburg were currently able to produce. He stopped reading and laid the newspaper aside.

It was still morning when the express train pulled in to the station at Montparnasse. Lorenz hailed a cab and asked to be taken to Place Vendôme where a smart hotel had been appropriated for the exclusive use of naval officers. In the foyer he ran into Kurt Gessner, an old friend who had recently been promoted to the rank of Korvettenkapitän, and they agreed to meet the following evening. After reporting his arrival at the reception desk, Lorenz was escorted to his suite by a porter whose humble office was aggrandized by a uniform decorated with epaulettes and lengths of gold braid. The rooms were equally ostentatious and furnished in a style that suggested eighteenth-century aristocratic opulence. Leaving the porter to unpack his suitcase, Lorenz left the hotel and strolled along the north bank of the river. On the Île de la Cité he paused to admire the Gothic extravagance of the cathedral before crossing the bridge that linked the larger island to its smaller companion, the Île Saint-Louis. A few minutes later he entered his favourite restaurant, where the proprietor welcomed him with much ceremony and seated him at a table by the window.

The food was beautifully prepared and extraordinarily flavoursome: onion soup, braised rabbit with gratin potatoes, followed by a moist apple tart. Lorenz had imagined himself seated in this exact spot on countless occasions during the preceding months. Looking out over the cold, inhospitable waters of the North Atlantic, he had anticipated this moment which he was now, at last, able to savour along with the agreeable aftertaste of his meal. A woman pedalled past on a bicycle with a basket full of bread: a simple, everyday occurrence, but over a month spent at sea had imbued such simple sights with inestimable charm.

Lorenz beckoned the proprietor and asked if he could use the telephone which was situated in a rear office. When he heard Faustine's voice he couldn't think of anything to say except, 'Hello, it's me.'

There was a pause, filled with the clatter of typewriters, before Faustine responded. 'Where are you staying?' She was breathy with excitement.

'Place Vendôme. Are you free this evening?'

'Yes, of course.'

It was decided that they would have dinner together at a well-known restaurant near the opera house. Before ending the call Faustine whispered, 'I've missed you.' He pictured her covering the receiver with her hand to ensure that she was not overheard by her colleagues.

Lorenz spent the rest of the day wandering around the streets of Paris like a seasoned boulevardier. His route took him through the Latin Quarter, across Saint-Germain, beneath the Eiffel Tower and up the Champs-Élysées. In the Jardin des

Tuileries he saw German soldiers buying homemade biscuits from a girl. The men were laughing and joking with her, provoking feigned desperation with their abominable French. She was smiling and demonstrating a precocious grasp of the relationship between flirtation and commercial success. By the time Lorenz got back to his hotel it was already dark.

Two hours later he was sitting in a private dining room, fitfully reading the menu and consulting his wristwatch. After a significant wait, the door swung open, he heard Faustine thanking someone, and suddenly she materialized directly in front of him. She was wearing a long coat with a fur collar and her beryl eyes seemed to glow from within like those of a cat. Lorenz stood up, walked around the table, and planted a kiss on her gloved hand. Her perfume reminded him of lily of the valley.

'I'm sorry,' she said in accented German. 'Monsieur Gilbert insisted that I finish typing all of his letters before I could leave.'

'It doesn't matter,' said Lorenz, freeing her arms from her coat sleeves and taking her hat. 'You're here now.'

As the food and wine were served, Lorenz listened to Faustine's fast-flowing talk with inordinate pleasure. She gossiped about her colleagues (one of whom was unmarried and pregnant), defamed Monsieur Gilbert, described the plots of numerous films she had seen, and complained bitterly about her feckless mother. She did not invite Lorenz to reciprocate because she understood that he was obliged to keep the details of his life secret. Even if the navy had made him uniquely exempt from the customary prohibitions, he would never have chosen to spoil their evening together by describing the horrors of submarine warfare. Occasionally, he would mention some of the more amusing incidents that had happened on patrol, like his discovery of the smuggled bra, but that was the limit of his openness. His contributions to their conversation were necessarily confined to bland generalities or harmless anecdotes.

After they had finished eating they walked back to Lorenz's hotel where they drank champagne and made love. Their mutual culmination was poignant and they both cried out, gripping each other tightly. A line of hazy street light showed where the curtains almost touched. He was dimly aware of Faustine smoking cigarettes; the sound of matches being struck, one after another, becoming increasingly distant.

When he awakened she had gone, but not without having written an affectionate note which he discovered on the bedside table. Her fragrances still clung to the pillow. He breathed in the smell of her perfume and the musk of her body and acknowledged that he was, in all probability, falling in love.

As he luxuriated in the moment, his thoughts were interrupted by unwelcome, intrusive recollections: the hardness of his mattress on U-330, the stink of the crew, burned faces and a sea of bodies. Returning to that hellish world was always a formidable challenge, but now the hardship and horrors of war were compounded by less tangible threats. Foreboding made his stomach churn. Lorenz turned his face into the soft whiteness of the pillow and groaned.

The Scheherazade Club was a high-class bar mostly frequented by submarine officers. Even Vice Admiral Dönitz was known to drink there when he was in Paris. A small band of musicians were playing arrangements of popular German songs and ice buckets were beginning to appear in significant numbers. Lorenz was waiting for Faustine at a corner table when he noticed a young girl approaching. As she advanced he remembered her from a previous visit. 'Siegfried?' Her voice was hesitant. She touched her neck self-consciously and the skin flushed. 'It is you – isn't it?'

'Yes,' he replied, standing up; somewhat embarrassed because he couldn't remember her name. 'I'm sorry, I can't quite . . .'

'Audrey,' she said, making a forgiving gesture to indicate that she was not offended. 'I was wondering . . . have you heard anything from Richard?' Lorenz suddenly remembered who she was: Richard Heppe's girlfriend. 'It's been such a long time,' she added.

'Oh, I'm sure he'll be back here soon enough,' Lorenz said encouragingly. In fact, Heppe's boat hadn't responded to signals from headquarters in over a month. There was always a slim hope that his name would show up on the roster of survivors that the British released occasionally, but this was very unlikely.

'Have you seen him?' Audrey rested a hand on the table-cloth.

'No.' Lorenz sighed. 'But that doesn't mean anything.' Audrey's brittle smile vanished and her eyes became moist. 'Look,' he continued, affecting cheery optimism, 'there's no need to worry. Not yet, anyway. Why don't you sit down? Let me buy you a drink?'

The girl shook her head and said, 'You're very kind, but . . .' Without finishing her sentence she took a few steps backwards, turned, and marched off in the direction of the toilets. A handkerchief appeared in her right hand as her pace quickened.

The band began to play the introduction to 'Lili Marleen' and the audience responded with appreciative applause. Lorenz was joined by two watch officers up from the U-boat base in Lorient. They were in high spirits and accompanied by a pair of sisters who tittered melodiously at every conceivable opportunity. Faustine arrived shortly after and the last vacant seats at Lorenz's table were taken by Karl Altmann, a fellow commander, and Altmann's fiancée, Catherine Varon, a French actress who had appeared in a Hollywood musical. Varon's stories about life in America and the excesses of famous film stars were quite amusing at first, but her tendency to dominate the conversation eventually became rather tiresome.

Lorenz's attention had started to wander and he found himself staring at a group on the other side of the room. One of the faces was familiar. Doubt was gradually replaced by increasing levels of certainty. The face Lorenz was studying belonged to Hans Friedrich, the SS officer who had supervised the transfer of prisoners from the cargo ship to U-330. 'I'm sorry.' Varon displayed mild irritation as Lorenz stood: she was in the middle of another anecdote. 'I've just spotted someone I really must talk to.' As he crossed the floor his pulse added syncopations to the steady beat of the music. Friedrich was sitting with an older man and two well-dressed female companions, one of whom had a white fur stole wrapped around her shoulders. When Lorenz arrived at their table the company fell silent. 'Obersturmbannführer Friedrich?' The SS man looked up. 'Kapitänleutnant Siegfried Lorenz.'

'Lorenz . . .' Friedrich repeated the name without confidence. Recognition, when it came, made him start. 'Lorenz!' He smiled nervously at his companions and rose from his chair.

'May I introduce Kapitänleutnant Siegfried Lorenz.' He then swept his arm over a floral centrepiece – 'Herr Ehrlichmann' – and extended the movement to include the two women, 'Mademoiselles Descoteaux and Lévesque.' Lorenz bowed. 'Well, well,' Friedrich continued. 'How unexpected – so, you are in Paris.'

'Could we talk?'

'Now?'

'Yes.'

'As you can see,' Friedrich indicated his group, 'that isn't possible.'

'I'll be brief.'

'Kapitänleutnant . . .'

'Very brief.'

Friedrich considered his options for a few moments and then nodded. The two men walked away from the table and stood by the bar area. Lorenz noticed that Friedrich was unsteady. He had obviously imbibed a large quantity of champagne.

'You know what happened?' said Lorenz.

'Yes,' Friedrich replied. 'Of course I know what happened.'

'You allowed an armed man to board my boat.'

'I can assure you it wasn't intentional.'

'Were you personally responsible?'

Friedrich frowned and raised an admonitory finger. His

death's-head ring was clearly visible. 'I don't know what you hope to achieve by importuning me in this discourteous manner, but I would strongly advise—'

'I demand an explanation!' Lorenz cut in. He was not going to be intimidated.

'May I remind you,' said Friedrich, his speech slurring, 'that we were involved in a special operation.'

'I could have lost men.'

A glimmer of sympathy softened Friedrich's eyes. 'I understand. I understand that you care about your crew. I respect that.'

'Who was Sutherland? What happened to his boat?'

'You know very well I am not at liberty to disclose more than you already know.'

'Grimstad was carrying a notebook. It was full of runes.'

'He was an archaeologist.'

'You said he was in possession of extremely sensitive intelligence.'

Friedrich swayed a little. 'Knowledge – he knew things – valuable things . . .' The SS man reached for the edge of the bar. He hadn't intended to say anything – the words had just slipped out. Anger made him stand up straight and speak with greater precision. 'Kapitänleutnant: your failure to return the prisoners to France was, I believe, allowed to pass. You have been fortunate – so far. Do not abuse our forbearance!' He turned to leave and Lorenz grabbed Friedrich's arm, preventing him from stepping away. The SS man glanced down at Lorenz's hand and then slowly raised his eyes. Something passed between them, a tacit acceptance that it was not in their interests to escalate hostilities beyond this point. Lorenz released his grip and Friedrich said, 'Enjoy the rest of your furlough, Kapitänleutnant.' He sashayed back to his companions and as he sat down Ehrlichmann asked a question. Friedrich dismissed the inquiry with a gesture before lifting a magnum bottle of champagne from an ice bucket. The woman wearing the white fur stole leaned against him and rested her head on his shoulder.

When Lorenz arrived at his table only Faustine acknowledged his return. She looked bored. 'Who was that?'

'Someone I had to speak to.' He shook his head as if to say it wasn't important. 'Shall we go back to my hotel?'

'No. Come to my apartment instead.' She lit a cigarette and exhaled a cloud of smoke.

'But I promised to meet a friend there later this evening.'

'Oh?'

'Gessner – Kurt Gessner. You haven't been introduced.'

'Come to my apartment,' Faustine repeated. 'You can always go back to your hotel after. I won't mind. I understand.'

'Why don't you want to come to the hotel?'

'I don't know.' She tapped the ash from her cigarette. 'Sometimes it feels . . .' Her expression was reproachful.

Lorenz nodded, recognizing her point immediately. He had been tactless, expecting her to come to his room every night like a whore and to endure the disdain of the concierge, the lewd smirk of the bellboy. 'Yes, you're right. Forgive me,' Lorenz conceded, 'I've been inconsiderate. I should come to your apartment more often.'

They left the Scheherazade Club and chose a route that avoided busy thoroughfares. It had been raining and the cobbles beneath the lamp posts were coated with a yellow glaze. Passing through a little square surrounded by quaint, shuttered houses, they listened to a turbulent Chopin prelude being played on a nearby piano. The effect was absurdly romantic. Further on, they turned into a narrow lane and came to a building with a rickety front door. Faustine pulled it open, switched on a hall light, and led Lorenz up a twisting staircase. The first floor landing was exceedingly narrow and chunks of plaster had fallen from the wall.

'Why don't you get this repaired?' Lorenz asked.

She produced a key and turned it in the lock. 'The landlord says it's too expensive.' They went straight to the bedroom where Faustine lit candles and attended to a cast-iron stove. On the window sill was a pile of creased paperback books, most of which seemed to be works of sensational fiction:

Fantômas, Arsène Lupin, Sherlock Holmes. There was also a copy of *The Double* by Dostoyevsky. Without preamble, Faustine began removing her clothes. Lorenz watched her as she folded her skirt and hung her jacket in the wardrobe. Her fastidiousness was enchanting. She placed one foot on the mattress, released her suspender fastenings and rolled a stocking down her shapely leg with slow grace.

When their lovemaking was over, Faustine opened her hand on his chest. 'Are you all right?' she asked.

'Yes,' he replied, stroking her hair. 'Why do you ask?'

'You seem . . . I don't know – a little different.'

'Oh?'

'Preoccupied?' She took his hand and brushed it against her lips.

'No,' he murmured. 'I am very contented, actually.'

The room was draughty and the agitated candle flames moved shadows across the ceiling. A ticking clock attracted Lorenz's attention and when he looked to check the time he discovered that it was later than he'd thought. Without much enthusiasm, he muttered, 'I'd better be going.'

Faustine got up and wrapped herself in a dressing gown. She tightened the belt and said, 'Why don't you come back? After.'

'No,' said Lorenz. 'You'll be asleep. Don't you have to get up early for work tomorrow?'

'Yes.'

'Well then.'

She lit a cigarette and he noticed that her hands were shaking. 'I'm cold,' she said, making her shoulders shiver excessively. 'Aren't you?'

'Not really.'

'Would you like to go to a concert sometime this week?'

'If you can get tickets . . .'

Lorenz collected his clothes together and carried them to the bathroom. He washed and dressed and when he returned he found Faustine, still smoking, her hair mussed and a smear of kohl beneath one of her eyes. Her dishevelled appearance was curiously alluring.

'I'm going,' he said, raising her chin with a crooked finger. He kissed her smoky mouth and when they parted she said, simply, 'Tomorrow.'

'Yes, tomorrow,' he repeated.

Lorenz stepped out onto the landing and rushed down the stairs, sliding his hand along the banister rail. When he reached the end of the corridor he pushed the flimsy door open and was momentarily startled by an impression of movement. Two shapes were rushing towards him. A glimmer of light on steel signalled that he was in mortal danger. His response to the attack was swift and instinctive. His left arm swung upwards and outwards, deflecting what might have been a fatal lunge and he delivered a kick that ended with his foot finding soft accommodation in his assailant's groin. Turning swiftly he landed a punch on the second assailant's jaw. It produced a loud, satisfying crack. He sensed rather than witnessed the figure teetering and falling. Lorenz charged towards the first assailant, who was doubled over in pain, and brought his knee up with considerable force. Cartilage crunched and he repeated the action several times until he heard the knife clattering on the ground. Then, he grabbed the collar of his assailant's shirt, raised him up, and rammed him against the wall on the other side of the road. Lorenz's fingers closed around a scrawny neck.

An image flashed into his mind: Sutherland as vengeful strangler.

Lorenz had been reminded of his homicidal dream only a few days earlier, when the lamps had failed on U-330 and Sutherland had appeared in his torch beam. Now their roles were reversed; now it was he, Lorenz, who was doing the strangling. An inner voice reminded him of what he had said to Sutherland, and what Sutherland had repeated in the dream: 'Destruction is *your* purpose as much as it is mine.'

For the first time he could see what his assailant looked like. He was young, no older than sixteen, and blood was pouring from his broken nose. The boy's eyes were wide open and his expression communicated surprise rather than fear.

Lorenz tightened his grip. Glancing over his shoulder at the boy's unconscious accomplice, he registered the slightness of the prostrate body and supposed that he was roughly the same age.

They had been waiting for him.

The boy began to make choking noises. Lorenz was tempted to squeeze tighter, but gradually, as his anger subsided he released his grip. Immediately, the boy started coughing, spluttering, and massaging his throat: he edged away, his back remaining in contact with the wall.

'Go,' said Lorenz in French, 'before I change my mind.' The boy looked at Lorenz in disbelief. 'Go!' Lorenz barked.

Startled into action, the boy staggered over to his comrade who was just regaining consciousness. He helped the dazed accessory to his feet and the two boys limped off as fast as they could, occasionally turning to make sure that they weren't being pursued.

Lorenz took a few steps and picked up the knife. He tilted the lambent blade and tested the sharpness of its edge. Had his reactions been a fraction slower it would have easily passed through the material of his coat and between his ribs. He re-entered the building, climbed the stairs and knocked on Faustine's door.

'Who is it?'

'Me.'

'Siegfried?'

'Yes.'

He heard the key turn and the door opened. 'Did you forget something?'

'Why?' he said bluntly.

She tilted her head to one side: 'What?'

'How could you?'

Faustine pushed a lock of hair off her forehead. 'I don't understand.'

'Please don't treat me like a fool.' They stared at each other. He saw her hand disappear behind the door. She was getting ready to slam it in his face if she failed to convince him of her innocence. 'Let go of the handle,' he said. 'For God's sake – do you really think I'd hurt you – even now?'

'I don't understand,' she repeated.

'Oh, I think you do,' said Lorenz, offering her the knife. 'Give this back to your patriotic friends. And tell them that next time, they should attack from behind – not from the front.'

She took the knife and stared at it. Then, her face crumpled and tears ran down her cheeks. 'They said they would kill me. They said they would kill me if . . .' He was tempted to take her in his arms and console her, but he knew that now there could be no going back. 'You don't know what it's like for us.' She sobbed, her shoulders shaking. 'You don't know what it's like. They send coffins – you open a letter and you find a tiny coffin inside with your name scratched on it.' Her anguish brought her to the edge of delirium, the threshold of ecstatic pain. She continued crying and her face became red and swollen. Suddenly, her legs buckled and she leaned against the jamb for support. When, finally, her sobbing became less violent she closed her eyes and said, 'What are you going to do?'

Lorenz buttoned his coat. 'I'm going to have a drink with Gessner.' As he made his way down the stairs he felt something snagging in the vicinity of his heart – and with every step the sensation became more intense.

Lorenz arrived in Berlin late in the afternoon and boarded a train bound for the northern suburb where his sister lived. Her house was situated in a pleasant, tree-lined street on the very outskirts of the city, only a short distance from woodland and a picturesque lake. Steffi opened the door and threw her arms around his neck, saying softly, 'I didn't tell them.' She released him from her embrace and shouted, 'Jan. Pia.'

A boy answered. 'What is it?'

'Just come out here – both of you – at once!'

Two children came running down the hallway and when they saw their uncle they both screamed. He scooped them up and they clung to him like monkeys. The customary charade, in which he pretended to have forgotten to bring gifts, was played out until little hands searched his pockets and discovered several chocolate animals and a beribboned packet of gingerbread biscuits. 'All right, children,' said Steffi, 'that's enough. Let your uncle through the door.' Lorenz stepped into the house and said, 'It's good to be here.' He lugged his suitcase up to the spare bedroom where he changed and allowed himself a few minutes rest before returning downstairs.

While Steffi cooked, the children continued to compete for Lorenz's attention. He found their antics and playful conversation strangely restorative and memories of Paris began to fade. After supper, Pia and Jan were prepared for bed and Lorenz was summoned to read them a story. Before turning the light off, he paused at the door. They were both looking back at him with wide, adoring eyes. Jan's hair was standing on end. The love that he felt for them was so visceral and deep-rooted, he could barely speak. 'Goodnight,' he said, before flicking the switch. He had to compose himself before descending the stairs.

When he entered the kitchen Steffi asked, 'Will you be staying for Christmas?'

'No,' he replied. 'I have to go back.'

'They're so inflexible. As if a few extra days would make any difference!'

Lorenz ran his finger along the grain of the tabletop. 'How is Elias?'

'We got a letter from him only last week.'

'Where is he?'

'On his way to Leningrad.'

Lorenz nodded, expecting his sister to say more. Instead, she remained silent, pressing her lips together until they became pale. He decided that it would probably be wise to talk about something else. 'I heard about the bombing: I was worried.'

'Actually,' Steffi relaxed, 'it wasn't that bad. There were a lot of planes but most of them got shot down, and there was very little damage – considering.'

They discussed the war in a roundabout, allusive manner, and when their talk dwindled Lorenz produced a bottle of perfume that he had bought for Steffi on the Rue du Louvre. She unscrewed the top, dabbed a little on her wrist and inhaled. 'Thank you – divine. Did your friend help you to choose it?'

'No,' Lorenz shook his head.

Steffi's eyes became slits. 'Sigi?'

'It didn't work out.'

'Oh, I'm sorry. What happened?'

'We just weren't right for each other.'

Steffi shrugged and replaced the bottle top. 'I know some-one who'd like to meet you. A school teacher: she's very nice.'

The next day Lorenz went for a long, solitary walk around the ice-fringed lake. He skipped stones like a boy and observed scudding clouds reflected on the water. Frozen leaves crunched beneath his boots in the forest. Entranced by the chilly still-ness of the winter morning he was overcome by an eerie sense of remove, of having entered some magical, timeless domain. This fantasy was shattered by the sudden roar of a low-flying plane. Lorenz had already called out the first syllable of the word 'alarm' before he recognized its redundancy. Looking up through a canopy of bare branches, he saw the underside of a Messerschmitt heavy fighter. Even after it had passed and the stillness was restored his heart was still hammering.

The days were passing too quickly. He didn't want to return to the boat, he didn't want to plunge deep into dark-ness, to endure yet another eternity of explosions, breaches and shrieking metal. And most of all, he didn't want to face the unknown. Eschewing the word 'ghost' in favour of vague abstractions helped to mitigate fear. He was still clinging to the notion of himself as a rational man. But the dread that he felt at his core was like molten rock, exploiting weaknesses, finding ways to the surface through chinks and fissures. Lorenz picked up a piece of ice and held it until the cold became pain.

He had arranged to have lunch with an old friend, Leo Glockner, and when he arrived at the restaurant behind St Hedwig's Cathedral, Glockner was already there, sitting at a table and reading a typed document. Glockner had been a thin, weak, myopic boy, always coughing, always poorly, and attracting the attention of bullies. Lorenz had been obliged to rescue him on countless occasions. Poor Glockner had compensated for his physical deficiencies with hard work: he became fluent in five European languages, including Russian and Greek, studied law, and went on to teach jurisprudence at the university, where his skills were valued and he was swiftly promoted to a very senior position. Glockner was also very well connected, which was surprising, because he was constitutionally shy and did not enjoy the receptions and dinners that he was frequently invited to attend. Looking at him, Lorenz didn't think that his friend had changed very much over the years. He was still thin, nondescript, and easily overlooked, the kind of awkward, unprepossessing, largely invisible man who might have made an excellent spy.

Their conversation was warm, jovial and punctuated by reminiscences. When they had finished eating and the coffees had been ordered, Lorenz said, 'Can you do me a favour?'

'Well,' Glockner replied, 'that depends . . .'

'I'd like you to find something out for me.'

'Oh?'

'I'd like you to find out about a professor who used to have a chair at the University of Oslo. He's dead now. Bjørnar Grimstad – an archaeologist. He may have been involved with the Norwegian resistance.'

'What do you want to know, exactly?'

'I want to know what he studied: I want to know if he was regarded as an authority on anything and I want to know what sort of a man he was.' Glockner looked over his glasses, sensing that Lorenz hadn't quite finished. 'And . . .' Lorenz lowered his voice, 'I want to know why the SS were interested in him.'

'Ah,' said Glockner. 'I see. Perhaps it would be wise to give me some background – a little context?'

Lorenz had not intended to disclose the full story of his involvement with the Schutzstaffel's special operation, but already he could see that total candour was necessary. He hunched his shoulders and leaned forward. 'We'd been sent up north to provide a weather report – idiotic use of a U-boat – and we were on our way south again when we received a triply encoded message from headquarters.' He continued, describing Sutherland and Grimstad's transfer, the shooting incident and Dönitz's reluctance to discuss the matter, and ended with an account of his meeting with Friedrich in the Scheherazade Club.

'Intriguing,' said Glockner. He removed his glasses and cleaned them with the edge of the tablecloth, 'How very intriguing.'

'But tread lightly, Leo.' Lorenz walked his fingers around his coffee cup. 'Friedrich was almost certainly telling the truth. His orders came from very high up.'

'I always do.'

'Even so . . .'

'And what do I get in return?'

Lorenz studied his friend's badly ironed shirt and crumpled tie. 'Steffi is setting me up with a pretty school teacher – I'm meeting her tonight. I'll ask her if she's got a friend, someone who likes opera and reading foreign poetry. Will that do?'

It was sad how little it took to make Leo happy.

That evening, there were two dinner guests: Monika, the school teacher, and an elderly doctor called Hebbel. Monika was young, attractive and respectful. She wore her blonde hair in traditional alpine braids and there was something about her appearance that suggested fresh-faced innocence, wholesome country living. Hebbel, a widower, was Elias's mentor and a longstanding friend of the family.

When they had finished eating, Lorenz was encouraged by Hebbel to step outside in order to sample one of his 'strong' cigars. The doctor claimed that the smoke that they produced was so pungent it would almost certainly irritate the delicate mucous membranes of the female nose. It was, as Lorenz suspected, a somewhat transparent pretext for a man-to-man discussion about submarine warfare. The doctor was particularly interested in the routine deprivations of everyday life on a U-boat: the mouldy food, the damp and stink – the cramped space and poor sanitation. He shook his head sympathetically and said, 'The nation owes you a great debt.' A limousine festooned with pennants rolled down the road and a face appeared in the black rear window. The vehicle slowed for a few seconds before accelerating into the night.

'A curious thing happened on our last patrol,' said Lorenz, affecting an attitude of casual disregard. 'We were transporting a British prisoner who unfortunately died before we could get him back to base for questioning. Shortly after, one of my mechanics had an accident – he banged his head on a diesel engine – and from that moment onwards he kept on babbling about having seen the dead man.'

'The brain is a remarkable organ,' the doctor responded. 'But uniquely vulnerable. The slightest concussion is sometimes all that it takes to disrupt its functioning.'

'Indeed. It's just . . . I was wondering . . .' Lorenz rotated his cigar in the air, producing a floating white hoop that gradually dissipated. 'Are hallucinations always connected with insanity?'

'Your mechanic suffered a brain injury. He didn't go mad, as such.'

'He was acting as though he was mad.'

'Yes, because of a lesion in his brain.'

'Don't *all* hallucinations come from the brain?'

'They do . . .'

'Then what's the difference?'

'You raise a very interesting point, my friend. Doctors have been arguing over such philosophical distinctions for a hundred years or more. I suppose, medically speaking, all hallucinations must be the result of some kind of lesion, but some lesions – such as those that are likely to result from banging one's head against a diesel engine – are more readily determined than others. Are you worried about this crewman?'

Lorenz ignored the question. 'Then you would say that hallucinations – if not always associated with insanity – are always associated with a . . . brain problem.'

'Well,' said Hebbel, his face showing the first portents of that singular form of irritation professionals are prone to exhibit when subjected to persistent questioning by laypersons. 'It's not quite as simple as that. There are some who have proposed other possibilities, other accounts that do not assume structural damage.' The doctor sucked on his cigar and when he exhaled, his features vanished momentarily behind a vaporous haze. 'I used to know a psychiatrist called Simmel. He founded the Tegel Palace Sanatorium not far from here. It was a very fine institution in its day.' Hebbel seemed to be engaged in the effortful process of forming a mental picture of those persons and places he was remembering. 'Simmel was a disciple of Freud and on those occasions when Freud came to Berlin, he usually came as Simmel's guest. I attended one of Freud's talks.' Hebbel's eyes became more focused. 'You know of Freud?'

'I've heard of him, of course.'

'His work has since been vilified for being un-German.' Again, Hebbel paused to draw on his cigar. 'I had many fascinating conversations with Simmel and the members of his circle. Some of his associates suggested that hallucinations have special meaning, and, like dreams, merit interpretation. Indeed, they spoke of hallucinations as if they were escaped dreams . . .'

'Escaped from where?'

'The unconscious: that part of the mind that is not accessible to introspection. Deeper and wider than any ocean you have explored, my dear fellow, infinitely deep. It is a concept that has become associated with Jewish psychiatry, but actually our own German philosophers have been discussing the hidden depths of the mind since the eighteenth century.'

'I'm sorry, Herr Doctor, my question . . .'

'Which was . . .?'

'Are hallucinations always a symptom of insanity?'

'In most cases, yes, but in others – perhaps – hallucinations might represent some kind of communication from the unconscious.'

'I don't understand: communication? What kind of communication?'

'That rather depends on the circumstance. But if a person were, let us say, in some kind of danger, then the hallucination might be construed as a warning.' The doctor dropped his cigar stub and crushed it beneath his heel. 'Come now, shall we go inside? It's cold and I am of the opinion that Fräulein Monika is eager to become better acquainted with you.' Hebbel smiled. 'You shouldn't be standing out here discussing philosophical aspects of psychiatry with an old man like me when there's a pretty girl like Fräulein Monika anxiously awaiting your company. That *would* be madness!' The doctor laughed at his own joke and resting a solicitous hand on his companion's back exerted just enough pressure to encourage movement. Lorenz tossed his cigar stub aside and said, 'In which case I had better prove my sanity before you call an ambulance.' Opening the front door he bowed and gestured. 'After you, Herr Doctor.'

★

Lorenz was sitting outside a cafe on Unter den Linden, sipping his coffee and flicking through the evening papers. The unseasonal mildness of the preceding day had caused him to doff his overcoat and drape it over an adjacent chair. After twenty-seven months, Germany was finally at war with America. Yet this momentous news had had no noticeable effect on life in the city: civil servants clutched their leather briefcases and marched briskly towards the Brandenburg Gate; well-dressed secretaries checked their makeup in hand mirrors as they clicked past on high heels; crowded trams rattled along tracks and Mercedes drivers hooted cyclists. The bustling capital seemed unchanged.

Leaning back in his chair, Lorenz estimated the size of the US navy and made some rudimentary calculations. It took up to 300,000 man-hours to build a Type VIIC U-boat – and the newer models took even longer. German shipyards would never be able to meet revised targets, not unless some of the work was given to steel mills and factories. Pressure hull sections and plating would have to be assembled by subcontractors. The task was colossal.

'Kapitänleutnant.' Lorenz turned to see who had spoken. The voice belonged to a boy of about fourteen years of age, dressed in the winter uniform of the Hitler Youth: a blue tunic, cap and black shorts. He was accompanied by an identically accoutred and smaller companion. 'Kapitänleutnant, we would be greatly honoured if you would sign our autograph book.' The boy produced an imitation-leather volume chased with gilt involutions.

'What?'

'Your autograph, Kapitänleutnant?' The boy signed the air to make his meaning clear.

'Listen,' said Lorenz. 'Why don't you run along to the nearest theatre, where I'm sure you'll find a gamesome actress who'll be only too pleased to sign your book. That would be a much better use of your time, believe me.'

The boys shared a moment of confusion before their simmering excitement came to the boil and they both started asking questions simultaneously: 'Where are you based?' 'What is the number of your boat?' 'What type is it?' The taller boy stopped talking but his friend continued. 'American sailors will be no match for our navy.' He looked somewhat moist and overwrought. 'Our group leader says that they have left it too late to enter the war, that the Americans are inexperienced and unprepared.'

Lorenz was relieved to see Monika approaching. When she arrived she smiled at the boys and said, 'Who are your friends?' Lorenz stood up and drew a chair out from under the table. She sat down and the taller boy said to her, 'We're collecting autographs.' When Lorenz sat next to Monika the boy placed the book and a pen on the table directly in front of him. Lorenz stared at the blank pages.

'Siegfried?' Monika prompted.

'The book contains the names of many heroes,' said the smaller boy encouragingly.

Lorenz recoiled. Observing his discomfort, Monika said, 'Kapitänleutnant Lorenz is a very modest man.' Then, catching his eye, she queried again: 'Siegfried?'

'I'm not . . .' Lorenz began an abortive sentence and then immediately failed to complete another. 'It's just . . .'

Monika stiffened. 'Siegfried, they're waiting.'

He didn't want to make a scene. Picking up the pen he scrawled his name and said, 'There!' The delighted boys gave him the party salute and said in unison, 'Good hunting, Herr Kapitänleutnant,' before rushing off with their prize.

'Why didn't you want to sign their autograph book?' asked Monika.

Lorenz shrugged. 'Where shall we eat?'

They found a pleasant, traditional restaurant in Kurfürstendamm but the tasteless, rubbery food was somewhat disappointing. Lorenz made a comment to this effect and Monika said, 'Well, nothing's quite as good as it was.' There was no awkwardness and their conversation flowed easily. Monika talked about the school where she worked, her love of teaching, and her hobbies, which were all, predictably, either healthy or meritorious: mountain walks, swimming, painting watercolours and singing in a choir. As the evening progressed, Lorenz realized that he had not fully registered the magnitude of her beauty. Her perfectly balanced features conformed to a classical ideal and her clear, powder-blue eyes were like those belonging to an antique doll. She was a sweet-natured creature, solicitous and sympathetic. Suggesting that they book a room in Hotel Fürstenhof for the night was not going to be acceptable.

'That boy,' said Monika, 'the shorter of the two who wanted your autograph. He was right, you know.'

Lorenz tried to make sense of the non sequitur but was unable to do so. 'I'm sorry?'

'You *are* heroes.' Her expression changed, quite dramatically, as though her features had suddenly been cast in a different light. Her elevated jaw suggested stoic pride and her striking eyes became filmed with emotion. Lorenz smiled politely. *Heroes.* A part of him was still standing on the bridge of U-330, watching men burning and screaming in an infernal sea. Monika reached across the table and covered his hand with her own and he noticed that her skin was remarkably soft and cool. 'You do your duty. And I am prepared to do mine.' There was no doubting her meaning.

Lorenz was shocked and for a moment quite speechless. In his mind, sex and patriotism were very separate entities and he wanted to keep it that way. 'You are most kind and I am genuinely touched by your generosity of spirit.' He captured the attention of a passing waiter and ordered another bottle of wine. 'But please . . . tell me more about your school.'

The following morning Lorenz wandered into the kitchen and found Steffi sitting at the table. 'Well,' she said. 'How did it go?'

'How did what go?'

'The district baking competition – what do you think?'

Lorenz was amused by her sarcasm. 'It went very well.'

'So, do you like her?'

'She's extremely good company.'

'But . . .'

'Could we continue this conversation after I've had a cup of coffee? I've only just woken up.'

The telephone rang and Steffi left the kitchen. She returned almost immediately.

'It's for you.'

'Who is it?'

'Someone calling from Brest.'

Lorenz went to the drawing room and picked up the receiver. 'Yes?'

'Good morning, Lorenz, it's Cohausz.'

'Good morning, sir.'

'I'm sorry to disturb you at this early hour but I have some bad news concerning your boat.' Cohausz hesitated before continuing. 'There was a battery explosion.'

'My crew,' said Lorenz anxiously. 'Were any of them injured?'

'No. But two electricians were killed and two firemen.'

'That's terrible,' said Lorenz. 'Do you want me to come back now?'

'No,' said Cohausz. 'There's nothing you can do – your return would serve no purpose. U-330 will be in dry dock for at least four or five weeks. What with it being so close to Christmas we've decided to extend your leave.'

'Thank you, sir. What caused the explosion?'

'We don't know as yet.'

'Is the boat very badly damaged?'

'I've been assured that everything can be put right.'

They speculated about the possible causes of the explosion for a few minutes before Cohausz said, 'Incidentally, we've found replacements for Hoffmann and Richter.'

'Are they experienced men?'

'Be realistic, Lorenz.' Cohausz didn't elaborate. 'And you've been allocated an extra crew member – a photographer.'

Lorenz sighed. 'They get in the way. Do we have to take him?'

'Yes. Enjoy the rest of your furlough.'

When Lorenz returned to the kitchen Steffi looked wary. 'What's happened?'

'An accident – a battery explosion on my boat – some people got killed.'

'Crew?'

Lorenz shook his head. 'Maintenance and firemen.'

'Must you go back?'

'No. I can stay in Berlin until after Christmas.'

Steffi stood up and embraced him tightly. 'I know I shouldn't say this – not given the circumstances – but that's wonderful.'

'Yes,' he said. 'It is.'

After eating a light breakfast Lorenz walked to the lake. Had the batteries been leaking chlorine? And for how long? Poisonous fumes could cause hallucinations; *that* was common knowledge. He was still searching for answers, explanations for his bizarre experiences, common-sense explanations that didn't implicate brain lesions or esoteric psychology or the reality of ghosts. The degree to which he wanted to believe that everything could be attributed to the pedestrian expedient of poisonous fumes was, he realized, a measure of his desperation. But the very fact that there had been yet another accident made the superstitious agitation of his crew seem less ridiculous – even warranted, perhaps. Lorenz picked up a stone and made it skip across the water.

'You know,' said Lorenz, as he tied a glass ball to one of the lower branches of the Christmas tree, 'I have a Christmas tree on my boat. In the control room there is a complicated assembly of pipes and red wheels. All U-boat men refer to this structure as the Christmas tree.'

'Do you hang things on it?' asked Jan.

'No. That would be dangerous. The red wheels are the flooding and bilge valves. We need to get to them quickly – decorations would slow us down.' Pia handed Lorenz a carved wooden angel blowing a trumpet. 'Last year,' Lorenz continued, 'when I knew that I was still going to be at sea on Christmas Day, I made sure that we had an artificial Christmas tree on board. We put it up on Christmas Eve and the cook made us a special Christmas dinner.'

'Did Father take a Christmas tree with him to Russia?' asked Jan.

'He didn't need to,' Lorenz replied. 'They have plenty of Christmas trees in Russia. I had to make special provision, you see, because Christmas trees are rather hard to come by in the middle of the Atlantic Ocean.'

When they had finished decorating the tree, they sat on the

floor and admired their handiwork. Lorenz pointed out how their reflections were distorted in the silver baubles and the children laughed. He wanted their laughter to last forever, because when they stopped laughing, another minute would have passed, and every passing minute brought him closer to the end of his furlough. A familiar dread rose up inside him, bringing with it memories of the torpedo room splattered with blood and brain tissue; a cold hand on his shoulder; Richter saying, *He tried to strangle me. While I was asleep*; Hoffmann's severed safety belt; and a face – as white as alabaster – momentarily illuminated by the sweep of a torch beam.

'Uncle Siegfried, what's the matter?' Jan was pulling at his jumper.

'I was just wondering what I'm going to get for Christmas, that's all.'

Later, Monika arrived and suggested to Lorenz that they go for a short walk. The streets were empty and tiny flakes of snow began to fall. Monika's talk was as easy and fluent as usual. They stopped beneath a street lamp and the crystals of ice on her eyelashes twinkled like stars. When she pouted Lorenz found that he could not resist kissing her.

'Can we go into town tomorrow night?' she asked.

'If you want,' Lorenz replied.

She laid a hand against the side of his face. 'I've booked a hotel.'

'Which one?'

'The Fürstenhof.'

Lorenz grinned. 'An excellent choice.'

Glockner ushered Lorenz down a dimly lit hallway and into a spacious living room: bookcases, escritoire, Grotrian-Steinweg upright piano, leather sofa and reading chair. Everything was the same. There were no ornaments, paintings or photographs, and the air seemed somewhat hazy, as if the contents of the room were being viewed through a fine mesh.

'You've started playing again?' Lorenz had noticed a Beethoven piano sonata on the music stand.

'Yes. It's gradually coming back.' Glockner wiggled his fingers.

'I don't know why you stopped.'

'Time,' said Glockner, 'never enough time. And I can't bear to play badly.'

Lorenz sat on the sofa, crossed his legs, and extended his arms along the back rest. 'Well, what did you find out?'

Glockner lowered himself into the reading chair. 'He was quite a character, your Professor Grimstad. You said he was an archaeologist.'

'That's what I was told.'

'He did supervise some archaeological digs in Norway and

Iceland, but these were undertaken without the approval of his university. In fact, he wasn't an archaeologist but an authority on Norse literature. He came to prominence early when his controversial translation of the Völuspá was published.'

'The what?'

'The Völuspá. The Seeress's Prophecy. Some believe it to be the greatest poem of the Germanic peoples.'

'I've never heard of it.'

'It's part of the Edda, which you *must* know.'

'We did it at school.'

'Indeed. Grimstad's reputation grew and for many years he enjoyed the respect of his colleagues; however, he began to attract criticism when he started writing about pagan cere-monies. It was all rather speculative and his peers began to question his judgement and it was about this time that he began to dabble in archaeology – a discipline in which he had no formal training or experience – presumably in the hope of discovering evidence that would support his theories. Things came to a head about four years ago. It seems that he per-suaded some of his students to participate in re-enactments of a pagan ritual and a subsequent scandal led to his dismissal from the university. I'm not sure what he got up to, precisely, but I believe that there were allegations of sexual impropriety.'

'Was he a member of the resistance?'

'After his dismissal he became involved with various folkloric groups, among whose number he was bound to have met staunch nationalists.'

'And the Schutzstaffel? Why were they interested in him?'

'I don't know. I wasn't able to find that out; however, Himmler – of course – is renowned for his peculiar ideas about the significance of Norse mythology. And he's very fond of runes.' Glockner hummed a jaunty introduction and sang a few lines of a famous SS anthem: '*We all stand ready for battle, inspired by runes and death's head* . . .'

Lorenz nodded in agreement and the two men fell silent. A clock was ticking and outside a car drove past. A sudden blast of wind rattled the windows. 'Thank you,' said Lorenz. He took a slip of paper out of his pocket and handed it to his friend.

'What's this?'

'A name and a telephone number.'

'Lulu Trompelt?'

'She likes opera and foreign poetry and she's supposed to be pretty – although I only have someone else's word for that.'

On returning to Brest, Lorenz was informed by Cohausz that Wilhelm had gone absent without leave. He remembered the young bosun's mate, clearing up the boat – anxious, scared –

handing him the British penny. 'He was due back three days ago,' said Cohausz. 'I've spoken to his parents. He spent Christmas with them in Hamburg. They said goodbye to him at the station.'

'Did they see him get on the train?'

'No.'

'He could be anywhere.'

'True. But eventually he'll be found and then . . .' Cohausz mimed aiming a rifle and pulling a trigger. 'What a fool. Do you have any idea why he's chosen to face a firing squad?'

'Well, we don't know that for sure, do we? Not just yet, sir.'

'He couldn't have got lost.'

'An accident possibly, Kommodore?'

'What? On the way down from Hamburg? I think that's highly unlikely, don't you?'

Some of the crew had already been interviewed and Lorenz learned that Berger was the last person to have spoken to Wilhelm before the errant bosun's mate had departed for Hamburg. Lorenz had the young seaman brought to his quarters.

'It was the day after the explosion,' said Berger. 'A group of us had got together in a beer cellar down in the port, Herr Kaleun. We'd all drunk too much. It was getting late and most of the men went off to the Casino Bar: Kruger, Peters, Stein,

Neumann, Arnold – and a few others – crew from different boats who I didn't know. I was left sitting at a table with Wilhelm.'

'How was he behaving?' Lorenz asked.

'He wasn't himself, sir.'

'What do you mean by that?'

'He was glum, moody: not very talkative. But then, all of a sudden, he started saying things . . .' Berger shifted in his seat as though he was experiencing some kind of physical discomfort.

'*Things?* What things?'

'It was difficult to understand him at first, sir. He wasn't very clear, because of the drink, I suppose – mumbling, cursing. Then he started saying that the boat wasn't right.'

'You mean unsafe?'

'No, he wasn't referring to a technical problem. More like the boat was . . .' Berger hesitated. 'More like the boat was jinxed. I suppose he was brooding about Hoffmann – and the explosion.' The young seaman ventured a tentative opinion. 'We *have* been unlucky, sir.' His expression was a tacit invitation for Lorenz to agree and his features sagged when the anticipated endorsement was not forthcoming.

'What else did he say?'

'Something about God and punishment, something about his mother meeting a gypsy in a wood, and Richter – he was going on about Richter being right. It was all very confused, Herr Kaleun.'

'It sounds like Wilhelm was frightened.'

Berger frowned. 'No, not really – I'd say upset. But it's difficult to say, sir. He was very drunk, Herr Kaleun. I didn't stay with him for long. To be honest, I was feeling a bit sick and wanted to lie down. That was the last I saw of him.'

After Berger was dismissed Lorenz summoned Sauer and Voigt.

'Do you think you can manage without Wilhelm?' he asked.

'If we have to,' Sauer replied. Voigt nodded his assent.

'Good,' said Lorenz.

'I can't believe he would have done such a thing, Herr Kaleun,' said Sauer.

Lorenz sighed and remembered how he had found Wilhelm standing outside the listening post – awkwardly positioned, his eyes wide and fearful. The boy had seen something. And like all superstitious sailors he had taken it to be a bad omen.

Lorenz was seated next to Graf in the lounge bar of the Hotel Café Astoria. The chanteuse with the plangent voice was singing a song about a cold-hearted lover, and her geriatric accompanists were performing with customary vigour.

'Are you satisfied?' asked Lorenz.

'Yes,' Graf replied. 'The new propellers are wonderful. Not a sound . . .'

'Hydroplanes?'

'The whole system has been taken apart and put together again: you couldn't find a speck of rust with a magnifying glass.'

'Engine mountings?'

'Solid as a rock.'

'Ah,' said Lorenz, 'there they are.' An administrator was standing by the door and scanning the room. By his side was a handsome, square-jawed young officer, whose permanent half-smile communicated condescension rather than good humour. The administrator spotted Lorenz, raised his hand, and advanced with his companion through the smoky haze.

'Kapitänleutnant Lorenz, Oberleutnant Graf. May I introduce Leutnant Max Pullman, the photographer assigned to your patrol.' The young officer saluted and Lorenz invited him to sit. 'I'll get more drinks,' said the administrator. Lorenz asked Pullman about his prior experience of U-boats and he was surprised to discover that the lieutenant had already been out on one (albeit uneventful) patrol. 'My photographs appear regularly in magazines,' he said proudly, 'and one of them was chosen to be on the front cover of the *Illustrated Observer*.' He was, as Lorenz had expected, intelligent and well-informed. They talked for a whole hour before the administrator announced that he had orders to take Pullman back to the academy. The photographer had been engaged to take some formal portraits of Cohausz. As the administrator and Pullman elbowed their way through the crowd, Graf leaned towards Lorenz and said softly, 'Well, what do you think?'

'He's a Party man,' Lorenz replied. 'He'll be keeping a close eye on us. You'd better warn everyone.'

'That's what I thought,' said Graf.

The following evening the crew of U-330 were assembled on the deck in readiness for the commander's customary pre-departure speech.

'All hands present or accounted for,' said Falk.

'Well,' said Lorenz. 'Here we go again. There are expectations, but we are prepared and able to meet those expectations.' He paused, grinned at the crew, and scratched the back of his head. 'A boat can only ever be as good as its crew, but its crew is only ever as good as its captain.' Pullman was positioned near the tower and the repetitive sound of a camera shutter echoed around the vast interior of the pen. 'I'll do my best – as I'm sure you will too. And together . . .' Lorenz filled his cheeks with air and let it out slowly. 'And together, we shall prevail. Dismissed.'

The photographer sidled up to Graf and said, 'That was his speech?'

'Yes,' said Graf. 'His longest yet. He may have spun it out for your benefit.' Although Pullman maintained his habitual half-smile, he was not able to conceal his disapproval.

Thirty minutes later U-330 floated out of the bunker and followed a tug boat through the obstacles in the military harbour. Lorenz was on the bridge, calling engine and rudder orders through the communications pipe. The sky was not covered with an even distribution of stars: barrage balloons produced ominous areas of blackness – sharp-edged voids. Hulks materialized out of the gloom like cursed ships and the air smelt of oil and sea weed.

'No brass bands,' said Graf. Lorenz nodded. Further expansion was unnecessary. They were clearly leaving in secrecy because of renewed suspicions of an intelligence breach.

Lorenz thought of his family, the quiet courage of his sister and the small, perfect hands of his niece and nephew. He thought of Monika, her upturned face beneath the street lamp – tiny ice crystals landing on her eyelashes; Leo Glockner in his study, and finally Faustine – beautiful, sensuous, elegant

Faustine – who he would never see again. Would he see any of them again?

An escort vessel was waiting for U-330 outside the sea wall. It led them through the Goulet de Brest, along the coast, and past the Pointe de Saint-Mathieu. They continued west and on reaching the 200-metre contour Lorenz cleared the bridge. Just after midnight he gave orders to dive and the boat slipped beneath the waves. In Lorenz's pocket, a British penny was continuously rotating between his fingers, and each revolution seemed to accumulate dark presentiments of increasing intensity.

Patrol

Two days passed, the watch-rotation progressed through its inexorable cycles, and the lookouts stared over an unchanging, empty wilderness of foamy ridges. The monotony of their vigil was broken only once by the appearance of a flotilla of wooden crates. Lorenz, ever curious about the detritus carried between continents by the sea, ordered that one of the containers should be opened. Inside were a number of identical yellow velvet ball gowns. They were so old fashioned they could have been made by a seamstress in the nineteenth century.

'Shall we keep one?' asked Falk.

'Yellow isn't your colour,' Lorenz replied. 'You're far too pale.'

'I meant for luck, sir,' said Falk, stiffening as the men standing around him began to smirk.

Lorenz shook his head. 'We don't have room.'

The boat was crammed with provisions. Loaves of bread-filled nets were drawn across the engine room, the crew quarters looked like a butcher's shop, and one of the heads was completely full of coffee, tea, chocolate powder, and fruit juice. Moreover, the deck in the forward compartment had been raised to accommodate the reserve torpedoes, making the already confined space even more cramped than usual. There really wasn't any room for a ball gown. Even so, if there had been even the slightest possibility of stowing it somewhere, Lorenz would have given his consent. The atmosphere on board U-330 had been subdued and uneasy. This was not only because of the photographer's unwelcome presence but also because of Wilhelm's desertion, which was viewed by many as yet another bad omen. A lucky charm, Lorenz recognized, might help to counteract the general feeling of despondency. 'I tell you what,' said Lorenz, swiftly reviewing his decision, 'cut out one of those embroidered flowers and pin it up somewhere in the control room.' His compromise was welcomed by sighs of satisfaction.

The following day, Arnold and Engel reported symptoms of venereal disease.

'So,' said Lorenz to the two shame-faced penitents, 'I suppose you spent most of your leave upstairs at the Casino Bar?'

'No, Kaleun,' said Arnold indignantly. 'I've been seeing a local girl, that's all.'

'Me too,' said Engel. 'Her name's Marie. She's very chaste. She goes to church every Sunday.'

'When are you idiots going to learn?' Lorenz asked rhetorically. 'Venereal disease is a British secret weapon. The local women carry it especially for the likes of you. I suppose they succumbed to your amorous advances as soon as you told them you were about to leave. Well?' Arnold and Engel looked down at their boots. 'It's a strategy. Don't you see? A method of interfering with the efficient running of U-boats at sea.'

'Is that really true?' asked Pullman.

'Yes,' Lorenz replied.

'Then we must take the names of these women,' said Pullman, reaching for a notebook, 'and radio Brest at once.'

'It's not something we can prove.'

'Be that as it may . . .'

'Pullman, it isn't possible to arrest women for carrying venereal diseases. Not yet, anyway.'

'They could be questioned.'

'There are more important things we should be worrying about.'

A few days later Lorenz consulted Ziegler concerning his patients.

'They've both got gonorrhoea – I think. Arnold is responding to the albucid cure but not Engel.'

'So what are you going to do?' asked Lorenz.

Ziegler shrugged. 'The old method, I suppose, permanganate of potash in a urethral syringe.'

Pullman turned pale.

'There's something you should record for posterity,' said Lorenz, addressing the photographer. 'Take a picture of that and it'll be sure to make the front cover of the *Illustrated Observer*.'

The sun was setting when Lorenz was given the decrypted message. Another vessel of the 1st Flotilla, U-112, was pursuing a convoy just north of U-330's current position. He consulted Müller at the chart table, who, on seeing the co-ordinates, exclaimed, 'We can catch them up in a matter of hours.' Immediately Lorenz gave the order to change course.

When darkness fell the night was moonless and impenetrable. Visibility was so poor Lorenz resorted to sniffing the breeze for traces of oil.

'Can you smell anything?' asked Falk.

'No,' Lorenz replied.

The boat raced north at full speed, cutting diagonally across waves of increasing size. Two hours passed.

Lorenz was peering over the bulwark when something on the forward section of the deck drew his attention. A portion of the darkness seemed to become detached, to separate from its surroundings – a deeper black against the general blackness that enveloped the bow. He watched its slow progress, a figure walking beneath the radio antenna, and when it arrived at the

8.8 cm gun it came to a halt. An involuntary sound escaped from between Lorenz's lips: a dipping and rising note that expressed surprise and disbelief.

'Kaleun?' said Falk.

The edges of the shape blurred and whatever it was seemed to dissipate and become absorbed into the darkness. 'Nothing,' said Lorenz. 'Keep your eyes on the horizon.'

One of the lookouts coughed and said hesitantly, 'Fifty degrees starboard. I'm not sure – but I think . . . I think I can see a steamer.'

Lorenz struggled to remain focused. He dismissed the figure from his mind and when he raised his binoculars he spied a smudge against the faintly phosphorescent sky. 'Yes,' he responded, 'I see it.' He gave further course directions and U-330 continued to jounce across the water with both diesels thumping.

As they approached the convoy, officers began to assemble on the bridge: Juhl, Müller, Graf and Pullman. Falk was looking through the aiming device, reeling off numbers – target speed, range, angle – and in the conning tower, Sauer was entering data into the computer. Some corrections were made and Falk felt a flush of satisfaction when the large shadow he was observing became aligned in the cross hairs. Indistinct forms, no more than vague penumbra, suggested other craft beyond his principle mark. Two fan shots followed. U-330 turned to evade the nearest escorts and after a brief interval there was a massive explosion, a great tower of flame rose up from the sea and the men on the bridge felt the shock wave inside their chests. Pullman's camera shutter was clicking. The torpedoes had been spread out in order to optimize the chances of sinking any other steamers in the vicinity, but this ploy had not proved effective. They had either passed harmlessly between hulls or they had, yet again, failed to detonate. Lorenz wondered if the new G7e torpedoes were going to be as unreliable as the old ones. Suddenly the sky was ablaze with star shells and parachute flares. A large silhouette loomed out of the middle distance directly ahead of them.

'Shit!' Falk cried. 'Where did that come from?'

Lorenz yelled, 'Alarm!'

The lookouts and the spectating officers leapt into the tower. Lorenz was the last to leave the bridge and he shouted, 'One hundred metres,' as he closed and dogged the hatch. When he stepped off the ladder in the control room the deck was angled and Graf was standing behind the hydroplane operators studying the manometer dial. 'Hard port turn.'

Twenty metres, twenty-five metres, thirty metres . . .

'Dead slow – continue to turn.' U-330 doubled back to run parallel on the attacker. Lorenz climbed through the bulkhead and squatted next to Lehmann who was already listening through his headphones and rotating his wheel. The boat levelled. 'Well?' Lorenz asked. Lehmann whispered a bearing, gave an estimated range, and added, 'Heading straight towards us.' Soon, everyone could hear the thrashing of propellers. The escort passed overhead and there were two splashes. The noise of the propellers faded and the ensuing silence was so profound it was possible to hear the malignant ticking of the depth charges, becoming louder and louder as they sank. A powerful blast rocked the boat and the lights went out for a few seconds. When they came on again Lorenz could see Pullman staring upwards, his hands cradling the lens of his camera. He did not look particularly frightened and his half-smile was still intact. Zealots had many faults, Lorenz reflected, but cowardice wasn't one of them. Addressing Graf he said, 'Another thirty metres.' The boat nosed down and levelled out again. More depth charges exploded but none of them were as accurate as the first. 'They don't know where we are,' Lorenz crowed. 'The Tommy commander must be inexperienced.' Lehmann confirmed that the escort was moving away and after thirty minutes Lorenz gave orders to surface and reload.

The night was still uncompromisingly dark but as they made their way back towards the convoy one of the lookouts spotted a light. Lorenz looked through his binoculars and saw that its source was a carbon arc lamp being aimed from the deck of a destroyer at a listing, burned-out carcass. Somewhere inside the wreck, a fire reignited and made the windows of the superstructure glow. The destroyer was clearly searching for survivors, although Lorenz couldn't see any.

'Is that our steamer?' asked Falk. 'The one we attacked? Or did U-112 do this?'

'It's difficult to say,' said Lorenz. 'We'll have to ask headquarters.'

They stopped at a distance of approximately 800 metres from the rescue operation. The destroyer was completely unaware of their approach.

'What shall we do?' asked Falk in a hushed voice.

The officers became restive as they waited for Lorenz's tardy answer. 'There's nothing more to accomplish here.'

'But the steamer, Kaleun,' said Falk. 'It's offering an easy broadside.' He glanced nervously at Pullman.

Ignoring Falk's remark, Lorenz spoke into the communications pipe. 'Turn the boat around. Ahead slow.'

'Herr Kaleun,' said Pullman. 'I don't understand.'

'What don't you understand?'

'Aren't we obliged to deliver a *coup de grâce*?'

'No – we are not.'

'But in the handbook it says quite clearly —'

'I don't care what the fucking handbook says!'

Pullman bridled. 'I was merely seeking clarification, Herr Kaleun.'

'We're turning around. Is that clear enough? And don't

ever question my judgment on *my* bridge again or I'll have you thrown over the side.'

The men on the bridge stiffened as they awaited the outcome of the altercation. After a long silence Pullman raised his hand and said, 'Permission to leave the bridge?'

'Granted,' Lorenz replied, adding under his breath: 'With great pleasure.'

When Pullman had gone Falk whispered, 'Has he gone to make notes?'

'That's very likely,' said Lorenz.

'Aren't you worried?'

'When we've finished this patrol and we're cruising through the Goulet de Brest then I'll start worrying. Right now, that feels very distant.'

The sea resembled the bleak desolation of a lava plain, a rocky mantle or crust. U-330 was travelling slowly, producing a trenchlike wake, as though its propellers were cutting a continuous channel out of basalt. Diesel fumes rose from the gratings and embroidered the air with black braids that unravelled to form a grey veil. The engine noise became louder and softer when the exhaust vents dipped in and out of the water.

'Odd,' said Pullman. 'We haven't been at sea for very long but—'

'It feels like forever,' Lorenz interrupted.

'Yes. Sometimes I wake up in the morning and I have no idea what day it is.'

'That's because it doesn't matter. Not really. One day is much like the next. And when we're under the water you can't tell night from day.'

The boat climbed up a freakishly large wave and slid down the other side. When the deck was horizontal again, Pullman asked, casually: 'What are your thoughts on the Lion's strategy? Do you think we should be doing things differently?'

'I don't have any thoughts on the matter,' Lorenz replied.

'But surely you must have an opinion, Herr Kaleun?'

'We all have opinions . . .' Pullman was expecting Lorenz to continue, but the commander pushed his cap back and walked away.

'I am interested in what you think,' he persisted.

'I try not to,' said Lorenz flatly.

Juhl glanced at Voigt and grinned.

Pullman raised his camera and took a close-up of Arnold, who was wearing a woollen hat with a large bobble on top. The self-conscious sailor adopted a heroic expression that was irretrievably undermined by his headgear. Play-acting was superseded by authentic emotion when Arnold's features suddenly convulsed and he screamed, 'Aircraft astern!' Lorenz looked up, judged that they had just enough time to escape and called, 'Alarm!' As he clambered into the tower he saw two fighter aircraft swooping in from the opposite direction. There was a burst of machine-gun fire as he closed the hatch and the boat had barely submerged when the first explosion almost rolled U-330 on its side.

Lorenz landed in a chaotic control room where men were sprawled on the matting, foodstuffs were flying through the air, and glass was shattering. The angle of descent was so steep he was thrown against the forward bulkhead. Another explosion shook the hull and it was more violent than anything he had ever experienced. It seemed implausible that so much power could be unleashed from a device made by mere mortals, that so much energy could be disciplined and contained in a small canister. The boat seemed to be spinning around in a vortex caused by an upheaval of cosmic proportions: collision with the moon or the death of the sun. A third and final explosion pushed the bow down and accelerated the boat's descent. Graf had managed to remain upright by holding onto the periscope halyard and he was requesting more speed in order to increase pressure on the hydroplanes. He hadn't registered that the motors had stopped humming. The forward hydroplane operator, his face incandescent with fear, turned and croaked: 'It's not responding – it's jammed.' From his position on the deck, Lorenz could see the needle on the manometer moving around the dial at an unprecedented speed.

Forty-five metres, fifty metres, sixty metres, seventy metres . . .

'All hands aft,' yelled Graf. The usual stampede did not ensue. Only a few men managed to stand and stumble up the incline towards the stern.

Several voices in different locations were calling out, 'Breach!'

'She's out of control!' shouted Graf. Then, facing his supine commander, he repeated more evenly, 'Kaleun, we're out of control.' His words seemed to travel through the boat in all directions, silencing every compartment. Apart from the sound of trickling water nothing could be heard except men breathing heavily. Lorenz felt as if he were falling through space. The manometer needle confirmed their predicament: *ninety metres, one hundred metres, one hundred and ten metres . . .*

So, thought Lorenz. *This is it.* He had never truly believed that he would survive the war and now he would only have to endure it for a few more seconds before the ribs of the boat buckled and the deck-plates and the overhead came together. The waiting had come to an end.

One hundred and eighty metres, one hundred and ninety metres . . .

Rivets shot across the control room and jets of water filled the bilges.

An apprentice mechanic was on his knees, mewling softly.

Lorenz thought he could hear the boy repeating the word 'Mother'. They were no longer a community of fate, a band of brothers, or proud Germans, but scared children. Personas were slipping like poorly tailored disguises. *This is where it all breaks down*, thought Lorenz. *This is how we die.* A man in the petty officers' quarters had started to wail an inarticulate plea to St Nicholas.

One hundred and ninety, two hundred, two hundred and ten . . .

Lorenz wanted to get it over with: he wanted the shell plating to peel open like a can of sardines and the cold black ocean to release him from all the terror and the pain and the guilt.

Two hundred and twenty metres . . .

Graf gestured at the manometer, awed by the boat's resilience. The set of his jaw suggested a certain patriotic pride in what had been accomplished by the shipbuilders of Kiel.

Two hundred and forty metres . . .

There was a loud boom and a jolt raised Lorenz's body off the rubber matting. Those who had managed to remain standing were knocked off their feet and the men in the aft compartments started screaming. More glass shattered, the hull began to vibrate, and a terrible screeching started up. There were bangs, crashes, then a low rumbling. For an indeterminate time it felt like the keel was being dragged along a basin filled with rubble. When the boat came to a halt the lights flickered and went out.

The apprentice mechanic stopped crying for his mother and the screaming stopped.

Lorenz's jacket was soaked through and cumbrous. He tried to stand but someone was crawling over his legs. There were yet more cries of 'Breach!' and a single torch beam appeared. When the emergency lights came on he saw pipes hanging off the overhead, hand wheels on the deck and members of the crew with blood on their faces. He stood up, peered through the cracked glass of the manometer and saw that the needle was stationary and pointing at a terrifying 260 metres. They were in the cellar, ten metres below the depth at which the pressure hull should have sagged and split open.

In spite of the devastation and the extraordinary danger they were in, order was quickly restored. Reports were delivered by pale, dazed men with sopping hair and torn shirts and Graf went off to supervise the stopping of the breaches. Timbers appeared and wedges were cut as a preliminary measure. Gradually, the sound of the water jets subsided but a constant dripping and trickling served to remind them of their extreme vulnerability.

When Graf returned, Lorenz said, 'Well?'

'We're very heavy,' the engineer replied.

'Then why aren't the pumps going?'

'They're broken, Kaleun.'

'Can they be repaired?'

'I think so.'

'What if we blew *all* of the buoyancy tanks?'

'Some of them are sure to be damaged.'

Graf stepped through the aft bulwark and vanished into the petty officers' quarters.

Lorenz sniffed the air and detected a distinctive, unwelcome smell. The batteries were leaking. Without batteries, the motors wouldn't work, and without motors, the propellers wouldn't turn. Schmidt was policing the crew, clapping his hands together and urging those who had been given jobs to work faster. Pullman – who had been standing by the engine telegraph – stepped towards Lorenz and said, 'Can I help?'

'There's nothing you can do,' said Lorenz. 'Go to your bunk. Only those undertaking repairs should be up. We need to conserve oxygen.'

Pullman nodded but did not leave. 'Where are we?'

Lorenz invited Müller to give the photographer an answer. The navigator picked up a chart, brushed off the excess fluid, and laid it out on the table. 'I think we've come down on the longest mountain range in the world.'

'What?' said Pullman, dismayed.

'The Mid-Atlantic ridge,' said Müller, smoothing the wrinkled chart with the palm of his right hand. 'It runs all the way from the southern hemisphere to the northern hemisphere, goes right up the middle of the Atlantic and rises out of the sea when it reaches Iceland. If we'd missed it we would have just kept going down. It saved us. You might not think so, but we've been very lucky.'

'When your number's up . . .' said Falk.

Lorenz shook his head. 'It was so . . . coordinated.'

'What was?' Müller asked.

'The aircraft: one from behind, two from the front – a pincer movement!' He illustrated his point by bringing his finger and thumb together. 'It was as though they knew exactly where we were.'

'Maybe they were lucky too,' said Müller.

'Kaleun,' said Pullman. 'Before I retire to my bunk may I take some photographs? Such acts of heroism deserve to be recorded.'

'Listen, Pullman,' said Lorenz. 'If I catch you trying to take a single photograph I'll have you inserted into one of the torpedo tubes. This isn't a propaganda exercise.'

Pullman saluted and walked off, his boots splashing in water that still appeared to be rising.

Lorenz climbed through the forward hatchway and saw Reitlinger, Hoffmann's replacement, and Martin, standing together and conferring anxiously. They had taken the cover off the battery and Reitlinger was holding a strip of litmus paper. It was obvious what had happened, the smell was enough, but Reitlinger still said: 'Cracked cells. The acid is leaking.' Sea water and sulphuric acid were combining to produce chlorine gas. Lorenz's brief conversation with the electricians was interrupted by a steady flow of reports: fractured pipes, blown valves, unidentified breaches. The downward tilt of the boat had caused serious flooding in the torpedo room and Kruger and Dressel were wading through water that had risen above their knees.

The crew appeared to be coping well, but Lorenz was not convinced by their stalwart industry. He was aware of too many small but reliable indicators of terror: crossed fingers, pulsing temples, trembling lower lips. Such signs betrayed what lay close to the surface. He sensed the threat of nervous breakdown – latent panic – the possibility of madness spreading through his boat – havoc, mayhem, anarchy.

Graf was rushing up and down the length of the boat, taking stock and issuing instructions. When he returned to the officers' mess the table had been covered with blueprints. He spread them out, frantically making notes with a pencil and mumbling like a lunatic. His hair and beard were matted with oil and he had stripped down to his vest. 'Chief? Chief!' Reitlinger attempted to capture Graf's attention, but the engineer was far too engrossed. The word had to be repeated several times before Graf turned. Reitlinger spoke in a low, confidential tone that Lorenz was unable to hear. He saw Graf respond by rolling his eyes and entering several crosses in a row of boxes on the blueprint. They represented the battery cells. An earlier thought returned to Lorenz in the form of a mocking, playground chant: no cells, no batteries – no batteries, no motors – no motors, no screws – no screws, no movement. The fate of the boat and its crew was now entirely in the hands of the chief engineer.

Lorenz still had a role to play, but it was largely symbolic. The men would be studying him closely, looking for signs of weakness, and his outward composure would check their wayward emotions, calm the constantly simmering dread that might so very easily boil over and become hysteria. Lorenz ordered the control-room mate to fetch him a book from the library and when Danzer returned he was clutching a damp, cloth-bound novel. 'I'm sorry, Kaleun, all the books are wet. This is the best I could do.' Danzer moved aside to let two men carrying buckets of limewash pass. Lorenz glanced at the spine: a popular naval adventure. 'Good choice!' He peeled the soggy pages apart and held the book up high so everybody could see that he was reading. In fact, he was staring at illegible words printed with smeared ink on cheap paper. He listened to the limewash being poured into the bilges to neutralize the battery acid.

In due course Graf was ready to give his final damage

report: 'The main bilge pump and auxiliary pumps are broken. The starboard diesel has been knocked completely off its mounts and the bolts have sheared. The port diesel is loose. The forward hydroplane is stuck. The housing of both batteries is severely damaged and very few of the cells are serviceable. There are breaches in the torpedo room, control room and diesel room. Several valves on the Christmas tree won't open and the observation periscope is leaking. The gyroscopic compass—'

Lorenz exclaimed: 'Is *anything* working?'

'The auxiliary magnetic compass,' Graf replied. But after a short pause he added, 'Possibly.'

Lorenz laid his book on the table and drifted through the compartments, not in order to offer encouragement or stirring clichés, but to simply make his presence felt, to embody the indomitable spirit of the stricken U-boat. In the gloomy half-light, the crew looked more like a long lost tribe of troglodytes than sailors: streaked faces, bloodshot eyes, wielding wrenches like clubs and gripping spanners between exposed teeth, negotiating the narrow confinements of their forgotten underworld. In the torpedo room Kruger was searching for new breaches beneath the waterline. After filling his lungs with air, he squeezed his nostrils together and disappeared beneath the surface. A minute passed before he rose up again coughing and gasping.

On returning to the officers' mess, Lorenz lifted his book again and simulated reading. He turned the pages at regular intervals and allowed his mind to wander. Superimposed on the blurred text, his imagination supplied a limpid portrait of Faustine. Where was she? Asleep in her bed or sitting in an office typing letters for Monsieur Gilbert? Eating her breakfast in a cafe or watching the west facade of the cathedral turn gold in the afternoon. He didn't know what time it was. Faustine was in Paris and he was sitting in a metal tube, balanced on the summit of a mountain under the sea.

A voice roused Lorenz from his thoughts. 'Kaleun? All of the breaches have been stopped.'

Lorenz lifted his head and saw Graf standing over him. 'Is that the pump I can hear?'

'Yes. We just got it going again.' The two men smiled at each other, but the familiar grinding became laboured, the pitch dropped, and then there was silence. Exhausted, Graf leaned back against the woodwork and spat out his frustration. 'Shit!'

Breathing was becoming increasingly difficult. Lorenz felt as if a tight harness was constricting the expansion of his chest and his head ached. The levels of carbon dioxide in the atmosphere were perilously high. When he spotted some of the crew twitching he ordered Sauer to distribute the potash cartridges. After hanging the case around his neck, Lorenz placed a clip on his nose and bit on the 'snorkel' mouthpiece. The taste of rubber was strong and unpleasant. His headache receded but the mouthpiece made him produce excessive amounts of saliva. He was soon having to wipe away unsightly threads of drool from his chin.

Having previously taken on the appearance of cave dwellers, the cartridge 'snorkels' now made the men look like giant insects. The bunks resembled a hive, the result of some outlandish scientific experiment. This fanciful thought seemed to intensify the illusion and Lorenz shook his head to recalibrate his brain. He was tired, a bone-deep tiredness that made simple activities like raising a hand or just thinking effortful. He could feel the weight of sleep in his body, the pull of its shadowy mass. There was nothing more to do. He had lost count of how many times he had toured the boat, so he retired to his nook and lay down, resting the potash cartridge on his stomach.

At once, he was standing outside the boat on the Mid-Atlantic ridge. The peaks were jagged and stretched to the north and south. To the east and west, rocky slopes descended into dark obscurity. U-330 was leaning to one side and pointing downwards, its bow hanging over a wide chasm. The saddle tanks were dented, the deck rails were warped and twisted, and there were scorch marks on the tower. Lorenz could barely make out the scorpion emblem. The boat looked forlorn, almost abandoned – a wreck that would eventually rust away and vanish. Lorenz climbed over uneven ground and when he was next to the boat he slapped the hull, producing a low, resonant 'thump'. Some paint flakes were dislodged and they sank through the water in oscillating arcs like falling feathers. His examination of the battle-scarred hull was disturbed by the sound of thrashing propellers. He scrambled down the slope and stood on a flat ledge. When he looked up, he saw a wolf-pack of U-boats passing overhead, and beyond them, the merest shimmer suggesting the play of light on a surface too far removed to see. The wolf-pack travelled slowly through the green vastness and the spectacle of its progress was arrestingly beautiful. A giant squid swam by trailing long, suckered tentacles.

Lorenz removed his cap and waved it above his head and was surprised to feel the water resisting his movements. 'Help!' he called. His request was carried upwards by a single, irregular, wobbling bubble of air. 'Help!' he called again. Hydrophone operators would be listening: surely one of them would hear his call? He noticed a new phenomenon – an unhurried shower of black specks. As they descended they became more readily identifiable as depth charges. They began to explode and their continuous detonation resembled a fireworks display.

There were flashes, cracks, and smouldering streamers. One of the submarines was blasted out of the arrowhead formation and it dived towards Lorenz. He watched it gathering speed and he was tempted to run, but he was strangely transfixed and did not budge from the ledge. The boat sailed past him, demolishing the summit of a neighbouring peak, before plummeting into the darkness on the other side. A few moments later he saw a fireball ignite in the fathomless deep. The consequent shockwave woke him up.

The overhead showed through the fading vision and Lorenz became conscious of the weight of the potash cartridge on his stomach. He adjusted the mouthpiece and noticed that his beard was covered in spittle. The boat was remarkably quiet. So quiet, in fact, that he wondered if the crew had suffocated while he had been asleep and whether he was the sole survivor. He still felt incredibly tired and rolled his head to the side. Through the gap in the curtain he could see a figure, turned away, wearing a long coat – arms angled slightly and distanced from the body – a cap held in the right hand. The back of the man's head was missing. Instead of an occipital bulge, there was only a gaping cavity, the interior of which glinted beneath an unsteady emergency light. Splinters of bone bristled around the edges of the wound and runnels of cerebrospinal fluid trickled around the man's ears. Lorenz thought: *I am still dreaming.* But he knew that he wasn't. The sound of his shallow breathing was amplified by the 'snorkel'. Fear had dispelled the torpor of sleep and sharpened his senses.

Lorenz eased himself up so that his torso was supported by his elbows. He could not believe how solid Sutherland looked. When Lorenz raised himself higher, the dead commander tilted his head, as if listening. Blood had pooled around the stump of the brain stem. This minute movement caused a red cascade to spill over the jagged bone and splash down Sutherland's coat, creating an archipelago of dark stains. Something inside the cavity loosened and dropped and its wet impact on the base of the skull sounded like the parting of puckered lips. Lorenz blinked and the figure was gone.

The sense of time flowing forward was restored, he could hear men at work, voices, the clatter of tools, and these indications of life seemed to rush into his nook like air filling a vacuum. He pulled the curtain aside and saw Ziegler asleep in the radio shack. Rising from the mattress he walked across the gangway and shook the radio operator's shoulder. After removing the mouthpiece of his 'snorkel', Lorenz said, 'Wake up! Ziegler, wake up!'

Ziegler opened his eyes, mumbled something incomprehensible and removed his own mouthpiece. 'Kaleun?'

'How long have you been asleep?'

'I don't know – not long. I was in the middle of these repairs.' He gestured at a circuit board. 'I'm sorry.'

'Did you see anything?'

'Kaleun?'

'Did you —' Lorenz stopped himself and started again. 'Yes, yes . . . it's difficult, I know.' Glancing at the wall clock he noted that they had been submerged for sixteen hours.

Lorenz made his way towards the aft of the boat. In the petty officers' quarters he found Falk checking that the sleepers were breathing through their 'snorkels'. The cook was in the galley, trying to save food that had got wet or covered in dirt. In the diesel room, the deck plates had been taken up and the heavy machinery beneath was fully exposed. Every surface had been covered with lubricating oil: even the hull was slick and dripping. Fischer, the chief mechanic, was entirely black. The motor room had become a snakepit of tangled cables. Elsewhere, men were staggering around like drunkards, trying to accomplish difficult tasks while their organs and vessels became clogged with poisons. Time was running out.

On his way back to the officers' mess Lorenz was stopped by Lehmann. The hyrdrophone operator handed him a pair of headphones. Lorenz placed them over his ears and listened. He could hear the distant rumble of depth charges.

'Sounds like quite a battle,' said Lorenz. 'Are they coming our way?'

'No,' Lehmann replied, wiping saliva off his chin with his sleeve. 'It isn't getting any louder.'

Lorenz carried on listening. The acoustic changed and he thought that he heard the constant, even rhythms of speech. Was it English? He focused on the faint perturbations in the hiss, but whatever he had identified as language was almost immediately drowned out by more explosions. Lorenz handed the earphones back to Lehmann, sat down in the officers' mess, and pretended to read again.

Over twenty-four hours had passed. Lorenz was sitting with his head thrown back and his eyes closed, occupying a twilight state of consciousness somewhere between sleep and wakefulness. Nonsensical thoughts ran continuously through his mind and he was beginning to feel feverish. The clip on his nose had become extremely painful. He was tempted to rip it off but resisted the urge because he was obliged to lead by example. For some time he had been aware of a grinding sound, infiltrating his malaise, a sound that he had only identified as a non-specific background irritation, something preventing him from obtaining restorative sleep. Then it occurred to him that this sound, this familiar periodicity, was actually very significant and he forced his eyelids open. He saw Graf swaying on the opposite side of the table, ragged, filthy, his 'snorkel' tucked behind the cartridge strap. The engineer steadied himself and started speaking in a hoarse, cracked voice. 'We've pumped out most of the water. The batteries are working: we bridged the cells. The motors are ready. The forward hydroplane is ready – I think. Of course, we won't know for sure until we start moving. The diesels are secured and ready. The gyroscopic compass is ready.' Graf continued his lengthy recitation of accomplishments and at its conclusion he fell backwards. Falk caught him and raised him up again. Lorenz stood, his eyes glistening with emotion. 'What took you so long?' He squeezed out from behind the table, straightened his cap, and made his way directly to the control room where he switched on the public-address system. 'Well, before we left I said that a crew is only ever as good as its captain, but sometimes a captain is only ever as good as his crew. Prepare to surface.' A mournful, strangulated chorus served in lieu of a cheer.

The crew made valiant efforts to conceal their shattered nerves. Juhl had assembled the watch, Müller was poring over charts and Graf was standing at his customary post behind the hydroplane operators. The community of fate was beginning to repair itself. All of them, without exception, looked weary and haggard.

'Blow the tanks,' said Lorenz – angry, defiant – as if issuing a personal challenge to the forces of destiny.

Valves were opened and compressed air hissed. All eyes were on the motionless manometer needle. Lorenz was forced to consider again the enormous weight of water pressing down on the hull, the tiny mathematical margins that would determine whether they all lived or died. The hissing continued but the needle remained fixed. A scraping noise came up through the underside of the casing, there were groans, screeches, and a shrill whistle that became intermittent like Morse code. Everything began to shake and rattle and a shard of glass that hadn't been removed from one of the damaged dials dropped and shattered. Finally, the boat started to rock. The bow was rising and it continued to rise until the deck was horizontal. Further increments angled the boat upwards. There was more scraping, which stopped abruptly and allowed the hum of the electric motors to be heard. The manometer needle trembled and jerked back.

'Let's get off this rock-pile,' said Lorenz.

Two hundred and fifty-five metres, two hundred and fifty metres, two hundred and forty metres . . .

The ascent was slow and the stressed frame of the boat continued to complain. A minor breach had to be plugged at 190 metres, but the boat maintained its smooth upward climb without further incident. At fifty metres Lorenz consulted Lehmann. The hydrophones were still silent.

Forty metres, thirty metres, fifteen metres . . .

The observation periscope was raised. It was safe to surface.

'Tower clear!' Graf cried.

Lorenz climbed the ladder and opened the hatch. The cold, clean air burned his throat and seared his lungs; its frigid purity was almost intolerable. He felt dizzy, slightly delirious. The diesels started and released a cloud of black smoke. 'Quickly,' he said to the watchmen. 'Get into position – concentrate. That was all very diverting but now it's back to work.'

The weather conditions were much the same as they were when they had been attacked: intimidating clouds over a roughcast sea. It was as though their ordeal had happened out of time. He imagined the great mountain range 260 metres below the soles of his boots, its pinnacles and dark spaces – and shivered.

'Permission to come up.' It was Pullman.

'Granted.' Lorenz was feeling magnanimous.

The photographer appeared with his camera. He looked fragile, shaken, and less assured. 'May I?' he said, raising the lens.

'If you must,' said Lorenz. 'But I can't help feeling that I'm not looking my best.'

War Diary

10.13 Two aircraft sighted. Alarm.

11.00 Mist, light swell. The after starboard lookout has reported a faint shadow at 10° on the port quarter. We alter course and travel towards it at ¾ speed.

11.40 We sail ahead of shadow, our intention being to intercept later.

11.45 To the west and south the horizon is overcast whereas to the north and east it is bright. Average visibility, 5–8 nm. Gradually it becomes clear that the shadow is the conning tower of a submarine; however, it is impossible to establish type.

12.13 The submarine alters course hard a-port.

12.30 We dive as it is too light for a surface attack.

12.50 Through the periscope the submarine is identified: British T-class. Bearing 340° true. Course 220°, speed 10 knots, range 2,000 m. We alter course hard a-port to 270° and proceed at ¾ speed. The mist thickens. Contact lost.

13.15   The hydrophone operator reports propeller noises at
        320°. Enemy reappears, proceeding 60°, passing at a
        high speed, range of 200 m on our port beam. We
        alter course hard a-starboard to 60°. Port engine at
        ¾ speed. There are three watch men all of whom are
        looking away to port but without binoculars. No watch
        men on the starboard side. We prepare to fire, but the
        enemy submarine then turns about 150 m ahead of us
        and withdraws at an inclination of 180°.

13.37   We alter course to 90°. Port engine dead slow,
        periscope depth. The enemy submarine appears to be
        patrolling along a NE–SW course line. We will wait for
        it to return.

14.00   Mist thickens again. We lose sight of enemy. Course
        80°. Inclination 180°.

14.20   Bright, but cloudy. Light swell from the SW. Enemy in
        sight once again.

14.27   We prepare a single shot from tube I. The bow cap
        does not open.

14.35   We prepare a single shot from tube III. Torpedo speed
        set 30 knots, depth 10 m, enemy speed 8 knots,
        inclination 35°, bows left, range 600 m. Inclination
        now automatically updated by computer.

14.40   Enemy steers a straight course. I order the boat hard a-port, starboard engine ¾ speed. Enemy course 215°. We pull ahead of the enemy in order to keep the parallax angle small.

14.44   Just before firing we enter new data for enemy speed of 5 knots. Range 500 m.

14. 46   Tube III fire! Enemy speed 5 knots, inclination 70°, bows left, range 500 m, aim-off angle 8.7°. No aim-off adjustment required as enemy speed is slow. We keep the rudder hard a-port so that the enemy bearing is always 350°–10° ahead. After a running time of 34.7 seconds (= 520 m) a detonation. We feel the shockwave. A huge explosion can be seen with pieces of wreckage rising into the air. There is nothing more. Only a large patch of oil and air bubbles.

15.02   We retire, steering course 90°. Port engine dead slow.

15.04   I shall not complain, though I now founder, And perish in watery depths! Nevermore shall my gaze be cheered, By the sight of my love's star (Better not type this, Ziegler – the Lion doesn't like Ludwig Tieck. 'Despair' – a beautiful poem. The last words are 'I am a lost man'. We are all lost men – sooner or later.)

Siegfried Lorenz

Every member of the crew had become preoccupied and inward-looking. They only spoke to each other out of necessity, and when they did, their voices were hushed. The fact that the vessel they had just destroyed was a submarine magnified the usual considerations. Yes, they were British, but in all probability they were no different to themselves, with similar hopes and fears, doing their duty, obeying orders. The logical endpoint of such thinking was a meditation on personal vulnerability and the likelihood of meeting the same fate, a conclusion that was reinforced by superstitious propensities (an eye for an eye, a submarine for a submarine) and a belief in arcane laws that preserved primitive forms of natural justice.

Lorenz was seated in his nook. He had been observing Lehmann, who was listening out for enemy vessels. The hydrophone operator looked particularly troubled. His face seemed to be caving in, his cheeks were sunken and the skin beneath his eyes had sagged and darkened. Occasionally he would stop turning his wheel and just stare at the dial. It was obvious he wasn't registering the figures, but rather focusing on something that existed only in his imagination. Lorenz got up and walked across the gangway. As he approached, Lehmann turned. 'Kaleun?' The hydrophone operator knocked one of the headphones back exposing his left ear. Lorenz spoke in a hushed, confidential whisper. 'What is it, Lehmann?'

'What is it?' Lehmann repeated, confused.

'Yes. Something is bothering you.'

Lehmann sighed. 'I was listening after the torpedo detonated.'

'And . . .?'

'I heard them.'

'Who?'

'The British. Their screams.'

'That's not possible.'

'It wasn't for very long, just a few seconds.'

'No. You *think* you heard their screams.'

'Perhaps.'

'You have to remember, Lehmann, if the tables were turned . . .'

'I know, sir. It's just . . .'

'Unpleasant. Indeed.'

Pullman had been working on some of the younger members of the crew. He had sensed the change of atmosphere, their need for reassurance, comforting certainties, and he had seized the opportunity to preach his gospel. In the forward compartment, he was seated on a lower bunk, reading to Berger and Wessel: 'Everything on this earth is capable of improvement. Every defeat can become the father of a subsequent victory, every lost war the cause of a later resurgence, every hardship the fertilization of human energy, and from every oppression the forces for a new spiritual rebirth can come as long as the blood is preserved pure.' Pullman gazed at his disciples and offered them his durable half-smile. 'The lost purity of the blood alone destroys inner happiness forever, plunges man into the abyss for all time, and the consequences can nevermore be eliminated from body and spirit.'

Lorenz moved through the compartment and Pullman lowered his book. 'The words of the Führer.'

'I know,' Lorenz replied.

'They are uplifting, don't you think, sir?' Lorenz ignored the question and Pullman added, 'A corrective for . . .' his smile widened, 'defeatism.'

Lorenz detected a hint of criticism behind Pullman's missionary zeal.

'I'm sorry?' He glared at Pullman who shifted nervously.

'I was merely saying . . .' The sentence trailed off and the photographer cleared his throat. 'I was merely saying that there is solace in the Führer's counsel – hope, encouragement.'

Lorenz put his hands together around his mouth and shouted, 'Ziegler?'

The radio operator stepped through the doorway. 'Herr Kaleun?'

'Did any of the records survive?'

'Only a few: Glenn Miller – Wagner Overtures.'

'Put the Glenn Miller on, will you? And play it loud.' Without looking at Pullman he carried on walking between the bunks to the torpedo room. Graf was standing with the torpedo men.

'Don't tell me. You can't find anything wrong with Tube One.'

Graf shook his head. 'There are no faults.'

'The bow cap was being what then? Temperamental?'

'Just one of those things,' said Graf.

'Why did I know you were going to say that?'

The sound of the Glenn Miller Band started up, the slippery clarinets answered by muted brass, and beneath, the steady, strolling bass. Graf leaned towards Lorenz, tilted his head to one side to emphasize the music, and said, 'Was that wise, Herr Kaleun?'

'No,' Lorenz replied with evident pride.

Ziegler was changing the dressing on Peters' hand. A number of men had sustained injuries when the boat had been bombed and it was fortunate that none of these had proved serious. Ziegler pulled at the blood-stained bandages and Peters swore.

'Be careful, that hurt.'

Schmidt was also waiting to have a dressing changed. 'Don't be a girl, Peters.'

'I'm telling you, it fucking hurt.'

Ziegler smeared some cod-liver-oil ointment over the exposed cut.

'Hurt?' said Schmidt. 'You haven't got a clue, have you? When I was a boy I ran away and went to sea on a merchant steamer. God, what a rust bucket! Leaked like a sieve. Anyway, we'd just left this stinking port on the west coast of Africa and the boiler exploded. The stokers flew out of the engine room like demons out of hell but someone was still down there, shouting and screaming – trapped. The Portuguese captain paid no attention. I asked him if we shouldn't go down and help the man, but he brushed me aside and started to organize the lifeboats. The Chief Engineer was just the same. "It's only a black," he said. "We need to get off right now, without delay." Cowards, I thought. Cowards! So, I climbed down to the engine room on my own and there was this big black stoker with his foot stuck beneath a girder. Well, I tried to lift it, but I couldn't. The thing weighed a ton. The ship was going down fast and the water was rising. What was I to do? I spotted a big iron coal shovel, held it over the stoker's foot and nodded.

"Do you want me to? Yes?" He nodded back, as if to say: *Go on then, it's my only chance.* And with a downward strike I sliced his foot right off. Then I put him over my shoulder and carried him up onto the deck. I tell you, Peters, he didn't make a sound.'

'So what?' said Peters. 'What does that prove? He was a black. They don't feel pain like us.'

'Shut up, Peters,' said Ziegler. 'Is that true? He didn't make a sound?'

'Not a whimper,' said Schmidt. 'I often wonder where he is. I'd like to think he found a woman who wasn't put off by his stump and that he went on to raise a family. Perhaps he's sitting in some African village right now, bouncing children on his knee, telling them all about how he would have drowned that day, had it not been for a courageous German boy.'

'A nice thought,' said Lorenz from behind his green curtain.

'Oh, I didn't realize you were there, Kaleun,' said Schmidt.

'He'll very probably get to know more Germans in the fullness of time,' said Lorenz. 'But I can't help feeling he'll be disappointed. You may have given him unrealistic expectations, Schmidt.'

*

Lorenz couldn't sleep. Loud snoring issued from the crew quarters: a horrible, liquid respiration that came in short bursts separated by crackling, pulmonary interludes. Something in the food had caused many of the men to complain of abdominal pain and the heads had been in constant use throughout the previous day. A foul, cesspit smell hung in the air – rank, heavy and strong. Lorenz felt hot and agitated. The curtain that separated his nook from the rest of the boat gave him no real privacy. He wanted to get away from the snoring and the stink, to be on his own, to still his mind and order his thoughts. Sitting up, he swung his legs off the mattress, rested his elbows on his knees and lowered his head into his hands. Perspiration lacquered his forehead and when he massaged his temples he could feel salty granules beneath his fingertips. He felt nauseous and wondered if he had also eaten food that was going to make his stomach cramp and loosen his bowels. Gradually, the queasiness subsided and he stood up.

In the control room, a small number of men were at their posts keeping the boat on a steady course at a depth of thirty metres. Earlier, headquarters had sent an aircraft warning: Catalinas – probably out of Reykjavik. Lorenz examined the charts, exchanged a few words with the helmsman, and climbed up the ladder into the conning tower. He shut the hatch at his feet and experienced a sense of relief: quiet, stillness, solitude. His gaze took in the computer, the attack periscope, the narrowness of the space he occupied. Leaning against the ladder for support, he closed his eyes and an image formed in his mind – a miniature U-330, gliding through darkness. It was something he did routinely when the boat was being depth-charged, in order to visualize his position in relation to enemy destroyers. He dissolved the starboard armour plating, achieving a cut-away diagram effect that afforded him interior views of every compartment. Homunculi moved around the control room, and above them he saw a tiny silhouette, himself, in a bubble of yellow light.

The temperature was dropping and his breath produced white clouds in the air. Something was about to happen. He could sense inevitability, identical to the foreshadowing that had preceded the strange occurrences in Brest, when U-330 had been undergoing repairs. Lorenz felt dissociated, as if he were sitting in a theatre, watching a play that he had already seen. The future was no longer free to deviate. A palpitation in his chest signalled danger. This impression of peril was incontestable, almost overwhelming, and he was certain that it did not represent a psychological threat – something fantastic that might untether the mind, but rather the drawing near of a real, existential threat. A simple phrase clarified his intuitions: death is coming.

An irregular rhythm captured his attention; stopping and starting again, a faint squealing like a rusty hinge. It was difficult to locate at first, but in due course Lorenz raised his eyes. Several seconds elapsed before his brain identified the source of the sound. His eyes focused on the phenomenon and the full horror of its significance delayed his reaction. He remained completely still, looking upwards, in a state of frozen disbelief. Above Lorenz's head, the wheel that locked the bridge hatch was slowly turning. The miniature U-330 came into his mind again. He did not consider its illuminated interior, but rather the surrounding darkness, the immense weight of water pressing down on the other side of the hatch. A glistening rivulet progressed around the seal and droplets began to fall on his face. Icy detonations made him spring into action and he raced up the ladder and grabbed the wheel. He tried to reverse its rotation. After the first failed attempt, a second followed, and when he tried a third time his muscles weakened and the wheel slipped beneath his fingers. He tightened his grip and found some further reserve of power, but he could not sustain the effort. The nausea he had experienced earlier returned and he began to feel dizzy. Suddenly the wheel was receding and the conning tower went black.

When he opened his eyes he was in his nook and Ziegler and Graf were bending over him. His head was throbbing. He tried to prop himself up, but Ziegler said, 'No, Kaleun – lie down. You fainted in the conning tower.'

'Chief, go and check the bridge hatch.'

'For what?'

'It was making water.'

'Kaleun?'

'Just go, will you?'

'Please . . .' Ziegler encouraged Lorenz to lie back again.

'Very well,' said Graf. When the engineer returned he spoke with respectful neutrality. 'A little condensation, but everything's in order.'

'Are you sure?'

'Yes, Kaleun.'

Ziegler mopped Lorenz's brow with a damp cloth. 'I think your temperature's running high, sir. You've probably got the stomach complaint.'

The radio operator was right. It took two days for Lorenz to recover.

Leaning out of the radio shack Brandt called, 'Officer's signal.' Juhl excused himself from a card game and went to collect the decoding machine. He set it up in the officers' mess and Lorenz handed him the code for that day. After adjusting the settings, Juhl exhibited his customary tendency to exploit the dramatic possibilities of his role by cracking his knuckles and wiggling his fingers over the keyboard. He started tapping the keys and each strike made a letter on the lamp board glow.

Eventually, he laid his pencil aside and glanced back at Lorenz: 'For the commander only.'

'Ah,' Lorenz responded. 'I see.' He went to his nook to collect his special instructions. On his return he made a brushing movement in the air indicating that Juhl should move aside and after taking Juhl's place he reset the machine. The whispering that travelled through the compartments was like the soughing of the wind through branches, words carried on a breeze. Letters flashed and when the decryption was complete he stared long and hard at what he had written. U-330 was to rendezvous with U-807 as a matter of utmost urgency. No explanation was given and the coordinates (which Lorenz double-checked) were for a location above the 70th parallel. U-807 was a Type IXB, a heavier, larger submarine armed with twenty-two torpedoes. He wondered why such a rendezvous was necessary. The collection and transfer of prisoners seemed unlikely. If U-807 was carrying prisoners then it should proceed directly to its destination. A transfer would only cause additional delay. But what else could it be? And why so far north? At the end of the message were the code names assigned to U-807 and U-330. They were typically bombastic – 'Verdandi' and 'Skuld' – two of the three personifications of fate from Nordic legend.

Lorenz stood and walked to the control room where the men seemed to withdraw, stepping away as he came through the hatchway as if he were surrounded by a repulsive energy. He stepped over to the chart table and folding the piece of paper so that only the coordinates were visible he showed them to Müller. The navigator's eyebrows drew closer together. 'Can they be serious?' He pawed at his charts and when he had found the one he wanted he laid it out on the table. Dislodging some mould with his fingernail, Müller fussed with a torn edge. Lorenz lowered the lamp and both men leaned into its beam. The crew were listening intently. Müller pointed at a spot on the chart roughly between the north coast of Iceland and the east coast of Greenland. 'Why in God's name do they want us to go there?'

'I'm sure you can make an educated guess.' Müller was shaking his head. 'Cheer up,' Lorenz continued. 'They could have sent us to the rose garden.' He tapped the chart between Iceland and the Faroe islands. It was where British aircraft were in the habit of jettisoning unwanted bomb-loads. 'And you'll have no trouble seeing the stars. The nights are going to be very long where we're going.' Lorenz turned, ordered a change of course, and the boat veered north with diesel engines thumping at full speed.

Stormy weather forced them to dive. It was late, the lights were low, and Lorenz was sitting in the officers' mess on his own.

The door to the crew quarters was open and he could hear the men talking. As usual, they were discussing sex and trying to outdo each other with outlandish stories. He had noticed that when the boat was submerged their conversation became more extreme, as if physical descent was correlated with moral descent. After a while, it didn't matter who was talking. The voices became interchangeable.

'Have you ever fucked a dwarf?'

'Yes, I've fucked a dwarf. We were in this shitty brothel in Lübeck and all the whores were busy. They had this little midget woman there whose job it was to serve drinks. I got tired of waiting and asked the madam if I could hump her instead. It'll cost you, she said, but I was beyond caring.'

'Was she any good?'

'Well, I wouldn't say she was good – but she was very enthusiastic. When she was on top it was a bit like being part of a circus act.'

'Do you know Golo Blau? He fucked Siamese twins once when he was out in India. They were joined at the head and the hips.'

'Imagine it . . .'

'What about Kruger, though?'

'What about him?'

'He's fucked a pig.'

'Has he?

'Yes. Her name's Helga and she works in a bar in Wilhelmshaven. Isn't that so, Kruger?'

'All right . . . she was a little overweight maybe.'

'I'm surprised you could get anywhere near her.'

And so it went on, disembodied voices drifting through the open hatchway: a journey through the darkness of the ocean and the soul.

The light changed, the temperature dropped to minus fifteen, and ice began to accumulate: on the bulwark, the rails enclosing the rear of the bridge, the 2 cm flak cannon, the periscope housing, and the aiming-device pedestal. Within minutes of climbing out on to the bridge the lookouts were soaked and freezing, their foul-weather gear became stiff, restricting movement, and icicles ornamented their sou'westers. When they re-entered the boat the ordeal continued. Instinct compelled them to huddle around the electric heater but the return of sensation was excruciatingly painful, a horrible burning thaw that left them speechless and exhausted. Boots, filled with seawater, stuck to their feet. Nothing dried and they resigned themselves to sleeping in wet clothes beneath damp blankets. It got colder and to survive on the bridge it became necessary to wear knitted underwear and thick sheepskins, clothing so bulky and cumbersome it became difficult to squeeze through the hatch. Frequent dives were necessary to control the build-up of ice, but sometimes the mantle thickened so quickly that teams had to be sent out to smash it with hammers. The deck was slippery and the men had to be roped together like mountain climbers.

Lorenz stood firm, his face encrusted with rime, staring at the bow slicing through the floes. The noise it made was satisfying, a steady whoosh punctuated by thuds and crunches. He turned just in time to see Pullman struggling to remove a glove. 'What do you think you're doing?'

'I'm trying to get my glove off,' said Pullman. 'I can't operate my camera.'

'I'd advise you to keep it on. If you touch the bulwark with your bare hand the skin will stick to the steel. And if a plane appears we'll have to tear you off and I don't know how many fingers we'll leave behind.'

Pullman accepted the advice with a curt nod. 'How often are you ordered this far north, Herr Kaleun?'

'It's happened before – last time to provide a weather report.'

'My teeth . . .' Pullman winced. The cold was spleenful and malicious, nipping and biting, perversely inventive, almost inspired when it came to discovering novel pathways for the transmission of pain.

'They can crack in these temperatures. Perhaps you should get back inside.'

'I've never seen weather conditions like this. The other patrol I was assigned to went out into the middle of the Atlantic. Are we in very much danger?'

Lorenz laughed. 'If we need to execute a rapid dive we might discover that the ventilation tubes and the ballast tank purges are blocked – or the diving planes won't work. The ice makes us unstable. The cold can bend a propeller out of shape. Shall I go on? Yes, Pullman, we are in considerable danger and will continue to be for some time.'

When night came it delivered the spectacle of the Northern Lights. Luminous green veils travelled across the sky, folding and unfolding, brightening and dimming. Scintillating emerald cliffs collapsed and shimmering silver spires rose up from the horizon. The boat's foamy wake separated slabs of ice that appeared to be made from polished jade. Sparkling ribbons fluttered at the zenith and the constellations shone with frigid brilliance through gauzy undulations.

Lorenz had observed the Northern Lights many times before, but he was still entranced by the profligate genius of the natural world, the casual and indifferent but perfect flourishes that caused his chest to tighten with a hopeless, generalized yearning. He was tantalized by the possibility of meaning, but meaning inconveniently located beyond the reach of human intellect. Such beauty was so fiery and vivid and pure that it cauterized thought. He was nothing, consciousness bathed in green-white brilliance, a pattern of sensations, humbled and cleansed by intensive exposure to the sublime. The cold was no longer hostile, but fresh, vital and redemptive. He wanted to leave the earth and fly up into the sky, not to be commemorated like some ancient hero in a constellation, but to achieve the exact opposite, to be absorbed and dissipated by the dancing lights, to be strewn across the heavens until the distance between his thoughts made personal identity impossible. He dreamed of nullity, obliteration, escape. A sigh brought him back to earth. Müller was standing next to him. The navigator held his sextant against his chest and his face was tilted back. A tear beneath his right eye had collected enough light to shine like a jewel. Müller wiped it away and said, 'Are you coming back down now, Kaleun?'

'No,' said Lorenz. 'A little longer . . .'

'You'll freeze, sir.'

Lorenz reconsidered. 'Yes, you're right, Müller. I've been up on the bridge for far too long. Thank you.'

On the way to his nook, Ziegler leaned out to attract Lorenz's attention. 'Kaleun? The lights . . . they're playing havoc with the radio. I can't pick up any broadcasts.'

'All right,' said Lorenz. 'There's nothing we can do about that.'

He crossed the gangway, pulled the curtain aside and lay on his mattress. After closing his eyes he could still see the aurora borealis, glaucous cathedrals crumbling into dust before being blown away by a wind that had crossed the void between planets.

It was close to midday and the short-lived sunless glow that interrupted the polar night was revelatory. The ice floes were becoming larger and heavier and it became increasingly difficult to navigate a way through. When the bow met with resistance the pitch of the engines rose to a higher, labouring note that persisted until the obstruction was broken into smaller fragments or pushed aside. Thereafter, the boat lurched forward and the pitch of the note dropped to its prior default. The grim twilight seemed to collapse three dimensions into two, producing an effect that resembled a poorly executed oil painting – bleak vistas of a dead, colourless world.

'We can't go on like this,' said Graf. 'It's getting colder.' Lorenz responded with a bearlike grunt. He was reluctant to open his mouth, because whenever he did so his lower molars ached. 'What are we going to do?' Graf persisted. Lorenz bowed his head and a full minute passed before he spoke. 'Yes, you're right. We can't go on. It's absurd.' He descended into the conning tower, dropped into the control room, and marched straight to the radio shack where he found Brandt jotting down messages. 'Are you receiving signals again?' Lorenz asked.

'Intermittently,' said Brandt. 'There's nothing for us, though.'

'Is all the equipment working? Right now?'

'Yes.'

'Very well,' said Lorenz. 'Send this message to headquarters.' He grabbed a sheet of paper and scribbled a terse request: PACK ICE IMPASSABLE. HIGH RISK OF CATASTROPHIC DAMAGE. PERMISSION TO ABORT. Headquarters responded promptly. PERMISSION DENIED. RPT DENIED. DO NOT ABORT. RPT DO NOT ABORT SPECIAL MISSION. IMPERATIVE YOU CONTINUE. When he encountered Graf in the officers' mess the engineer said, 'Well?' Lorenz could only shake his head.

Within an hour the Northern Lights had rendered the radio useless again. Brandt offered Lorenz the headphones and said, 'Solar interference, Herr Kaleun.' Lorenz listened to what sounded like a high wind modulated by periodic changes of frequency. Below this 'rush' were sonic inflections that resembled a man chanting in an adjacent room. Short bursts of frenetic chirruping evoked mobbing birds. The overall effect was disturbing. Lorenz handed the headphones back to Brandt. 'It won't last forever.'

Progress was slow; however, that evening Müller completed

his calculations and declared, 'We've arrived.' Glittering curtains billowed across the sky and the reflective plain of ice acted like a mirror. The boat seemed to be suspended between two green conflagrations. In the distance, a floating mountain appeared to be illuminated from within by a flickering, coppery fire.

In spite of repeated attempts to clear ice from the deck, the boat was beginning to feel unstable again. Lorenz ordered the crew to their diving stations and called out 'Flood!' Graf studied the ballast-tank lights and said, 'Door number five isn't opening.' The diesels had already stopped. 'Come on!' Graf shouted. 'Open up, you bitch!' His anger seemed to have an effect. The light panel indicated that the water level in tank five was rising and the boat began to sink. They circled for three hours at twenty-four metres and then settled into a pattern of three hours up, three hours down. This seemed to be the solution to their problem, but on the following day door number five didn't open again. The ice floes had begun to fuse together and, as Lorenz had expected, the boat became trapped.

'Shit!' said Falk. 'If a plane flies over they'll just pick us off.' Looking up at the blazing nebulae he added, 'It's the dead of night and look how light it is!'

'We're not defenceless,' Lorenz replied, indicating the flak cannon. 'We'll just have to keep scraping the ice off.'

'It's minus twenty, Kaleun. And the 2 cm isn't very reliable at the best of times.'

'True, but what else do you suggest we do?' Falk pressed his hands together in an attitude of prayer. 'If I thought that would work,' Lorenz continued, 'then I would willingly request help from God, but I'm not convinced that we have his support.'

'Don't let Pullman hear you say that, Herr Kaleun.'

'Why? Pullman doesn't believe in God. He's a Party man. Give him half a chance and he'll be making sacrificial offerings to Odin.' Lorenz watched a pavilion of light collapse. Without removing his gaze from the dissolving sheets of radiance, he added: 'Get Sauer to organize a team, will you? To scrape the gun.'

Falk hesitated. 'Why are we here, sir?'

'I don't know,' Lorenz replied.

'Really, Kaleun?'

'Yes, Falk, really.'

'Special operations . . .' The first watch officer's expression resembled the sagging countenance of a blood-hound.

There was nothing to do except wait. The men played card games and listened to endless repetitions of Glenn Miller. Some competed in an impromptu chess tournament. A singing competition was won by Pullman.

The photographer possessed a fine tenor voice and he performed a Schubert song of such lyrical sweetness that even the most cynical members of the crew yielded to its charm. Poetry and a disarmingly simple melody conjured a pastoral ideal of babbling brooks, linden trees and naive, reckless love; a nostalgic vision of a German Eden purged of impurities and populated by beautiful maidens of peerless virtue. Lorenz was impressed by Pullman's skill, his unerring instinct for opportunity and weaknesses. Even he, Siegfried Lorenz, the stalwart outsider – stubborn habitué of the political margins – had been momentarily moved, albeit briefly, by nationalist sentiment. It had crossed his mind that there might be something worth dying for after all.

Time passed slowly.

At five o'clock in the morning – a morning as dark as the deepest night – Lorenz poked his head through the hatch and the first thing he saw was Juhl's grinning visage. 'We don't have to worry about aircraft any more.' The second watch officer was wearing so many clothes he was almost spherical.

'What?' Lorenz wondered if Juhl had gone mad. His demeanour was uncharacteristically cheerful.

'Not for a while, anyway.' Juhl pointed upwards. 'We're invisible.'

An opaque canopy had settled over the boat. It resembled the roof of a marquee.

'Falk said he was going to pray for our salvation,' Lorenz quipped.

After clambering out of the tower, Lorenz stood by Juhl's side. More fog was rolling towards them and there was enough shimmering light in the sky to imbue the advancing waves with a trace of exotic colour. As soon as he was satisfied that the fog wasn't a transient phenomenon, Lorenz said: 'It hardly seems necessary to maintain a four-man watch under these conditions. Juhl, Voigt, Arnold, get back inside and warm up. I'll stay out here with Wessel.' The young seaman was unable to conceal his disappointment. 'Don't look so hard done-by Wessel, it won't be for long.'

Wessel mumbled an apology.

When the other men had squeezed through the hatch Lorenz and Wessel stood back to back, staring north and south respectively. They made desultory conversation until the fierce cold made even superficial talk effortful. Lorenz was accustomed to desolation. The sea was a wilderness. But the interminable dark of the polar night and the green-white fog made him feel utterly isolated. There were forty-eight souls inside the boat, yet their proximity did nothing to mitigate his sense of unspeakable remove. Wessel and he were the last men alive. They had ventured too far and crossed some mysterious boundary from beyond which there could be no return. How could this forbidding, pitiless place be part of the same world in which waiters served wine in candlelit restaurants, small children laughed and lovers held hands? He had been visited by such thoughts on countless occasions, but never more acutely.

The ice was producing odd sounds, creaks and cracks; however, these relatively inconsequential noises were subsequently augmented by moans, groans and even a howl. Lorenz could sense Wessel's unease. The sounds continued, becoming increasingly reminiscent of human vocalizations. It was such a compelling illusion, Lorenz imagined that he could hear his own name being called. He did not expect Wessel to react, but the young man gasped, 'Kaleun?'

'Yes?'

'Did you hear it?'

'Yes, I did.'

'It sounded just like a person, shouting.'

'There's no one out there, Wessel. How could there be?'

'An animal perhaps?'

'We're too far away from the coast of Greenland. Nothing could make it out here.' Lorenz traced a horizontal arc over the bulwark with his extended arm. 'This is pack ice.'

'A polar bear?'

'No.'

'I thought . . .' The young seaman's sentence trailed off.

'What, Wessel?'

The young man muttered a few words and added, 'Nothing, Kaleun.'

Lorenz peered into the swirling fog and the flickering of the Northern Lights broke the continuous movement into a sequence of halted images, each one slightly different from its predecessor.

'Kaleun?' Wessel's voice was almost a whisper. 'Over there.' Lorenz turned abruptly and raised his binoculars. The mouth of a tunnel had opened in the wall of a fog bank and its vault was penetrated by shafts of silver light. Pools of luminescence mottled the ice. Lorenz couldn't see anything remarkable and certainly nothing that merited apprehension. 'There! Kaleun!' Wessel's voice was urgent, ascending to panic.

'What?' Lorenz demanded, glancing at his companion.

'There!' Wessel jabbed his finger at the tunnel. 'Something dark.'

'Where?'

'There!' The young man was emphatic. 'Coming towards us.'

Lorenz lowered his binoculars. 'I can't see—'

Wessel cut in, 'On the ice!' Suddenly the young man was less sure. 'It's . . . I . . .' The vault of the tunnel collapsed creating slowly rotating vortices. Eventually, the uniformity of the fog bank was restored and it acquired the appearance of a low chalk bluff. The two men gazed at the inscrutable whiteness, willing it to give up whatever secrets it was harbouring. 'I *did* see something,' Wessel added, more to himself than to his commander.

'Was it big? Small?'

'It's difficult to judge. There's nothing out there to make a comparison with. You lose perspective, sir.'

'Could it have been a periscope?'

'No, it was travelling on top of the ice.'

'The floes are still separated by water that way. We're at the very edge of the ice shelf.'

'It wasn't a periscope, Kaleun. It didn't move like a periscope; it moved like . . .' Wessel hesitated. He looked confused and alarmed. 'It moved like something alive.'

'A seal, perhaps?'

'Yes,' Wessel allowed with edgy impatience. 'Perhaps, Herr Kaleun.'

The air was filled with semi-transparent wisps and filaments. They collected together and twisted into loose braids or spiralled into snail-shell patterns. The atmosphere around the conning tower seemed to be in a state of restless agitation. High above, the distant, muted ordnance of the Northern Lights was unnerving; as if the contagious madness of war had now reached the citadels of heaven. At the very limits of audition he could hear muffled bangs, sputters and claps. Lorenz imagined the bloodied down of angels' wings descending and settling around the deck gun. The fog bank thinned and became diaphanous. Through the transparent escarpment the ice plate receded into an obscure distance dotted with sapphire and diamond glimmerings. Wessel breathed in sharply. 'There! Coming towards us.' He was gesticulating frantically and his protuberant eyes were wide open. Lorenz looked through his binoculars but was unable to detect the cause of Wessel's excitement.

'Calm down, Wessel,' Lorenz barked.

The young man stopped waving his arms around but he was breathing heavily and each forceful exhalation clouded the space between them. 'There! Kaleun! Surely you can see it.'

'There's nothing there, Wessel!'

The young man stepped past the flak cannon and leaned over the rear railings, his head craning forward. Tense cords of muscle had raised the taut skin of his neck. Lorenz looked through his binoculars again but all he could see was surging fog. When he turned to challenge Wessel the boy looked desperate and bewildered. 'There's a man out there.'

'Don't be ridiculous, Wessel.'

'I saw him, Kaleun!'

'You couldn't have.'

'He was wearing a long coat and striding towards us.'

Lorenz experienced a chill that superseded the polar cold

and penetrated his very essence. He addressed Wessel sternly: 'Pull yourself together, Wessel.'

The young man, chastened, stood to attention, pushing out his chest. 'I'm sorry, sir.'

'I think you should get back inside the boat, Wessel.'

'But Kaleun . . .'

'It's all right, Wessel.' The tone of Lorenz's voice was conciliatory. He reached out and gripped the boy's arm. 'It's all right, Wessel, really. You've been up here for too long. The cold – the dark – this . . . landscape. Sometimes it all proves too much for the brain.'

'I could have sworn . . .'

Lorenz pulled the hatch open. 'Yes, of course. Get some rest, eh? Ask Ziegler to give you a dose of something to help you sleep.'

'Yes, sir.'

'And ask Leutnant Juhl to come up.'

'Yes, sir.' Wessel began his descent. Their eyes met for a moment and Lorenz was perplexed by Wessel's expression. Did it show frustration or was it resentment? He couldn't tell.

While Lorenz waited for Juhl he noticed that his heart was beating faster. The fog bank had become fully opaque again.

Juhl appeared: 'What happened? What's wrong with Wessel? He looks terrible.'

'I don't know, he had some sort of . . . panic. He started seeing things.'

'Do you want me to come up again?'

'No, send Voigt. I want you to organize a two-man rotation. Let's not have anybody exposed to this cold for more than an hour.'

'The cold doesn't make you see things, sir.'

'Where did you study medicine, Juhl?'

'I haven't studied medicine.'

'That's what I thought. We can go back to a four-man rota when the fog lifts.'

Werner had managed to prepare a surprisingly tasty stew from tinned meat and the last bag of potatoes. Condensation trickled down the wooden panels and the spicy fragrance that filled every compartment briefly masked the underlying stench of body odour and mould. Everyone in the officers' mess agreed that a good cook was a godsend and Pullman, visualizing a heart-warming magazine feature on the unsung heroes of the navy, hurried off to the galley in order to memorialize Werner on film.

'What are we going to do?' asked Graf.

Lorenz glanced at Falk. 'Are you still praying?'

'Yes,' Falk replied.

'Keep it up. And while you're at it, ask God to make the North-Atlantic Drift a little warmer. A degree or two should suffice.'

'I don't think God responds to specific requests, Herr Kaleun,' said Falk.

'Is that your plan?' asked Graf, looking over at Lorenz.

'We're stuck in pack ice,' Lorenz replied. 'That's all. If the North-Atlantic Drift brings us a little more heat then there will be a thaw and we'll be free.'

'And if the sea doesn't get any warmer?' Graf licked a cold dribble of stew from his spoon.

'The fireworks can't go on forever. When the radio starts working we can ask headquarters to send a boat to cut us out.'

'A rescue mission may take a long time to get here,' said Graf. 'We've been lucky so far. But . . .' He passed his hand over his plate like a low-flying aircraft.

'Falk's prayers have been exceptionally effective,' Lorenz responded. 'I have every confidence in him.'

Graf put his spoon down and said, 'That's all right then.'

No one smiled.

'The flak-cannon teams are working well,' said Falk, ignoring the irony of his superiors. 'We're ready to respond to an attack at any time – at least, theoretically.'

'Excellent,' said Graf. 'It's always reassuring to know that – at least *theoretically* – there's nothing to worry about.'

Falk would not be bated. He turned away and stared into the eyes of the portrait of Vice Admiral Dönitz.

Later, the majority of the crew, made lethargic by Werner's generous portions of stew, loosened their belts and retired to their bunks. The red dark-adaption lights were switched on and the boat became hushed and womblike. Conversation was unusually restrained. Quiet speech was succeeded by intermittent whisperings which were finally lost in the slow build-up of huffs and wheezes preceding sleep. Soon the air was resonating with snores and mumbles.

Lorenz was recumbent in his nook, passively observing a mental slideshow of Faustine: her feral eyes, her seductive smile, her slim wrist circled by a simple silver chain, the classical proportions of her nose, the vertical seams of her stockings that divided her calves and connected the hem of her skirt with the heel of her shoes. He remembered the mellow, lilting musicality of her voice, her books and her perfume, the scarlet impression of her lips on cigarette paper, and the paradox of their ecstatic union which always contained elements of anguish and despair.

Sleep washed over him in immense slow waves and he was carried onto the deck of U-330 and into a dream that replicated reality. The boat was trapped in a frozen sea and the sky was rippling with green light. He looked in wonder at the 8.8 cm deck gun, which appeared to be buried in a large viridescent gemstone. Among the ice floes in the middle distance he saw the raft approaching through black channels. He saw Sutherland and Grimstad in their customary positions – one standing, the other seated – and a third figure, a woman, pressing her body against the British commander. When Lorenz raised his binoculars he recognized Faustine. Her right arm was extended across Sutherland's chest and her fingers were splayed over his heart. One of her legs was raised and the angle of her knee had made her skirt ride up to reveal her suspenders. She rested her head on Sutherland's shoulder and gazed at Lorenz. The coruscations in the sky found chromatic resonances in the beryl of her eyes and she looked demonic. Attached to her back were two black wings that arced so high they almost met above her head. She opened her mouth and a scorpion crawled out.

Lorenz awoke. He pulled the curtain aside and looked across at Ziegler. The radio operator was sitting forward, elbows on the table, his chin supported by his interlocked fingers. Lorenz let go of the curtain and his privacy was restored. The boat was not entirely silent. There were men talking in the control room and he could hear drops of water falling into the bilges – a constant, regular beat. The hull was creaking like a sagging floorboard. He recollected standing outside his sister's house, smoking a cigar and talking to Hebbel. What had the doctor said? Something about dreams meriting interpretation . . . Lorenz couldn't remember precisely. What did this dream mean? Why had his brain cast Faustine as the Angel of Death and delivered her into the arms of Lawrence Sutherland?

Suddenly there was a loud bang – a sharp detonation. Lorenz sat up and his first thought was that they had finally been discovered by the British or Americans. He quickly changed his mind. There was no strafing or gunfire, the lookouts were silent, and more importantly, there were no further 'explosions'. He got up and stepped into the gangway.

Ziegler looked startled. 'Sir? What was that?'

Lorenz ignored the radio operator's question and entered the control room, where he found Schulze and Krausse standing by the periscope, looking like stuffed shop mannequins. They had been conducting some routine maintenance work and Schulze was clutching a large wrench.

'You heard it?' Lorenz asked.

'Yes,' said Schulze.

Lorenz climbed to the top of the ladder and opened the hatch. The cold flayed his face. 'Is everything all right?'

Müller peered down, his sou'wester silhouetted against a luminous mist. 'Yes.'

'Did you hear anything?'

'Only the fireworks. Why?'

Lorenz shook his head – *it doesn't matter* – and closed the hatch again.

As soon as Lorenz was back in the control room there was another loud bang. The sound seemed to have come from the forward end of the boat. Lorenz exchanged puzzled glances with Schulze and Krausse before he swung through the bulkhead and marched past the hydrophone and radio cabins. He ducked under a hammock, stepped over a pile of discarded clothes, and when he straightened up a slimy side of ham slapped against his cheek. Men were stirring in their bunks. He arrived in the torpedo room and noticed that the chains of the lifting gear were swinging slightly. A torpedo had been pulled out for servicing. Lorenz sniffed the air. He couldn't smell burning, only a foul combination of body odour and grease. He studied the swaying chains. There was no draught, the boat hadn't rocked, and no one could have tampered with them before his arrival. He reached out, grabbed the links and released them when they had stopped moving. Once again, there was another bang. It was close enough and loud enough to make his ears ring.

Falk, Juhl and Graf appeared.

'What's going on?' asked the chief engineer.

Lorenz paused before answering. 'Perhaps the ice is fracturing.'

He made his way back to his nook, donned his cap and

leather jacket, and ascended to the bridge. Looking over the bulwark he saw that some of the ice around the bow was uneven. Jagged pavements had risen out of the water at an angle. He addressed Müller. 'Are you sure you didn't hear anything?'

'The fireworks,' Müller replied. 'Only the fireworks.'

'How about you, Arnold?'

'I didn't hear anything . . . unusual, Kaleun,' Arnold responded.

'The ice . . .' said Lorenz, pointing beyond the cable cutter. 'It seems to have moved. You haven't seen it moving, have you?'

'No.' Müller's expression was perplexed.

'Nor me,' said Arnold.

'What did you hear, Herr Kaleun?' asked Müller.

'Three loud bangs,' Lorenz replied. 'I suspect the sound was transmitted through the hull. Odd though: odd that you didn't hear anything.'

When he dropped back into the control room a small crowd had gathered. In addition to Falk, Juhl, Graf, Schulze and Krausse, he also saw Schmidt, Sauer, Pullman, Voigt, Fischer and Danzer. They were looking at him expectantly.

'There has been some displacement,' Lorenz informed them. 'Some cracking and lifting, but none of it conspicuous enough to attract Müller and Arnold's attention.'

'Well,' said Graf. 'There's nothing wrong with the boat. Everything seems to be in order.'

'In which case,' said Lorenz, 'you might as well go back to sleep.' His gaze travelled around the ring of faces. 'All of you.' The 'all' was emphatic.

Back in his nook, Lorenz could hear the men quietly conferring. It took them a long time to settle and the boat was not returned to its former, satisfied, tranquil silence. The new silence was brittle and uneasy. Tensed beneath their fetid blankets, the men were not sleeping but thinking, and Lorenz suspected that most of them were thinking much the same thing. The noises that they had heard did not sound like breaking ice. They sounded much more like gunshots.

The temporary twilight at midday was accompanied by a rise in temperature and fissures began to infiltrate the ice field surrounding the boat. It became easier to scrape the rime off the flak cannon and curling strips fell away from the barrel like decorative paper. Darkness returned but the fog continued to reflect and refract the flamboyant sky.

After eating his lunch, Lorenz went up to the bridge and surveyed the eerie desolation. It seemed as if the boat had been plucked out of the sea by a mischievous giant and deposited in the middle of a lifeless salt plain. He turned to Falk and said,

'I'll take over. I want you to check the torpedoes and fire-control systems. If the thaw continues we might get away sooner than we thought.'

'Sir, isn't that rather . . .' Falk hesitated before he found the courage to add, 'optimistic?'

'You sound surprised, Falk,' Lorenz responded.

Falk returned an uncertain smile, saluted, and disappeared down the hatch. It wasn't really necessary for Falk to check the torpedoes and fire-control systems. The first watch officer had been quite right to raise the issue of prematurity and Lorenz could just as easily, and more properly, perhaps, have given the same order to the chief torpedo man's mate. In actuality, Lorenz had wanted Falk to leave the bridge so that he could be alone with Sauer.

Sauer was responsible for the crew's clothing, the daily cleaning rotation, and – during surface attacks – the entry of data into the boat's computer. He was also expected to perform custodial duties: supporting the younger sailors, offering them paternal guidance, and resolving any disputes before they came to the commander's notice. If Lorenz wanted to gauge the mood of the crew, then there was no better way of doing so than to discuss them with Sauer.

'So . . .' said Lorenz. 'How are they?'

Sauer raised his hand and tilted it from side to side. 'Not bad. But not good either.'

'Jittery?'

'Yes, largely because of Wessel. And last night didn't help, Kaleun.'

'What has Wessel been saying?'

'That he saw a man walking on the ice.'

'Does Wessel think he saw anyone in particular?'

'When he talks like that it reminds the men of Richter.'

'Yes – yes . . .'

'Last night,' said Sauer, his voice acquiring a concerned tone. 'It was peculiar, wasn't it, sir?'

'I'm not so sure.' Lorenz touched his ear. 'Listen.' The ice field was groaning softly. 'I remember going for a skiing holiday in Austria a few years ago and at night the glaciers were almost singing.'

'Did *you* see anything, Kaleun?'

'I'm sorry?'

'When you were up here with Wessel?'

'No. Not a thing.'

'The boy must have been tired.'

'Yes, he was.'

'Not used to the cold.'

'Who of us is?'

'I try to reason with them, Kaleun. But they get such ideas . . .'

'I know, Number One. I know.'

The two men fell silent. After a lengthy interlude, Lorenz cleared his throat and said, 'Pullman?'

'What about him, Kaleun?'

'Is he fitting in?'

'As well as can be expected, for a new officer, which is to say – no – but the men tolerate him. He can be irritating at times and he gets under our feet, but what can you do?'

'Has he converted any of the heathens yet?'

'He's been working hard on Berger and Wessel.'

'I've noticed. Anybody else?'

'Well, he's raised the subject of politics with pretty much everyone except the officers, of course. But I don't think he's making much progress.' Sauer indicated the swirling mist. 'We've been lucky with this cover, Kaleun. I heard an aircraft fly past about half an hour ago. They had no idea we were here.'

The ice stopped groaning and the silence that followed was curiously gravid. They both held their breath as if waiting for something to happen – but nothing did.

Lorenz exhaled and folded his arms. 'Will you have a word with Wessel?'

'I already have. But I can do so again if you wish – and I can be a little firmer, Herr Kaleun.'

'Thank you.'

*

Perpetual night and silence made it difficult to keep track of time. Lorenz looked at his wristwatch but the hours of the day had lost all meaning. There were no more card games and singing competitions. When the routine maintenance jobs had been completed the men went back to their bunks and slept. Eating was the only activity that brought the crew to life. Half past six: breakfast; midday: lunch; 5.15: light dinner. They would talk and joke, but most attempts at humour were forced and feeble; behind the fixed grins and artificial posturing lurked boredom, nervousness and suspicion.

Brandt was sitting in the radio shack, leaning forward and listening intently.

'Any change?' asked Lorenz.

The radioman shook his head and offered Lorenz the earphones. Lorenz took them and covered his ears with the speaker pads. The sounds were identical to those he had heard before, a rushing noise like wind, constantly changing to suggest a repeating cycle, interrupted by sudden flurries of high-pitched whistles and tweeting. It was while he was listening to the rushing sound that he imagined he could hear again the inflections of speech. The low mumbling suddenly clarified and a voice declared in measured English, 'How often do opportunities like this arise? How often do we get a chance to speak with our opposites? What harm will it do – a little civilized conversation?' He recognized his own words. They no longer sounded cordial, but like a taunt. Lorenz wanted to rip the headphones off his head and stamp on them. Even so, he forced himself to remain still. The rushing continued, becoming louder and softer, and as it diminished he heard, very faintly, as if the speaker were receding at speed, 'A penny for your thoughts.' It was a British idiom that he was familiar with. A woman he had once met in London had been overly fond of employing it. Like an automaton, Lorenz removed the headset, handed it back to Brandt, and said, 'Tedious, I know. But stay vigilant.'

Lorenz collected the British penny from the drawer in his nook and went up to the bridge. Juhl and Thomas were standing like bookends, staring into featureless embankments of mist. Lorenz brought his arm back and hurled the coin over the starboard side of the boat and onto the ice. 'My thoughts are not for sale,' he whispered in English.

'I'm sorry, what did you say, Kaleun?' Juhl asked.

The world was still and silent. Throwing the penny had been an act of defiance but Lorenz did not feel stronger or more resolute as a consequence. In fact, he felt the very opposite: deflated, defeated, overcome by doubts – as if he had made some final and irreversible surrender, as if he had pressed a coin into the palm of the ferryman and paid for the transport of his soul across the black water of the Styx to Hades. 'I'm sorry?' Juhl repeated. A large icicle fell from the radio antenna and shattered on the deck.

'Did you see that?'

'Yes.'

'Promising . . .'

Lorenz could hear Pullman preaching to his disciples but he wasn't listening to what the photographer was saying; instead, he was thinking about the night he had spent with Monika in the Hotel Fürstenhof and wondering whether Glockner had found the courage to telephone Monika's friend, Lulu Trompelt. There was something about Pullman's pulpitry that seemed to demand more attention; it kept on insinuating itself into Lorenz's consciousness until eventually he was forced to attend more carefully to the content. As soon as he did so, Lorenz understood why the monotony of the photographer's ecclesiastical cadences had been so distracting. Pullman was talking about runes. 'The Sonnenrad or sunwheel is the Old Norse representation of the sun and it is used by the Waffen-SS divisions Wiking and Nordland and the Danish branch of the Allgemeine-SS. The Tyr-Rune, also known as the battle rune, is used to represent leadership. It is commonly used by the SS as a grave marker instead of the Christian cross. Tyr was – of course – the god of war.' Lorenz stepped out of his nook and walked to the crew quarters. Pullman was sitting on the edge of a bunk with Berger, Wessel and Thomas at his feet. The photographer was holding up an open notebook in which he had drawn the symbols he was describing. As Lorenz approached, Pullman stopped speaking and the others turned their heads. They all stood.

'You know about runes?' Lorenz asked.

'Yes, Herr Kaleun,' Pullman replied.

Lorenz held out his hand, indicating that he wanted to look at the notebook. He flicked through the pages and saw various angular symbols. 'Have you studied Norse literature?'

'No,' said Pullman, affecting modesty. 'I'm no scholar.'

'You must have learned all this from somewhere?'

'I've read books – that's all.'

Lorenz jerked his head to the side, inviting the photographer to join him in the officers' mess. 'What books?'

'I'm sorry?'

'What books have you read?'

'Guido von List's *The Secret of the Runes*, the works of Karl Maria Wiligut . . .'

'Have you read Grimstad?'

'Who?'

'Professor Bjørnar Grimstad?'

'No, I'm afraid not.'

'Tell me, what does this mean?' Lorenz opened the

notebook on a clean page and drew the symbol that he remembered from Grimstad's stone.

'I believe that is Thurisaz. A very powerful rune – it represents a reactive force, or the direction or channelling of power. Are you sure that you have drawn it correctly, Herr Kaleun?'

'Yes.'

'Quite sure?'

'Yes. Why do you ask?'

'You've drawn it upside down, which alters its meaning somewhat. When a rune is reversed it is described as a *merkstave*.'

'*Merkstave?*'

'The literal translation is "dark stick".' Pullman traced his fingertip over Lorenz's pencilled figure. 'You have drawn a vertical line and a triangle pointing to the left. Usually the triangle of Thurisaz points to the right. This reversal signifies a darker meaning, the channelling of malice, spite, hatred. Where did you see this, Herr Kaleun?'

'What do you mean by that? "Channelling" . . .'

'Many people – educated people – believe that runes can be used to release powers. Some believe that these powers are nothing more than dormant human potential, but others believe that they are objectively real.' Pullman repeated his question. 'Where did you see this rune, Herr Kaleun?'

'Do you believe all this? Powers, magic . . . spells.'

Pullman closed his notebook. 'I do not think a man of vision like Reichsführer Himmler would concern himself with such things without good reason.'

'I'm not asking about Reichsführer Himmler, I'm asking you.'

'We should use all the powers at our disposal to further our cause.'

'But when you talk of the channelling of malice, spite, hatred – what do you mean?'

'The mental direction of destructive power.'

'Yes, but how would that actually work?'

'It was once believed that spirit agents could be harnessed and commanded to do one's bidding. They might be bound, and forced to perform a service.'

Lorenz recalled Grimstad waking from his trance, the triangle he had traced in the air with one hand while clutching the *merkstave* in the other. Did he know that Sutherland was carrying a gun and how the British commander intended to use it?

'And you really believe that is possible?'

'I believe that the universe is large enough to accommodate many secrets, Herr Kaleun.'

Had Grimstad trapped Sutherland's spirit on the boat? Released him from corporeal limitations and set him on the crew like a hunting dog? *The fetters will burst and the wolf run free, much do I know and more can see.* The SS were obsessed with the occult. Himmler and his friends sat in their storybook castle at Wewelsburg, presiding over ceremonies in which muscular blond-haired youths processed around sacred fires and invoked Teutonic deities. Of course the SS would be interested in a man like Grimstad. *He knew things* – that's what Friedrich had said – *valuable things.* Lorenz walked away from Pullman without acknowledging his final, creedal affirmation.

The night that followed was warmer and at midday one of the fissures in the ice field had widened and reached the rear of the boat. By late afternoon the surface of the sea to the south was full of separated floes with uneven edges. The crew came onto the deck in large numbers with hammers and whatever tools they could use to smash the thick, glassy mantle. When the underlying metal was exposed they rushed back into the boat and assembled at their diving stations.

Lorenz gave the order to flood and to everybody's amazement the vents opened. There were a number of cracking sounds as the bow broke free from the melting crust; the manometer began to move and the motors started up. The boat was a little unstable but with some skilful trimming it soon levelled out at forty metres.

Four hours later they surfaced, completely free of ice, and the radio started to work again. Brandt sent a message to headquarters explaining that they had lost contact because of solar activity and that they had been trapped in pack ice. Headquarters replied with an officer's signal that Juhl was obliged to pass on to Lorenz: 'Commander only'. When Lorenz unscrambled the brief communication he couldn't stop himself from swearing out aloud. It said: ABORT SPECIAL MISSION. Soon after, a standard message was picked up containing new coordinates – thankfully well below the 70th parallel.

'Well,' Lorenz said to Graf. 'That was an interesting excursion.'

'Yes,' Graf replied. 'A truly inspired deployment. I wonder how things would have turned out if we hadn't got stuck? What they had in store for us?'

'Who can say? But I'm prepared to guess that, whatever it might have been, our safety wasn't very high on their list of considerations.'

Lorenz wandered through the compartments, talking to the men and making sure that everything was running smoothly. He found Falk in the torpedo room.

'All good?' asked Lorenz.

'All good, sir,' Falk replied.

Pullman appeared and raised his camera. 'Herr Kaleun?'

There were some flashes and Lorenz said irritably, 'Not now!'

The photographer apologized and withdrew.

Lorenz rose early the following day. He went to the bridge to see dawn breaking. Pink-and-lemon bands appeared above the eastern horizon. It was a welcome return to normality. After the mineral glow of the Northern Lights, the rising sun, even when dulled by cloud, seemed humane and benevolent. The leeward ocean was dark grey and divided by wavering belts of silver and although the wind was freezing it was not vindictive.

War Diary

12.00   Day's run: 139 nm on the surface, 0 nm submerged.
Moderate swell, showers, variable visibility. Wind
veering gradually to starboard.

12.38–13.22 Test dive. Minor manometer problems.

14.30   Mast emerges from squall bearing 50° true, quite
prominent on the horizon. It is no longer safe to
proceed on surface. We decide to attack without delay
and dive. Periscope useless because of strong swell.
Lose sight of enemy but hydrophone operator reports
propeller noises at ship's bearing 180°. Also Asdic-type
pulses described as sounding like 'drops of water
falling onto a hotplate'. We assume a course of 50°
and at 14.55 re-establish visual contact, inclination 0°.
The approach of the vessel in our wake and the fact
that the inclination of 0° remains constant suggests
that we were discovered on the surface by their
hydrophones and that they are now attempting to
establish an underwater fix. We withdraw at 140° to

create some distance on her surface beam and then change course to a parallel 230°. Extremely difficult to keep the boat steady in the heavy swells but in the end able to identify the vessel's principal features: a cargo steamer with passenger decks. Two 10.5 cm forecastle guns. Forward of the bridge on both port and starboard sides there is what appears to be a platform on which anti-aircraft guns are mounted. It is not possible to determine the number of aft guns. The ship has camouflage painting. I believe it is an auxiliary naval vessel stationed here to perform combined roles of armed merchant cruiser, U-boat hunter and weather-reporting vessel.

15.10   Change to an attack course of 320°. Asdic-type pulses have ceased.

15.16   We fire a spread of three torpedoes from a range of 800m. Strong, erratic swell, less cloud. The periscope dips beneath the surface. After 50 seconds we hear two detonations. When the periscope re-emerges only the stern of the steamer can be seen. The boat dips below the surface again. Two powerful detonations separated by 30 seconds. The first is probably the boiler (after which can be heard the sound of collapsing bulkheads). The second is very likely the armed depth charges. Severe turbulence. Temporary loss of control; however the trim is soon restored. Through periscope no sign of the steamer nor any traces on the water.

16.00   We surface close to where the ship went down. Three men have managed to escape in a small rubber dinghy. The rest are struggling for their lives. There is virtually no wreckage to cling to.

16.10   Strong swell, cloud. I scoff at the raging gales, Scorn the fury of the flood . . .

16.30   We haul away to carry out patrol sweeps.

21.05   Calm sea. Moon, bright night, very good visibility. We have returned to the location of the sinking. A massive oil slick extends for several miles. We come across two rubber dinghies tied together. Inside are eight survivors. Two white men. The others are black. Americans. They are all wearing overalls with built in life-jackets. Some wear helmets (members of the gun crew?). We attempt to carry out an interrogation but it is hopeless. They all try to answer at the same time or shout each other down. Their ship was called the *Arapo – Arapaho –* or something similar. When asked about tonnage their answers range from 3,000 to 7,000 grt.

22.05   Again we haul away.

22.20	Aircraft with searchlights flying low over sea. Alarm!
23.10	Hydrophone contact at bearing 170° true and then another at 200°. Silent speed.
23.15	Hydroplane making loud grating noise which is remedied by lubrication.
23.35	Contact lost.
23.40	So thunder down the mountainside
23.50	And rage at me, you storms
23.58	So that rock shatters on rock!
00.00	I am a lost man.

Siegfried Lorenz

Storm clouds gathered in clumps around the horizon; they bubbled and climbed until it seemed that the ocean was hemmed in by huge mountains. Rutted, lumpy peaks were rising and expanding. The upper circle of the sky, still grey and luminous, shrank until its disappearance plunged the world into darkness. Seismic rumblings promised formidable violence, lightning flowed into the sea, and the wind whipped up great spirals of foam that spun in the air until they were torn apart by their own wild energies. Soon the boat was labouring to ascend twenty-metre waves and the lookouts were being battered to the point of insensibility.

Lorenz sealed the hatch, dropped into the control room, and did not let go of the ladder. The boat heeled and he heard crashes and moans and the smack and splash of vomit. A metal bucket rolled out from behind the master gyrocompass. Müller, Schulze, Keller and Arnold, who had preceded him, were lying on the matting in their oilskins. They had all been thrown off their feet. Water sloshed in the bilges as everything tilted to the left. 'That's it!' Lorenz shouted at Graf. 'Enough!

Take us to forty metres – sixty if necessary. Flood the tanks!'

The customary orders and confirmations followed.

'Clear air-release vents.'

'Clear air-release vents.'

Solemn voices and repetition imbued the procedure with a liturgical quality.

'Forward plane hard down.'

'Forward plane hard down.'

The pounding and roaring receded and the boat levelled off.

'Forty metres,' said Graf. Everyone stood still, gauging the boat's stability. There was no rolling or lurching. 'That should do it.'

'Saint Nicholas preserve us,' muttered Müller. He removed his sou'wester and raked back his soaking hair. 'That was hell.'

Two hours later most of the exhausted crew were in their bunks.

Lorenz slipped beneath his damp, mould-covered blanket and closed his eyes. He pictured U-330 sailing over submerged summits and valleys; the seabed strewn with rotting galleons and broken hulks; a creature with heavy claws scuttling into a crevice; fish disturbed by the sound of the boat's rotating screws. Most of the men had fallen asleep and would be dreaming. Where were they, Lorenz wondered? Where had they gone? Kruger would be enjoying the expert ministrations of a whore in the Casino Bar, Berger would be whispering endearments into the ear of his sweetheart, Müller would be walking in the woods with his wife (a carpet of dried pine needles underfoot, the air fragrant with resin), and Pullman would be attending a function at the Chancellery.

The boat was not only carrying men through the deep, but also their dreams.

Lorenz turned on his side and opened his eyes. He was facing one of the wooden panels and even though the lights were dim something caught his attention. He sensed its significance before his brain had fully comprehended what he was looking at. Someone had scratched the letters L and S into the varnish. Inevitably the name Lawrence Sutherland sprang to mind. The scoring was so superficial the signatory might have employed the point of a pin to leave his mark. Lorenz traced over the L and the S with the tip of his finger. He hadn't thought about it before, but his initials and Sutherland's shared the same two letters. The fact that they were reversed had uncomfortable resonances – reflections, mirrors, alter-egos. He remembered Faustine's bedroom, the pile of creased paperback books on the sill, Fantômas, Arsène Lupin, Sherlock Holmes and *The Double*. Lorenz could hear the movement of blood in his ears, the acceleration of his heart. A shred of fear fluttered through his soul.

He tried to persuade himself that the similarity between the scratches and the letters of the alphabet was accidental, but the L was so carefully executed, the vertical and horizontal strokes forming a perfect right angle.

Lorenz sat up, reached for his jacket and removed his pen-knife. He placed the blade on the wood and with a single movement removed a sliver of varnish. The letters were no longer visible.

Two days after the storm a message was received from head-quarters: PROCEED INTO AL 59. CONVOY EXPECTED GENERAL COURSE EAST-NORTH-EAST TWELVE KNOTS. LIGHT DEFENCE. GOOD HUNTING. Lorenz went to the chart table and consulted Müller.

'Not too far,' said the navigator, opening a compass on the warped, mildewed paper.

'We could be there by tomorrow morning,' Lorenz remarked.

Müller picked up a pencil, the end of which had been heinously chewed, and made a few calculations in the margins. 'Only if the weather stays calm and we can maintain maximum speed.'

Lorenz looked at Graf who nodded and said, 'I'll go and see Fischer.'

U-330 raced through the night, bouncing from one foamy

crest to the next, the noise of the engines penetrating all compartments: thumping, straining – pistons, crossheads, connecting rods, cranks – intake, compression, combustion, exhaust – prodigious mechanical power pushing the bow forward. The sea had the appearance of ruckled silk and a crescent moon was encircled by stars. They arrived at their designated position earlier than expected, just as the sun (still buried and burning beneath the ocean) began to haemorrhage crimson light into a clear sky. Only a few rounded heaps of cloud floated above the horizon. Lorenz was just finishing a strong, bitter coffee when Juhl called down from the bridge, 'Smoke, bearing three hundred.' Leaving his empty cup on the chart table, Lorenz climbed up the ladder and inhaled the fresh, antiseptic breeze. He aimed his binoculars dead ahead and saw an indistinct smudge. As they drew closer the smudge broadened, becoming a thick charcoal band, and soon after, it was possible to discern mastheads and stacks.

'They didn't tell us it was going to be an armada,' said Juhl. Lorenz counted the destroyers. There were three of them zigzagging ahead of the convoy. Juhl's voice shook with frustration. 'The message from U-boat command said they were lightly defended.'

'Yes,' Lorenz replied, 'excellent intelligence.'

'Perhaps we were given the wrong coordinates?'

'Ah!' Lorenz extended the exclamation enough to communicate not only surprise but also apprehension. 'To starboard, thirty-three degrees relative. If I'm not mistaken that's a fourth destroyer.'

'What? Over there?' Juhl raised his binoculars and made a whistling sound through his teeth. 'Yes, that *is* a fourth destroyer.' After a thoughtful pause he added, 'And we're on our own?'

'Indeed.'

'No more messages from headquarters?'

'No more messages.' Lorenz called down the hatch. 'Half speed.'

U-330 was low in the water and approaching from the east. The rising sun would hide the conning tower in its glare. Lorenz considered the situation to be relatively safe and judged that he had sufficient time to establish positions and identify targets before diving. The sun duly appeared and was obligingly bright. He was keeping a judicious eye trained on the fourth destroyer when Juhl said, 'God, they're fast.' The other three warships were considerably closer and producing high bow waves.

'Yes,' Lorenz answered, revising his plan and deciding to err on the side of caution. 'Perhaps we'd better get out of their way.'

'Shit!' The voice belonged to Voigt and its tone was incredulous.

Lorenz wheeled around and saw a thick black cloud rising from the back of the boat. Below, men were coughing and shouting: more smoke started to rise out of the hatch. Lorenz drew back and watched a swirling cyclone of smuts twist high above his head.

'They'll see us,' said Juhl, looking anxiously over the bulwark.

More smoke welled up from the hatch, almost liquid in its consistency. Lorenz watched it flowing through the rails and cascading onto the deck. It ran over the sides of the boat and dispersed over the water. The air became inky and opaque. Lorenz could hardly see Juhl, Voigt and the other two lookouts, and within seconds his eyes were blind and stinging. The boat was still travelling towards the convoy and the shouts from below were beginning to explore new registers of desperation. Lorenz snatched the communications pipe, removed the stopper and hollered, 'Chief? Chief? What's happening?' There was no reply, the hull juddered and the engines fell silent. Lorenz waved his hand impotently from side to side, trying to create an opening in the obfuscation through which he might see the destroyers. 'They'll fire at us soon as we're in range.' Only one course of action would prevent them from being utterly obliterated by heavy shelling. He leaned over the hatch and cried 'Alarm!'

Voigt was just about to jump into the tower when Graf's head appeared at his feet like a ghoulish creature emerging from a cauldron. The engineer's face was coated with filth. 'Kaleun, the boat's unfit to dive!'

'Unfit to dive?'

'Yes. There's a fire.'

'Where?'

'Somewhere aft – the engine room, I think. I was trying to get there when you called.'

'We've got to dive!'

'But we're on fire.'

'Listen: there are four destroyers heading our way. We can't just sit here sending up smoke signals. We'll just have to put the fire out when we're submerged.'

'But we need to keep the hatch open, Kaleun. The men will suffocate.'

'Then distribute the emergency breathing apparatus!'

When Lorenz landed in the control room he could see very little. The lights were glimmering weakly, emitting a dull brownish glow. Men were holding handkerchiefs or hats over their mouths. Everyone was coughing or retching. Contorted faces, eyes streaming, came forward out of the darkness and vanished again. The atmosphere became even more impenetrable now that the bridge hatch was closed. Lorenz grabbed Sauer. 'Where's the breathing apparatus?' For a moment Sauer appeared to have lost the ability to comprehend German. Lorenz shook him and said firmly, 'Number One! Distribute the breathing apparatus. Do you understand me?' Sauer nodded and as he stumbled away the smoke closed behind him like two stage curtains. Lorenz's mouth tasted of oil and his lungs felt as if they had been filled with concrete. A fit of coughing seemed to dislodge an obstruction from his throat and he was finally able to shout 'Flood!' He hoped that the crew had returned to their posts.

Graf's disembodied voice initiated the dive protocol. 'Clear air-release vents.' Lorenz felt a wave of relief when the reports followed.

'One.'

'Two clear.'

'Three – both sides.'

'Four.'

'Five clear.'

'All vents clear.'

Lorenz couldn't see anything. He felt disorientated and then strangely isolated. The status reports and general commotion were growing fainter. His convulsive breathing swamped the other sounds and the blackness became absolute.

A figure stepped out of the pitchy void; an apparition

bathed in the flickering illumination of its own dim aurora. Its long open coat was garlanded with thick rubbery straps of sea weed and a squidlike creature had made a home in its exposed ribcage. A thin tentacle slithered out from beneath its sternum, which was encrusted with conical limpet shells. Its skull retained remnants of loose, swollen flesh around manically grinning teeth, but the orbital ridges and frontal bone were covered in barnacles. This massy, bulging extrusion suggested deformity or the projecting forehead of a Neanderthal. There were no eyes, only holes through which it was possible to see the interior of a blasted, incomplete cranium. Lorenz's mouth opened involuntarily and he expected his giddy terror to become a scream; however, as in a nightmare during which all cries for help are stifled, he produced only a long, wheezy exhalation. The horror that he experienced was extraordinarily physical and resembled a sustained electric shock. It passed through his body and welded his feet to the deck. The present moment, usually so fluid and motile, became fixed and obdurate. He feared that he might become trapped in this dark limbo, doomed to keep Sutherland's rotting, skeletal remnant company for all eternity.

An instant later the noises of the submarine rushed into his ears and it was Sauer who was standing in front of him, saying, 'Kaleun, Kaleun – the breathing apparatus.'

'Thank you,' said Lorenz.

The boat tilted and Graf called out, 'Bow planes down fifteen, stern up ten.'

'Keep going,' said Lorenz. He couldn't see the manometer so he had to estimate the boat's depth by listening to its creaks and groans. 'Hard a-port.' When they reached what he guessed was fifty or sixty metres, he added, 'Level the boat, chief.'

'Planes at zero,' said Graf.

Lorenz bit on the mouthpiece of the breathing apparatus. The vision of Sutherland had left him feeling stunned and vacant. He felt as if he had just received a hard blow to the head. The smoke seemed to be clearing and the lights were like yellow orbs suspended in the gloom. There was a sense of a crisis having passed, but this was very short-lived. Within a few minutes Thomas had called out – 'Propellers, getting louder' – and soon they could all hear the thrashing of the destroyer's approach.

After removing his mouthpiece Lorenz responded: 'Ahead slow.'

Men were still spluttering, heaving and retching. The more distant coughs were sharp and clear like the repetitive chipping of a stonemason's chisel. Percussive sounds such as these would carry. Lorenz hissed, 'Shut up! Control yourselves.' Others repeated his command in hushed, anxious tones and the hacking was replaced by muffled grunts and whimpers. A desperate, childlike sob floated through one of the hatchways, but everyone was too focused on inner visions of detonations and surging water to be concerned about its source.

The thrashing was right above them and they tensed when the first icy pulse of the ship's underwater detection system chilled their blood and invited them to contemplate oblivion. It sounded like a wetted finger moving around the rim of a wine glass and pausing after each revolution. The crew awaited the inevitable: splashes, the ticking descent of depth charges, bowel-loosening thunder. But the inevitable never came. Instead, both the thrashing propellers and the Asdic pulses faded. The smoke had cleared sufficiently for Lorenz to see across the control room. He climbed through the forward bulkhead, knelt beside Thomas and looked up at him quizzically. Thomas shrugged and whispered, 'They've gone right over us. And they're not turning round.' Stepping back into the control room Lorenz caught Graf's attention, 'Carry on, Chief. Steady on course.'

'What happened?' said Graf softly. 'Why didn't they hammer us?'

'They must have been following the smoke we left behind. Perhaps the wind blew it away and they're still chasing it.'

'But the Asdic? They knew we were right beneath them!'

A depth charge exploded – then another – and another. The boat rolled a little; however, they were no longer in any danger. Charges continued to explode but the roaring diminished as they pulled away at two knots.

After forty-five minutes the air was hazy and foul-tasting but breathable. Every pipe and dial and valve wheel was covered in black soot. After consulting Thomas, Lorenz looked through the observation periscope and called out, 'Prepare to surface.' They ventilated the boat for twenty minutes and then, because the convoy was still in view, submerged again for another hour, during which cleaning materials were distributed and the crew set about making the boat habitable once more.

An investigation followed and Neumann, one of the mechanics, offered an explanation for what had caused the fire. 'I'd left some oily rags on the ledge over where the exhaust pipe bends. I do it all the time. Well, we all do – it's not just me, Herr Kaleun.' A note of defiant indignation hardened his voice. Lorenz gestured for him to proceed. 'I can remember the exhaust was really hot,' Neumann continued, 'because we'd been going so fast for so long. In fact the bend in the exhaust pipe was glowing. Red hot, it was. I think the rags must have fallen onto the pipe, caught fire, and dropped into the bilges. There's a lot of oil swilling around in the diesel room.' He made a silent, wide-eyed appeal to Lorenz and Graf. 'It can't be helped.'

'When we opened the outside ventilation valve,' said

Fischer, the chief mechanic, 'and we flooded the bilges, the blaze went out immediately. In fact, the fire only lasted a few seconds but it produced a huge quantity of smoke.'

'So why did the engines cut out?' asked Lorenz.

'They didn't,' said Fischer. 'It was chaos back there,' he jabbed his thumb over his shoulder in the direction of the diesel room, 'so I switched everything off. It was unsafe to leave the engines running when we couldn't see anything. Someone could have got trapped in the machinery – lost a limb – or worse, sir.'

'And what Neumann just said,' Lorenz frowned. 'Is that true? Your men always leave dirty rags on the ledge above the exhaust pipe?'

'Not always,' said Fischer. 'But it happens.'

'Have *you* left rags there?'

'Yes,' said Fischer. 'It was bad luck, Kaleun. The rags fell at just the wrong moment, just when the pipe was hot enough to cause a fire.'

'It's never happened before, Herr Kaleun,' said Neumann.

The men looked at each other and something passed between them, an uneasy acknowledgement of the fact that Fischer had employed the words 'bad' and 'luck'. The uniqueness of the event suggested agency, intervention, forces at work that might possibly create 'bad luck'.

'It's never happened before,' Graf repeated, largely to end

the tense, protracted silence. 'And it probably won't happen again, Kaleun.'

'Even so,' said Lorenz, addressing the two mechanics, 'you'd better stop leaving rags on that shelf in future. Just in case.' Fischer and Neumann nodded their heads in vigorous agreement.

'Kaleun?' Schmidt asked. 'With respect, are you going to recommend any disciplinary action?' The Master-at-Arms was holding a pencil over the page of an open notebook. His pained expression showed that it was his reluctant duty to raise such issues.

'No,' said Lorenz, shaking his head. 'I don't think that will be necessary.'

'The Admiral might take a different view,' said Pullman.

Lorenz hadn't realized he was there. He turned slowly to face the photographer. 'I beg your pardon?'

'The rags *did* cause the fire. And Neumann *did* leave them there.'

'I don't recall asking for your opinion on this matter, Pullman. Did I ask for your opinion?'

'No, Herr Kaleun.'

'Then would you kindly keep your mouth shut?'

'I was only seeking to be of service, Kaleun. Others may see things differently.'

'Pullman, I'm not interested in what you think.'

'What I think is of no consequence, sir; however, I was merely pointing out that Admiral—'

Lorenz hit the hull with the side of his fist. 'Enough!' Those gathered around him all flinched at once. 'God in heaven, Pullman, you test my patience!'

The photographer bowed his head and apologized.

Lorenz looked at each man in turn before speaking. 'It wasn't Neumann's fault. It wasn't anybody's fault.' Would Sutherland's spirit ever give up? Or would it carry on trouble-making, denied rest, until it finally succeeded in sinking U-330?

Neumann sighed and wiped the perspiration from his brow with his cuff. 'Thank you, Herr Kaleun.'

A message from headquarters reminded Lorenz that the Führer would be giving an important speech that evening in Berlin. At the appointed hour Lorenz stood outside the radio shack, even though there was little point in this, because the broadcast was going to be fed to every compartment of the boat through the public-address system. Pullman was also drawn to the same area, accompanied by his acolytes, Berger and Wessel. It was as though being close to the radio receiver was somehow the equivalent of sitting in the front row of a theatre. The sustained noise of an adoring multitude blasted out of the speakers. Lorenz pictured the scene: thousands of raised arms, flags waving, dramatic pillars of light rising into the night sky. He wondered if Monika had managed to get a seat in the stadium. For a moment he was distracted by a memory of her pale, naked body stretched out on red sheets.

The crowd fell silent and the Führer began his address. 'My fellow German countrymen and women, my comrades!' Pullman clasped his hands together and pressed them against his heart. 'At present everybody speaks before the forum which seems to them the most fitting. Some speak before a parliament. I believed that I should return again today from whence I came, namely to the people!' The stadium erupted: rapturous applause and cries of 'Sieg Heil'. The Führer resumed with calm authority, but his delivery became increasingly agitated, his language more plosive, until he was railing against British hypocrisy, American lies, and the iniquities of Bolshevism. After each outburst of incontinent rage he paused and the jubilant crowd cheered. Pullman nodded slowly, his hooded eyes and half-smile resembling the expression of an ecstatic flagellant. The Führer praised Germany's allies and concluded by paying tribute to the army. 'Thus we feel the entire sacrifice which our soldiers are making. Who can understand that better than myself – who was once a soldier too? I look upon myself as the first infantryman of the Reich. I know without doubt that the infantryman fulfils his duty. I fulfil my own duties also, unmistakably, and I understand all the sorrow of my comrades and know all that goes on with them. I cannot therefore use any phrase which they will misunderstand. I can only say one thing to them, the home front knows what they have to go through. The home front can well imagine what it means to lie in the snow and the frost in the cold of thirty-five degrees below zero and defend our homes for us. But because the home front knows it, they will all do what they can to lighten your fate. They will work, and they will continue to work, and I will demand that the German patriots at home work and produce munitions, manufacture weapons, and make more munitions and more. You remain at home, and many comrades lose their lives daily. Workers: work, manufacture, continue to work so that our means of communication, our transportation facilities, can take them to the front from behind the lines. The front will hold, they will fulfil their duty.'

When they heard the crowd erupting for the last time, Pullman gave the Party salute and clicked his heels. Berger and Wessel copied him, although when Lorenz looked at them his scrutiny made them self-conscious and uncomfortable.

'Well, Herr Kaleun?' said Pullman, offering Lorenz an opportunity to demonstrate his confidence in the Führer.

'Well . . .' Lorenz repeated without emotion.

'Inspiring,' Pullman persisted. 'Wasn't it?'

Lorenz's face was blank. He glanced at Graf, who was silently imploring him to say something positive.

'I share the Führer's pity and sympathy,' said Lorenz, 'for our countrymen who are serving on the Russian front.' Then, before Pullman could say anything else, Lorenz stepped into his nook and yanked the curtain along its rail.

Engine vibrations conducted through the boat and made the slip of paper that Lorenz held in his hands tremble. He had been instructed to intercept a convoy and participate in a coordinated attack with three other U-boats. The convoy, according to intelligence sources, was large but inadequately defended.

'Have you noticed,' said Lorenz to Juhl, 'how communications from U-boat headquarters are becoming increasingly sanguine? They are inclined to conclude that British and American defences are either light or inadequate even when the evidence available would strongly suggest the contrary.'

Juhl, standing next to Lorenz, reached out and drew an imaginary line under a phrase with his finger: 'Only three destroyers.'

'Exactly,' said Lorenz. '*Only* three destroyers, they say – and some corvettes. Well, that's all right then. I like that – *some* corvettes – hardly worth counting them.' He walked off to the control room, muttering imprecations, and set about plotting the new course with Müller. After this, he switched the public-address system on and spoke into the microphone. 'We're on our way to intercept a convoy. Müller believes we can reach them before sunrise. U-329, U-474 and U-689 are also coming to the party. Diesel room: we'll be racing through the night again. So please be careful where you put those dirty rags.'

As dawn was breaking, Müller requested Lorenz's presence on the bridge. The entire western horizon was dark with smoke. 'Well,' said Lorenz, 'headquarters *did* say the convoy was large . . .'

'How many ships do you think are out there?' asked Müller.

Lorenz scanned the horizon with his binoculars. 'We must be looking at twenty-five merchants – or thereabouts.'

'No, more than that,' said Müller. 'Nine columns and they're moving very slowly – seven knots, perhaps – and producing that much smoke? Thirty or more, I'd say.'

'At least intelligence got the size of the convoy right,' Lorenz huffed.

'How many destroyers are you expecting?'

'Three . . . but I can see four.'

'And the frigate?'

'Yes. Plus two corvettes.'

'No, three corvettes. Two points forward of the port beam.'

Lorenz rotated the thumbscrew. 'Three then ... and I wonder how many warships are still below the horizon?' He let the binoculars hang down against his chest and the barrels seemed to weigh heavily on his ribs. A bad feeling solidified in his stomach, a bolus of fear and premonitory misgivings.

The staff officers at headquarters had planned an attack in two stages. First, U-329 and U-474 were to advance and fire on the convoy, then – after a short interval – it would be the turn of U-330 and U-689. Lorenz gave the order to dive, and, maintaining 'periscope depth', the boat sailed north to await further instruction. One hour later Thomas reported faint detonations and these were followed by a message from headquarters stating that U-329 had been disabled by aircraft and had had to be scuttled. After more detonations a subsequent message declared with pithy indifference: RADIO CONTACT WITH U-474 LOST. 'A hundred men,' said Ziegler softly.

'*I shall not complain,*' whispered Lorenz, '*though I now founder and perish in watery depths! Nevermore shall my gaze be cheered by the sight of my love's star. I am a lost man.*'

Ziegler recognized the lines. 'Kaleun?'

'Yes?' Lorenz stirred from his lyric meditation.

'I haven't been typing out the poetry. You usually put a note in the diary telling me not to. But lately you haven't been doing that.'

'Haven't I?'

'No, sir. So I've assumed that you don't want me to type it out.'

'Yes. That's right. Thank you.'

'Kaleun?'

'Yes.'

'Why are you doing it – quoting poetry?'

Lorenz didn't feel obliged to supply Ziegler with an answer. He didn't really have one.

When night fell, U-330 and U-689 were ordered to take up battle positions. U-330 fired two torpedoes at a steamer and missed. While Falk was giving Sauer revised figures to enter into the computer they were spotted by a destroyer and a corvette. Lorenz shouted 'Alarm' and U-330 slid smoothly beneath the waves, but for the next three hours he was obliged to manoeuvre the boat through a corridor of violent explosions.

The following morning headquarters sent another message ordering Lorenz to attack once again, but this time he was to target only the escorts. Lorenz suspected that more U-boats were on the way and that it had been decided that the convoy's heavy defences should be weakened prior to their arrival. The moon coasted between patches of cloud and laminated the waves with silver. A clot of shadow was observed on the port bow and as U-330 drew nearer the ill-defined shape became increasingly recognizable as a Flower-class corvette. Falk was standing behind the aiming device, eager to repair his injured pride. The fact that he had missed the steamer the previous day had made him somewhat nervous and irritable. Lorenz caught his eye and said calmly, 'We're not in a hurry.' Falk nodded before peering through the lenses.

A fitful breeze brought with it the smell of diesel fumes and a hint of bacon. Lorenz couldn't help thinking, as he always did, of ordinary sailors sitting around a breakfast table, talking about nothing in particular and drinking tea. The corvette was over sixty metres long, sitting low in the water, with a blockish superstructure situated just in front of a conspicuously high central funnel.

'How many tons?' asked Pullman.

'Just over nine hundred,' Lorenz replied. 'Four-inch deck gun, Asdic. It'll be quite fast – sixteen knots – perhaps more.'

Falk had already begun his numerical incantations: range, bearing, speed, torpedo-speed, angle of dispersion . . .

Suddenly a flare ignited in the sky above them. The faces of the men on the bridge became vivid and white, the unnatural, brilliant white of rice-powdered geisha girls or clowns in a circus.

'Shit!' said Juhl.

Müller threw his head back and gazed up into the sizzling

glare. It looked like a vengeful archangel descending from the heavens. 'Someone aboard that ship has very good eyesight,' he muttered.

Falk fired two torpedoes and Lorenz shouted into the communications pipe, 'Hard about. Reverse course, full speed.' An enormous explosion followed and where the corvette had formerly floated there was now a column of flame rising up to an extraordinary height. Its size and vertical energy suggested the handiwork of a minor god. They could feel the heat of the conflagration on their cheeks and hear the roaring of rapid, chemical transformations – the vaporization of iron and flesh, the sound of something becoming nothing. Lorenz considered the number of warships in their vicinity and the brightness of the flaming column. The conning tower would be highly visible. Leaning over the hatch he shouted 'Alarm!'

U-330 descended at a fifteen-degree angle, travelling at five knots. At twenty metres Lorenz said, 'Rudder, hard over to starboard.' The boat accelerated to seven and a half knots. 'Level out at thirty metres, Chief – silent speed.'

'Planes at zero,' said Graf.

After a few more course-changes, Lorenz ordered the boat up to periscope depth. The corvette was still burning and in the distance he could see another flickering red light. The work of U-689, he supposed.

'Let's just circle around here,' said Lorenz to Graf. 'One of the other escorts will come along soon enough looking for survivors. It's getting light now so we'll be able to mount a submerged attack.' As he said these words Lorenz was sickened by the moral turpitude of war. It felt cowardly to attack a rescue ship, even more so given that it was extremely unlikely that any of the British crew could have escaped the inferno he had witnessed. Ordinarily he would have ordered their stealthy departure. But this was a joint operation and if word got back to headquarters that he had acted in a way incompatible with the mission's objectives then there would be consequences.

After only twenty minutes a large, heavily armed destroyer appeared. Lorenz offered the periscope to Graf whose pensive grumbles eventually became intelligible: 'Must be two thousand tons.'

'I think it's a Tribal,' said Lorenz.

'Yes,' Graf agreed. 'Automatic mountings and substantial anti-aircraft armaments. A real beauty.'

Lorenz climbed into the conning tower and sat at the attack periscope. After switching on the motor he raised the 'stalk' and applied pressure to the pedals with the balls of his feet. He swung around to the left, and then to the right, until the burning corvette came into view. The huge column of flame had been replaced by a roughly equivalent volume of black smoke. Leaning off the saddle he called into the control room, 'Ten degrees starboard.' Falk was already tapping the dials and buttons of the computer, performing his preparatory rituals.

The wind changed direction and the column of smoke leaned towards U-330. It collapsed onto the water like a demolished building.

'Damn!' Lorenz growled.

'What?' asked Falk.

'I can't see anything. There's too much smoke. We'll have to wait for it to clear.' After several minutes the situation had not improved. A solid black cliff was travelling across the crests and troughs and if the wind continued to assist its progress the periscope would soon be enveloped and blinded.

Graf called up: 'Lehmann can hear propellers, getting louder.'

Lorenz depressed the right pedal and rotated the saddle a full 360 degrees. Smoke – empty horizon – smoke. There were no enemy vessels approaching from behind.

'Getting louder,' Graf called again.

A grey V-shaped bow cut through the cliff face and suddenly the destroyer was ploughing towards them at high speed. Lorenz was momentarily stunned. Surely the British lookouts hadn't spotted the periscope hood through the smoke. That was impossible! Yet the destroyer's course was direct. Was U-330 leaking oil? Had a passing aircraft reported their location? If they didn't get out of the way quickly they would be rammed and sliced open.

Lorenz snapped out of his confused state and shouted, 'Destroyer! Hard a-port, take her down to thirty!'

The boat began its descent and Lorenz and Falk dropped into the control room. Almost immediately there were splashes and detonations. As the boat levelled, Lorenz climbed through the forward hatchway and stood next to Lehmann. The hydrophone operator had his eyes closed and he was not turning his wheel. Aware that Lorenz was standing next to him he said, 'They're following us.'

'We must be leaking, chief,' said Lorenz. Graf whispered some orders and two seamen removed their boots and went off in opposite directions. Lorenz passed through the hatchway again. 'Hard a-port, another ten metres. A Tribal has a top speed of thirty-five knots. Losing it isn't going to be easy.'

At first, the sound of the destroyer's propellers could be heard through the hull as a soft, rhythmic patter, but a swift crescendo soon amplified this distant, fluid rattle into a brazen declaration of formidable propulsive power. Each revolution suggested the cyclonic movement of vast quantities of water. Every man on board checked the flow of his breath. The destroyer's underwater detection system filled the air with transparent, gelid pulses. Lorenz watched Falk reach out to touch the 'lucky' flower they had cut from the ball gown at the beginning of their patrol. It was no longer bright yellow, but a repellent brown colour, soiled by smuts from the fire and repeated fondling with filthy fingers. This particular talisman hadn't brought them much luck, Lorenz reflected, and Falk's pathetic, naive gesture emphasized the terrible extremity of their predicament. Men were biting their knuckles, cowed, already reduced to quivering helplessness. A faint acridity in the nostrils betrayed private terror, fear so great that it stripped a man of his dignity and returned him to the nursery. Splashes – then ticking. Time slowed and it seemed to Lorenz that he was standing next to a prodigiously resonant clock. He gripped the valve wheel above his head with both hands and readied himself for the inevitable.

The ensuing blasts were so loud, the experience of hearing felt strange and unfamiliar. He understood, intellectually, that he was listening to detonations, but the experience did not *feel* as if it were being mediated by sense organs. Sound was no longer an ordinary, physical phenomenon, but something endowed with supernatural potency. It was demonic and took control of his mind and body.

When the roaring finally stopped Lorenz felt hollowed out, empty, as if the inside of his skull had been scoured like a saucepan. The control room was in darkness and it wasn't until the ringing in his ears had lessened that Lorenz realized the motors were no longer humming. He could smell burning, flames appeared near the matting, and a series of bangs echoed through the compartments – bottles of compressed air splitting open. Water spurted across the control room and there were cries of 'Breach!' The emergency lights came on and Danzer smothered the flames that lapped around the engine telegraph with his jacket. Lorenz looked at the manometer.

Forty metres, forty-five metres, fifty metres . . .

A metallic keening that none of the men had ever heard before arrested all movement. Graf tilted his head to one side and said, 'I think . . .' He swallowed and could barely bring himself to continue. 'I think one of the ribs has been fractured.'

There was no hope of keeping the boat stable without the electric motors working. A submerged U-boat had to move forwards otherwise it would sink. Long before the electricians had started to undertake repairs the overhead and hull would be bulging inwards.

Another two depth charges went off and the lights flickered. Through the haze Lorenz could see anxious eyes looking at him, expecting orders or a plan for their salvation expressed with epigrammatic concision. When Lorenz failed to say anything, Graf coughed and said, 'Kaleun, we've got to surface.'

Ninety-five metres, one hundred metres . . .

The boat was creaking and groaning.

'Herr Kaleun?' Falk prompted. 'What do you want us to do?'

If the boat continued sinking then all of the crew would be dead in a matter of minutes; however, to surface next to a speedy destroyer was practically suicidal. Lorenz considered these two grim alternatives, and supposed there was a slim chance, with respect to the latter, that some men might survive in the water and be taken prisoner. He took a deep breath and said, 'Blow the tanks, Chief! Distribute lifesaving gear.'

There was a great commotion as the compressed air began to hiss.

Reitlinger poked his head through the aft-bulkhead hatchway. 'The bilges in the motor room are making water fast.'

Graf uttered a string of obscenities before addressing the hydroplane operators. 'Forward up twenty, aft down five.'

One hundred and fifty metres . . .

Lorenz shouted through the forward hatchway: 'Lehmann? Ziegler?' The two men jumped out of their respective rooms. 'Smash up the code machine and destroy all manuals and documents.' Turning to address the navigator, Lorenz added, 'Müller! Rip up all plans, diaries and charts.' Another detonation rocked the boat and Lorenz wondered whether the implementation of standard security procedure would, in the final instance, prove to be entirely redundant. The manometer needle was still moving in the wrong direction and it had passed from the orange arc into the red.

Two hundred metres, two hundred and ten . . .

They were heading for the cellar again.

Nerves were as taut as piano wire. Lorenz could sense his crew struggling to retain their sanity as dark waves of fear and panic threatened to sweep away reason. He had rehearsed this ending many times in his nightmares. The loss of his authority, men scratching at their own faces, gibbering and weeping, tearing bloody clumps of hair from their heads – the boat transformed into a lunatic asylum as the lights dimmed and the iron ribs snapped: a community of fate become a fated community.

The manometer needle slowed down and stopped at two hundred and forty metres, but Lorenz experienced no relief. Perspiration trickled into his eyes and his heart felt swollen and heavy. The tortured metal of the boat was surprisingly vocal, discovering in its vibrating internal structures the means to produce a long, drawn-out lamentation. This was accompanied by the percussive cracking of woodwork under strain. Lorenz thought of finely balanced scales, trembling indecisively, such that even a sigh might make one side heavier than the other. Were they too heavy to ascend?

Graf growled at the manometer and raised his arms, pressing his palms against an invisible lintel. 'Now!' he commanded. 'Up, up, up!' The sheer extremity of his emotion endowed his will with magical properties and bizarrely, the boat obeyed, beginning an uncontrolled, vertical ascent. Slow at first, but gathering momentum, U-330 took off like an unstable barrage balloon released from its tether. It twisted and jolted through more turbulence as two more depth charges exploded.

Men were piling into the control room, wearing their escape gear – combined breathing devices and life jackets. Lorenz shouted through the aft hatchway: 'Pump the diesels.' The order was relayed back through the boat; each repetition taken up by a different voice and attenuated with distance. He wanted the engines to start without a second's delay, as a moving target would be more difficult to shell than a stationary one. 'Breaking surface!' Graf's declaration silenced the hubbub. U-330 had risen like a cork and its subsequent movements were so violent many of the crew were thrown to the deck. As the engines coughed into life, Lorenz scrambled over the bodies and climbed up the ladder. When he reached the top, he opened the hatch and leapt out onto the bridge. Over the bulwark he could see the destroyer. It was only a short distance away: two hundred metres or less. Lorenz shouted a new course direction and watched as the destroyer's deck gun started to revolve. 'Quick, get out! Before they start firing on us.' U-330 did not turn away from the destroyer as Lorenz had instructed. The rudders were jammed and the boat had begun to describe a tight circle. Men were already erupting through the hatch. They clambered down the conning tower, ran towards the bow and jumped into the sea. Ziegler emerged and addressed Lorenz. 'I've sent a message to headquarters and they know we're in trouble.' Lorenz gripped the radio operator's arm. 'Good man,' he said. 'Good man.' When Lorenz let go, Ziegler scaled the bulwark and accomplished a graceful, athletic dive that carried him comfortably clear of the ballast tanks.

Where were the shells? Why wasn't U-330 getting blown out of the water? Lorenz gazed at the looming destroyer. It was so close the forward mountings could not be sufficiently depressed. The frustrated British gun crew were shaking their fists and hollering curses and insults. One of them, however, was hoisting a stripped Lewis automatic rifle over the bridge screen. Lorenz ducked as bullets strafed the side of the boat and the conning tower. Through the rear railings he saw men tumbling and lying prostrate on the deck – clouds of red mist hanging in the air. Lorenz peeped over the bulwark and saw that the destroyer was trying to achieve an optimal ramming position.

Pullman climbed out of the hatch and Lorenz noticed that the photographer was clutching a small bag made from a green rubberized material. 'What have you got in there?' Lorenz asked.

'Film rolls,' Pullman replied.

'Don't be a fool!' Lorenz shouted. 'Worry about saving yourself – not your photographs!'

Pullman declined Lorenz's advice with his ludicrous half-smile and slid down the conning-tower ladder. He sprinted across the deck through a hail of bullets and while those around him were participating in a deadly ballet – throwing up their arms and spinning before collapsing in lifeless heaps – he continued determinedly and leapt into the water un-harmed.

U-330 had now completed a full circle and Lorenz saw members of his crew swimming to get out of the way. Some of the bobbing heads, propped up by the inflated collars of the life preservers, were surrounded by expanding, ruddy diffusions in the water. The boat's continuously changing orientation exposed Lorenz to gunfire, and bullets ricocheted off the internal curve of the bulwark. He jumped into the hatch, grabbed the ladder rails, and slid down into the control room.

It was the chief engineer's responsibility to open the sea-cocks and hatches and set the scuttling charges. Lorenz could hear water gushing into the compartments, a loud noise, like a cascade pouring over several deep tiers. Torn sheets of paper were floating on a river that seemed to be flowing out of the petty officers' quarters.

'What are you doing here?' asked Graf. 'The boat will go down in ten minutes. You really should leave. I'm finished.'

'Leave then,' said Lorenz. 'I won't be long.'

'But Kaleun,' Graf pleaded.

'I want to make sure that all my personal documents have been destroyed.' Graf's eyes narrowed with suspicion. 'Go!' Lorenz barked. 'Keep your head down and choose your moment carefully. If you can, wait until the conning tower is between you and the destroyer before attempting to get to the deck — and jump as soon as you can.'

'Thank you, Kaleun.'

'Now hurry!'

'Kaleun?'

'What is it now?'

'You're not wearing your escape gear.'

'Is this really a good time to start impersonating my mother?'

The engineer waded to the bottom of the ladder, placed his foot on the first rung, but hesitated before beginning his climb. He looked at Lorenz and his expression was curiously transparent. It was obvious that he had, albeit for a fraction of a second, considered saying goodbye. In the end he had thought it best to remain silent.

Lorenz watched Graf's ascent until the engineer's dripping boots disappeared into the conning tower. A sustained discharge of bullets made Lorenz cringe. He strained to hear Graf's progress but the gushing water was far too loud. Lorenz looked around the control room, registering the pipes and devices: the array of dials above the big hydroplane wheels, the Christmas tree, the vertical air compressor, the master gyrocompass – all useless now, all destined to rust on the seabed. He imagined how it would all look in a year's time, and then in fifty years, and then a hundred years. Shoals of fishes entering through the fore-bulkhead hatchway, everything transformed, barnacle-encrusted surfaces, gaping holes, fronds of seaweed swaying in the deep-sea currents . . . Lorenz splashed through the rising water and went to his nook, where he unlocked the metal box in which the Mauser was stored. He made sure that it was loaded and then continued, making his way forward between the empty bunks. The sound of bullets strafing the exterior had stopped and he hoped Graf had managed to escape from the boat unharmed.

In the torpedo room he leaned against the doors and felt overcome by exhaustion. The light bulbs buzzed and flashed a valedictory SOS before going out. He could see a faint glow in the distance emanating from the control room and he closed his eyes. When he opened them again Sutherland was standing in front of him. The British commander was wearing his cap and his coat was hanging open. Lorenz glanced down nervously to see if Sutherland's ribcage was visible, but there were no horrors to discover, no scraps of decaying flesh or bloated internal organs. All that he could see was a British naval uniform. Sutherland's skull was undamaged and the corners of his eyes were creased with compassion. Although Sutherland's lips did not move, Lorenz could hear the British commander's voice, as if its point of origin was in his own head. 'Let's get out of this prison.' Sutherland raised his right hand. The index and middle fingers were held straight and rigid, while the ring and little fingers were bent back. When he stretched his thumb it looked like a cocked gun. 'You know what to do.' Sutherland touched the tips of his extended fingers against his temple and added, 'You know what you *want* to do.' The figure began to fade until all that remained was an implied outline, a subtle mismatch between what had just been obscured and what had always been in view. Then Lorenz found himself staring into darkness. The bow dipped and he felt the angle of the deck change. The water had risen up to his chest and was lapping against his chin. He pushed the barrel of the gun into his mouth and as he did so he did not feel as if he had been defeated. He did not feel beaten, humiliated or vanquished; quite the contrary, he felt the wild elation that comes with a decisive victory. The metal tasted good, like a fortifying tonic. He applied a little pressure to the trigger and felt a fractional shift. The old doctor, Hebbel, had been right to marvel at the strange workings of the human unconscious, because for no apparent reason, Lorenz found himself remembering Friedrich Wilhelm Bessel, the astronomer who had proved that the star 61 Cygni was located 64 trillion miles away from the earth. He found the notion of such vast distances comforting. In such a boundless universe, there would always be distant corners beyond the reach of evil. He applied a little more pressure.

Two weeks later

Whenever he was alone, memories flooded into his mind. They were not ordinary memories, but vivid and cinematic: collecting his film rolls together and stuffing them into a waterproof bag, joining the other men beneath the conning tower, pushing, shoving, wondering whether a shell would hit U-330 before he was able to get out, climbing up to the bridge, Lorenz's exhortation – 'Don't be a fool! Worry about saving yourself – not your photographs!' – running while bullets whistled through the air and rang against metal. He squeezed the flesh of his forearm until the pain was intense and the mental pictures faded.

It was a bright, clear morning and Pullman was sitting at a window seat in a coffee house near the ministry. Traffic intermittently obscured the shop fronts on the other side of the road. One of them – *Cohen & Sons* – had been boarded up. He focused on the gold lettering but it was not enough to keep the past at bay. The memories were more real than the passing cars. Once again he was in the freezing water. Although his eyes were registering *Cohen & Sons*, he was actually watching

U-330 moving away, and when he inhaled, he couldn't smell coffee any more, but diesel fumes. He was floating in the middle of a ring of familiar faces: Wessel, Sauer, Juhl, Brandt. They were all dead and their blood had leaked out of their wounds and coloured the water. He was nudged from behind and when he turned he found himself looking into a mess of gelatinous adhesions, one displaced eye, and a gaping lower jaw full of broken teeth. Who was it? He had no idea. The abomination's arms were threatening to embrace Pullman so he kicked against the current and swam wildly until exhaustion forced him to stop.

The destroyer was preparing to ram U-330. He watched it gathering speed and then there was a dreadful explosion and pieces of hot metal rained down all around him. Every impact hissed and created a cloud of steam. The destroyer was on fire. He had no time to observe its demise because U-330 had completed another circuit and was coming straight towards him. His limbs felt heavy and weak and his extremities were numb with cold. He did not have the energy to start swimming again. The effort required to secure his survival was simply too much.

U-330 was getting closer and Pullman braced himself. The bow was beginning to plough a deep trench between the waves. It continued nosing downwards and eventually the deck was submerged up to the 8.8 cm gun. The conning tower appeared compressed and a frothy crest rose up around it. Then there was nothing to see except a whirlpool of swirling bubbles. Pullman felt his legs being sucked downwards, an unpleasant dragging sensation as the submarine passed beneath him. This traction eventually weakened and he turned his attention back to the destroyer which was being consumed by flames. Some thirty metres away another conning tower broke the surface and Pullman registered a white emblem. Graf bobbed up beside him and said, 'Looks like a polar bear, must be U-689. Quick, we can make it – start swimming.' Figures were looking over the bulwark and one of them pointed in their direction.

On returning to Berlin Pullman was treated like a hero by his colleagues. Only twelve crewmen had survived and the fact that he was one of them reflected well on the ministry. In addition, he had managed to save all of his film rolls and this was viewed as an act of outstanding professionalism. 'Well done, Leutnant!' his immediate superior in the Press Division had exclaimed while vigorously shaking his hand. 'Commendable! We can make something of this!' Subsequently, Pullman had been whisked from one social function to another – morning, noon and night – and introduced to numerous high-ranking Party officials and their immaculately dressed wives. It was even rumoured that he might be invited to a special gathering at the Kaiserhof and presented to the Führer.

Pullman had been so very busy, he had only been able to develop ten of the twelve film rolls he had saved. Moreover, none of the photographs he had developed so far were – in his opinion – very good. He had produced much better work on previous patrols. 'Ironic,' he muttered to himself. An over-eager waiter mistook the utterance as a request for attention and Pullman had to wave the man away.

At ten thirty the door opened and Herr Marbach entered the coffee house. He was a man in his early fifties and his hat and coat were clearly very expensive. His movements were unhurried and when he reached Pullman's table he greeted the photographer with genuine affection. 'Good to see you, my boy! Good to see you!' They had originally met at an art exhibition and had become friends on account of a shared interest in early photography. Marbach owned one of the finest collections in private hands. It included numerous daguerreotypes and some charming street scenes by Eugène Atget, Michael Frankenstein and Oscar Kramer. Marbach was a wealthy industrialist with Party connections and he had done a great deal to advance Pullman's career. These benign intercessions were not entirely altruistic for Marbach had three unmarried daughters between the ages of nineteen and twenty-four and he was always on the lookout for right-thinking husbands-to-be. His plan was to cultivate a circle of potential suitors and encourage a spate of romances just after the war's successful conclusion. This policy had been decided upon in order to insure against the possibility of premature widowhood. He was a doting father and couldn't bear the thought of any of his daughters having to endure a broken heart. Pullman was second in line for the hand of Marbach's middle daughter, Helga.

The two men sat down and Marbach ordered more coffees and an apple strudel. 'So, you've returned in triumph. Tell me all about it.' Pullman recounted the story of the scuttling of U-330 – for the umpteenth time – and when he had finished, Marbach expressed his admiration in the form of an extended eulogy seasoned with words like 'courage' and 'valour'. Pullman was quick to reject any charges of heroism, knowing full well that Marbach was always impressed by a show of modesty.

'I hear that you've been invited to the Kaiserhof?' Marbach raised an inquisitive eyebrow.

'That hasn't been confirmed yet.'

'But it seems likely.'

Pullman shrugged and sipped his coffee. 'I really don't know.'

Marbach studied his young companion and wondered whether he should elevate him to the position of first in line for his daughter's hand. He was, after all, a handsome fellow with a winning (if somewhat incomplete) smile. An invitation to the Kaiserhof was a great honour. This boy could go places ...

They continued talking about life on board U-330.

'He was something of a maverick, I hear.' Marbach sliced his apple strudel with the edge of his fork and raised a piece up to his mouth. 'Siegfried Lorenz.'

'Yes,' Pullman replied. 'A good man, but one who had succumbed to unhealthy levels of cynicism. He certainly didn't believe in our cause. In fact I doubt he believed in anything, really. He was a man without convictions.'

'I heard that he fouled up a special operation.'

'Did he?'

'Yes.'

'How did you find that out?'

'Through a business associate of mine – Ehrlichmann. We have joint interests in Paris.' Marbach savoured his apple strudel and swallowed. 'Ehrlichmann knows an SS officer who had some involvement.'

'Oh? What happened?'

'Well, as far as I understand it, Lorenz was supposed to transport some important prisoners back to France. One of them was a scholar, a Norwegian academic, who, if the rumours are true, was a man possessed of unusual gifts – a kind of psychic, who Himmler wanted taken to the castle at Wewelsburg. This Norwegian was supposed to have an encyclopaedic knowledge of runes, so you can imagine how keen the Reichs-führer was to meet him. I believe some tests of his ability were planned ... Anyway, the prisoners escaped or died, I forget which, so the mission ended ignominiously. And it was all Lorenz's fault.'

'That surprises me. He didn't strike me as incompetent, merely uncommitted.' Pullman gazed out of the window but was distracted by his own reflection occupying a table on the pavement outside. 'I suppose we shouldn't judge him too un-kindly. He wasn't exceptional in this respect. U-boat men are a peculiar breed. They do their duty but they can't seem to see very much beyond simple patriotism. They lack vision. One wonders why?'

'Compared with the army the navy has always been less ... ideological.'

'Well, things have got to change – and soon. Wars aren't won with indifference.'

'Indeed.'

Pullman's half-smile folded into an ugly sneer. 'You know, sometimes, I detected in Lorenz not only cynicism but also a dreadful weariness. It was as if he had grown tired or bored ... of everything.'

'Oh?'

'It was as if he didn't want to go on.'

'I abhor defeatism.'

'There was something about him that I can only describe as –' Pullman hesitated before completing his sentence contemptuously – 'decadent.'

'A man like that deserves to be exposed. I hope you'll be putting all this in your report.' Pullman produced a short burst of false, histrionic laughter. Marbach was baffled by the young man's reaction. 'What?'

Pullman looked around anxiously. 'I'm going to have to ask you not to repeat any of this . . .'

'As you wish – I can respect a confidence. Needless to say, you will respect mine. Ehrlichmann and so forth . . .'

Pullman nodded and continued: 'It's been suggested that Lorenz should be awarded a posthumous Knight's Cross.'

'That's ridiculous.'

'In actual fact he was a few thousand tons short, but no one will be poring over the figures or raising any objections.'

'Given what sort of a man he was . . .'

'It'll make a good story. And good stories are good for morale. Lorenz's sister lives in Berlin – and there's a niece and a nephew. His brother-in-law is fighting the Russians – a medical man who has been decorated twice for bravery. We'll be able to hold a ceremony for the family and place touching photographs in various publications.'

'Yes, I suppose you're right,' Marbach sighed. 'One has to be pragmatic.'

They discussed the war and mutual acquaintances, and then made small talk. Marbach invited Pullman to dinner at his townhouse and casually dropped into the conversation that Helga would be there that night. He was pleased by Pullman's response. 'And I must show you my latest acquisition,' he continued, 'an exquisite album of Viennese street portraits taken around 1902.'

Later that morning Pullman walked back to the ministry and discovered, to his great relief, that he was not required to attend a social function that afternoon. An engagement had been arranged but due to unavoidable circumstances the dignitary he was due to meet had had to cancel his visit. For the first time that week Pullman was left to his own devices. The fact that, so far, none of his U-330 photographs had been very good was preying on his mind. He was eager to develop the last two rolls in the hope that he would find a few images of merit.

When he had finished in the darkroom his mood was much better. Most of the pictures on the last two rolls had turned out to be rather good. There were several compelling portraits of the crew. Only one image was spoiled. It was the photograph that he had taken of Lorenz in the torpedo room. Lorenz was standing in front of the doors and looking directly into the camera; however, he must have moved just at the wrong moment. There seemed to be another commander standing next to him, a man of identical build with the same, intense expression. Pullman looked at the photograph more closely. He was unsure how the image had been produced. There was no blurring, no evidence of motion linking Lorenz and his ghostly double. It was rather irritating, because in all other respects this particular photograph was extremely effective. The camera had really captured Lorenz's character. With some regret, Pullman screwed up the image and allowed the ball of crumpled thick paper to fall from his hand and into a bin.

Sources and Acknowledgements

I would like to thank Wayne Brookes and Geoff Duffield for their encouragement when I initially proposed writing a novel about a haunted U-boat. I would also like to thank Wayne Brookes (a second time), along with Catherine Richards, Clare Alexander, Steve Matthews and Nicola Fox for their comments on the first and subsequent drafts. I am indebted to Lieutenant Colonel Michael Pandolfo, USAF (ret.) for reading through the second draft, offering advice with respect to a host of technical matters, pursuing military contacts with specialist areas of expertise, and responding with saintly patience to my follow-up questions that were so numerous as to almost constitute harassment. Thank you also to Colonel G. Knox Bishop, USAF (ret.) for providing information on British and American Air Force activity around Iceland from August 1941 to January 1942; and finally, Kapitän zur See Jurgen Looft (Federal German naval attaché, Washington DC) for resolving the thorny linguistic issue of whether or not German sailors refer to their 'neuter' boats using the feminine pronoun, and advising on naval ranks and titles. Needless to say, any errors are entirely my responsibility.

Writing in English about people who are speaking in German is fraught with difficulties. Nautical terminology complicates matters even further. I've tried to get the best fit with respect to the tone of exchanges and the technical vocabulary, but this has necessitated a certain amount of licence.

The Passenger was inspired by the story of U-65, a 'real' haunted U-boat launched in Hamburg on 26 June 1917. The best known account of the haunting of U-65 was published in July 1962 in *Blackwood's Magazine* and the author was G. A. Minto. The sea is the perfect metaphor for the unconscious. Ernst Simmel (as remembered by Hebbel) was a German psychoanalyst who knew Sigmund Freud. He emigrated to the United States in 1934 to escape Nazi persecution and died in 1947.

The War Diary sections of *The Passenger* are almost literal transcriptions and wherever possible I have based attacks, biographical details, and crew conversations on passages that appear in U-boat memoirs. The only fictional element in this book is the ghost. Everything else is – to a greater or lesser extent – authentic.

While researching *The Passenger* I made extensive use of *Das Boot* by Lothar-Günther Bucheim. Indeed, I think it's probably fair to say that I wouldn't have been able to write this book without it. *Das Boot* served as my essential model and I willingly confess to ransacking its detail-rich pages. In addition to being a matchless document of day-to-day life on a Type-VIIC U-boat, *Das Boot* is also an outstanding antiwar novel that deserves favourable comparison with works such as Remarque's *All Quiet on the Western Front*. Unfortunately *Das Boot* has been somewhat overshadowed in English-speaking countries by Wolfgang Petersen's impressive film adaptation. The novel, however, possesses all of the virtues of the film and a great deal more besides.

Other books that I found extremely useful were: *U-boat Crews* by Jean Delize, *Type VII: Germany's Most Successful U-boats* by Marek Krzyształowicz, *U-boat Attack Logs* by Daniel Morgan and Bruce Taylor, *The Official U-boat Commander's Handbook* edited by Bob Carruthers, *Grey Wolf: U-boat Crewmen of World War II* by Gordon Williamson (illustrated by Darko Pavlovic), *U-boat Tactics in World War II* by Gordon Williamson (illustrated by Ian Palmer), *U-boat Crews 1914–45* by Gordon Williamson (illustrated by Darko Pavlovic), *U-boat Bases and Bunkers 1941–45* by Gordon Williamson (illustrated by Ian Palmer), *First U-boat Flotilla* by Lawrence Paterson, *Neither Sharks Nor Wolves: the Men of Nazi Germany's U-boat Arm, 1939–1945* by Timothy P. Mulligan, *Teddy Suhren Ace of Aces: Memoirs of a U-boat Rebel* by Teddy Suhren and Fritz Brustat-Naval, *Iron Coffins: a Personal Account of the German U-boat Battles of World War II* by Herbert A. Werner, and *Hirschfeld: the Secret Diary of a U-boat* by Wolfgang Hirschfeld (as told to Geoffrey Brooks). In addition to the above, I also made use of: *USN Confidential (declassified) report 2G-9C S14, Former German Submarine Type IX-C-40* (Portsmouth Naval Shipyard, Portsmouth, N. H., March 1946).

On the subject of Nazi mysticism, *Unholy Alliance: a History of Nazi Involvement with the Occult* by Peter Lavenda was highly informative. Wewelsburg, a Renaissance castle in Westphalia, was the 'cult' headquarters of the Schutzstaffel (SS). The marbled floor of the Obergruppenführersaal is decorated with a runic symbol known as the sun wheel (or black sun). It was supposed to mark the centre of not only the castle, but also the entire Germanic world empire, and reflects the extraordinary significance given to runes (and their perceived power) by Himmler and his circle. Prior to the outbreak of war, Himmler had authorized missions to Iceland, the purpose of which was to search for pagan relics. Although such missions were carried out ostensibly as historical and racial-heritage research, many Nazi mystics were convinced that the acquisition of occult 'tools' would prove to have practical value.

'Wir Alle' is the SS battle hymn in which the phrase 'inspired by runes' appears. Runes used by the SS are tabulated in *Hitler's Elite: the SS 1939–1945* (edited by Chris McNab).

Adolf Hitler's words, when quoted, are taken from *Mein*

Kampf and a translation of one of his speeches. The translation of Ludwig Teick's poem 'Despair' was taken from *The Book of Lieder* by Richard Stokes.

The real U-330, a Type-VIIC, was a non-commissioned U-boat (cancelled on 22 July 1944 and broken up). Apart from U-39, all the other U-boats referred to were also non-commissioned or never laid down (see www.uboat.net for details). I did this to minimize dissonance for readers familiar with commissioned numbers, their commanders, crews and war records.

U-boat men were notably superstitious, but a great deal of their 'bad luck' was attributable to Alan Turing and the code-breakers of Bletchley Park.

Forty thousand men served in U-boats during World War II. Thirty thousand never came back.

F. R. Tallis,
London, 2014

picador.com

blog
videos
interviews
extracts